About the Author

MARGARET KAINE was born and educated in Stoke-on-Trent, the famous industrial area which inspired the setting of her page-turning and heart-warming historical novels. 'The Potteries Girls' sagas are set across the 1950s-70s following the lives of young women and families in the Midlands, and each can be read as a stand-alone novel. Her debut novel won the Society of Authors' Sagittarius Prize and Romantic Novelists' Association New Writer's Award.

Also by Margaret Kaine

A Daughter's Wish

A Family's Bond

The Price of Loyalty

A Light in the Dark

A Broken Heart

Hope from the Ashes

A Mother's Regret

Margaret Kaine

avon.

Published by AVON
A division of HarperCollins*Publishers*
1 London Bridge Street
London SE1 9GF

www.harpercollins.co.uk

HarperCollins*Publishers*
Macken House, 39/40 Mayor Street Upper
Dublin 1, D01 C9W8, Ireland

A Paperback Original 2026
1

First published under the title *Ring of Clay* by Poolbeg Press Limited (Dublin) 2002.
First published in Great Britain in 2003 by Hodder & Stoughton, an Hachette UK company.
First published under the title *A Mother's Regret* in Great Britain by
HarperCollinsPublishers 2026

A catalogue copy of this book is available from the British Library.

ISBN: 9780008838270

Typeset in Goudy Old by Palimpsest Book Production Limited, Falkirk, Stirlingshire
Printed and bound in UK by CPI Group (UK) Ltd, Croydon CR0 4YY

For my mother, to whom the publication of this novel would have meant so much.

'And from Love's shining circle
The gems drop away.'

T Moore

Chapter 1

The soldiers exploded into laughter, startling the six-year-old child crouching between the barley-twist legs of the dining-table. Hidden by the heavy folds of the chenille cloth, Beth drew up her knees to avoid their huge black boots. The worn green linoleum was cold to her bare legs but she didn't mind that. She was hiding from their Gordon – he'd threatened to give her a Chinese burn. She hated Chinese burns, even more than she hated having her arm twisted painfully behind her or her plaits tied to the back of a chair, all amusements devised by her nine-year-old brother to torment her. Well, he wouldn't find her under here, not with Uncle Charlie and Uncle Bob waiting to have their tea.

They weren't her real uncles, of course. Given the

choice of evacuees from London, or soldiers from the nearby army administration barracks, her mum had opted for the latter.

"That London's a den of iniquity," she declared. "I'm not having you two picking up bad habits."

The arrangement had worked well, the two middle-aged men, conscious they were lucky to have such a good billet, making themselves useful around the small semi-detached house.

"Wait till I tell you what that daughter of yours did today, Rose," Charlie shouted through to the kitchen, and Beth stiffened in horror.

Please, Baby Jesus, don't let him! Her cheeks flamed with shame as she stuffed her fist into her mouth, her blue eyes huge in her small, pale face.

"Crossing the main road we were, and what happens when we get to the middle? Her knickers only fell down! I've never been so embarrassed in me life!" he guffawed.

Bob gave a huge belly-laugh. He was a mountain of a man, and Beth could imagine how his chins would be shaking with mirth. Squirming, she heard him chuckle.

"What did you do?"

"I had to stop, didn't I, with a bus coming at me. The lass just stood there. I tried to get them off, but the clasps on her sandals got caught up in them. I felt a right fool! Anyway, in the end I picked her up, pulled them off and stuffed them in my pocket."

"What a shame," Rose said, as she brought in the men's meal. "I suppose I should have fetched her from school myself, but it seemed daft, with you passing the gate. Her elastic must have gone."

Beth's eyelids pricked with tears of humiliation. It had been a dreadful day, starting in the playground, when that fat bully Sammy Platt had jeered, "Show us your knickers then, Beth Sherwin!" Of course she hadn't; everyone knew that was rude. Then, to have to stand there in the middle of the main road, with people watching!

"I bet it's not the first time, eh, mate, that a young lady's dropped her 'you know whats' for you!" cracked Bob.

"That's enough of that sort of talk," Rose snapped, and suddenly bending, lifted a corner of the tablecloth.

"I thought as much, young lady. Come on out of there! What have I told you about eavesdropping?" Rose reached in and took hold of Beth's arm, pulling her out.

'Why aren't you outside, playing?"

Beth hung her head. Everyone knew you didn't tell tales – besides, her mum didn't have much patience with what she called kids' squabbles. She'd only threaten to knock their heads together, a prospect which alarmed her even more than the threat of a Chinese burn.

Rose sighed. "Oh, all right then. You can sit over there and read your comic until bedtime. But I don't want to hear a peep out of you, mind!"

Beth tried to bury herself in the adventures of Keyhole Kate, but there was too much noise. She frowned, trying to hear what the grown-ups were saying. It wasn't like her mum to sit talking like this – she was usually doing her 'Make Do and Mend', which she learned down at the Institute.

"It'll be tomorrow. That's what I've heard," Uncle Charlie was saying.

"Please God you're right. I just daren't let myself believe it's all over. As for Hitler committing suicide, well, that I find hard to swallow," Rose declared. "He'd be hung, drawn and quartered if I had my way."

"You and millions of others," Charlie said grimly.

Rose stood up. "Beth, go and tell Gordon he's to come in for bed. Hurry up now. It's going to be a big day tomorrow – I want you both in bed early."

"Why, Mum, what's happening?"

"You'll find out."

But Beth thought she knew already – everyone was talking about it. The War was going to be over.

The following day, she and Gordon sat on the

pegged hearth rug to hear Mr Churchill say so on the wireless.

Rose, in a rare show of affection, hugged and kissed her children and then, weeping tears of relief and joy, rushed out of the house and into the street. Beth followed and all the neighbours came out, laughing, crying and hugging each other.

"Come on, everyone," Mrs Ward, who lived three doors away called. "Let's collect for a bonfire!"

Soon, people were streaming from all the streets on the small estate of rented houses, carrying bits of wood, old broken furniture, and anything else they could salvage. Then, at dusk, they built a huge bonfire on a field bordering Mill Lane, which ran along the end of the small cul-de-sac. Allowed to stay up late, it seemed to a thrilled and excited Beth that the whole world had turned into fairyland.

She'd never seen streetlights before, and as she trotted by Rose's side along the narrow road heading for the bonfire, she caught tantalising glimpses of other people's homes, as the golden light poured out from uncurtained windows. It was as though people wanted to open their homes to the world, to celebrate that after nearly six years of blackout, life was beginning again.

Standing at a safe distance, the children watched the sparks shooting high into the sky, and ran laughing around the back of the crowd, playing tick with their friends.

Beth never forgot that night. Everyone was there from the maze of streets, old and young alike, and when the bonfire died low, they roasted potatoes in the embers. Smoke-blackened and scalding hot, she thought she'd never tasted anything so delicious.

"The war in Europe is over! Do you know what that means? Now your dad might come home!" Rose caught Beth by the waist and whirled her round.

Beth couldn't remember her dad – all she knew was that he was in a foreign country called Italy.

"Does that mean we're safe now, Mum?"

Although she'd only been small at the time of the air raids, Beth remembered their threat well. Sometimes, when the weather was cold, Rose had refused to get the children out of their warm beds to go down into the shelter.

"You've got more chance of dying from pneumonia than from Hitler's bombs," she grumbled. "Anyway, they're heading for the munitions factory at Swynnerton, not us!"

Uncle Charlie said that when the Jerries flew over the Potteries they didn't bother unloading their bombs as the amount of smoke hanging over the area from the potbanks, and all their marl-holes fooled them into thinking it had already been blitzed! It was true that their town suffered only minor war damage compared to cities like Coventry and London, but to Beth, lying on her narrow camp bed listening to the heavy persistent drone of aircraft overhead, the dread of bombs dropping on the house had been very real.

The euphoria continued over the next few months. There were street parties to celebrate VE day, the women making tremendous efforts to provide a good spread, even though it meant using up a week's food rations. Beth loved it although she didn't like it so much in the evening, when the fireworks began. Hating the bangers, she spent most of her time hiding from Gordon and a crowd of other boys. They were having a whale of a time stealthily lighting Jumping Jacks behind the skirts of the girls, and whooping with delight at their shrieks.

Eventually, Charlie and Bob got their longed-for demob papers, and packed their kit bags in readiness to leave Stoke-on-Trent and rejoin their families. Beth and Gordon stood at the gate and watched the two soldiers walk briskly to the end of the street, then turn and, with a wave, go out of their lives. Beth wasn't sorry to see them go. She wanted her dad to come home; then at last they could be a real family.

It was a month later when Rose had gone round to Mrs Ward's to borrow a knitting pattern, that Beth was alone in the house, hiding behind the settee. She and Gordon were playing hide-and-seek, but he'd been away so long she began to suspect that he'd gone off to play with his pals. Once she'd stayed upstairs in the wardrobe for nearly an hour! Well, she wasn't daft, even if she was small, and she began to wriggle out when the back door opened and a deep voice called,

"Anyone home?"

A tall man in army uniform came in, dumped his bulging kit bag and removing his cap stood still, looking around him. There was no fire in the grate as Rose was trying to save coal, and in the silence the clock on the mantelpiece ticked loudly, emphasising the emptiness of the room.

Beth shrank back as he crossed to the door leading to the stairs and shouted up,

"Where is everyone?"

He waited a few seconds and then, shrugging wearily, slumped into an armchair and fumbled in his pocket for a packet of Woodbines. He struck a match and, lighting up, inhaled deeply.

Hidden from his view by the large kit bag, she peeked around the corner of the settee, wondering who he could be.

He wasn't her dad, that was for sure. This man had a dark skin and a black moustache; he looked nothing like the snapshot. What was he doing in their house?

Her heart pounding, she began to feel scared. What should she do?

The soldier finished his smoke and went over to the old upright piano in the corner, tinkering with the yellow ivories. He began to pick out a tune. Beth knew it. It was the one Vera Lynn sang on the wireless, "*We'll meet again . . .*"

She jumped suddenly as the stranger crashed down the lid and turning, savagely kicked the kit bag, muttering, "Bloody hell!"

Beth's eyes grew round with shock. Her mum didn't allow swear words! She heard the man cross the room, open the door and go upstairs, his heavy boots thumping on the threadbare carpet.

This was too much! Scrambling from her hiding-place, she raced out of the back door and ran breathlessly round to Mrs Ward's.

Bursting in at the back door, she stopped, her breath coming in ragged jerks.

"Hey, what have I told you about knocking!" Rose scolded her.

"Mum! Mum! There's a strange soldier in our house!" Beth gabbled, her voice loud and shrill. "He's got a dark skin and a moustache and he played a tune on our piano!" She paused and then announced dramatically, "He's gone up our stairs!"

Rose looked up swiftly from the knitting patterns,

her brows drawn together. It couldn't be, could it? Her eyes met those of Mrs Ward and an unspoken message passed between them. Jumping up, Rose ran from the house. Beth went to follow her, but Mrs Ward grabbed her arm tightly.

"No, duck, you stay here with me."

"But –"

"No buts! Now, where's your Gordon?"

"He's outside, playing football." Beth had seen him in the distance as she ran along the street, the toad!

"Well, go and fetch him, and tell him if he comes straight back here with you, I'll make you both some toffee apples!"

Rose hurried along the street, her breath coming in shallow gasps. Harry here? She walked quickly up the path to the side of the house and then stopped, leaning against the wall, her legs trembling. Four years it was, four long worrying years since she'd seen him. She patted her hair, pushing the grips firmly into her front roll, and smoothed down her frock. All those hours she'd daydreamed of Harry's homecoming! How she'd have a special meal prepared, the house full of appetising smells, the children dressed in their best waiting to welcome him. She'd even saved her clothing coupons to make a new frock and here she was without a touch of lipstick!

On an impulse, she turned and crept round to the

front of the house, stealthily peering through the window. It was Harry! He was sitting in the armchair staring into space – thinner, deeply tanned and he'd grown a moustache – but it was him!

Feelings of relief, joy, excitement and trepidation, all warred together! She couldn't wait to see him, hold him, tell him how much she'd missed him. Her pulse raced and she was just about to move when Harry suddenly dropped his head into his hands, his shoulders shaking, and, to her horror, Rose saw her husband was weeping.

With sudden insight she realised what a terrible anticlimax his homecoming had been. 'Keep the home fires burning' went the song, and Harry hadn't even had that, just an empty house after travelling all that way, in who knew what conditions. In an upsurge of love and compassion she turned swiftly, and ran round to the back door, her face wet with tears,

"Harry?" she called as she opened the back door.

Harry jumped out of the chair and she flung herself at him, holding him close, crying and laughing at the same time.

"Oh, Harry, I wanted to give you such a welcome, but we didn't know you were coming. Your last letter said it would be another month!"

"I know, old girl. It doesn't matter!" Harry passed the back of his hand across his eyes and looked down at his wife, at her pleasant open face and frank blue eyes, luminous with tears. A man of few words, Harry Sherwin knew he was lucky to have Rose as a wife. He'd had no worries about her messing with other blokes while he was away. She wasn't the sort, not like some fellows' wives. The things he'd heard would make your hair curl. All through the lousy war, the only thing which had kept him going was the thought of coming home to Rose and the kids.

"It all happened so sudden, and I was going to send you a telegram, when I got this offer of a lift and there wasn't time," he explained.

Rose drew away, feeling suddenly shy.

"How're the kids?" Harry asked, taking out a handkerchief and blowing his nose.

"Oh, they're fine. Gordon's the spit of you, and wait till you see Beth. She's bright as a button!"

"Where are they?"

"At Mrs Ward's." Rose hesitated, and then said with a grin. "Beth was here when you arrived. She didn't know you with the tache! You should have heard her when she rushed round to tell me a strange man had gone up our stairs!"

Harry stared at her. "Well, I'll be blowed! Go on, Rose. Go and fetch them."

Gordon arrived first, dashing into the house like an

express train, only to stop short at the sight of the tall, dark-skinned man.

"Dad! You look different!"

"You remember me then?"

"'Course I do. Are you back for good?"

"No, not yet, lad. A week's leave."

Harry ruffled his son's hair, feeling proud at the sight of the sturdy, brown-haired little boy. Rose was right; he was the spitting image of himself at the same age.

Beth came in shyly, holding Rose's hand.

Harry crouched down, and limpid blue eyes looked into weary brown ones.

He gazed with wonder at the dainty little girl and reached out a hand, fingering one of her dark, shiny plaits.

"I didn't know I had a little princess for a daughter."

She blushed with pleasure.

"Give your dad a kiss!" Rose prompted.

Beth put her face up and then giggled. "It tickles!"

"Did you kill many Germans, Dad?" Gordon demanded, his eyes already glowing with hero-worship.

Rose saw Harry's face change, the smile fading and lines of strain deepen around his eyes which slid away from the boy's open gaze.

There was an awkward silence before Rose said briskly, "Your Dad doesn't want to be bothered with a lot of questions about the war, Gordon. I bet he's dying for a cup of tea – I know I am."

That night, as she lay beside her husband, listening to his regular breathing, Rose knew there were difficult days ahead. Oh, she and Harry had talked once the children were in bed, she'd brought him up to date with news of family, neighbours and friends, but there was a constraint there, a divide of four years' separation. She had become used to making her own decisions as head of the household. And Harry? An ordinary working man, whose horizons had stretched no further than watching Stoke City play football on a Saturday afternoon, he had been catapulted into a world of brutality he'd never dreamed existed.

As he'd climbed into their double bed, he'd simply leaned over and kissed her on the forehead, saying, "I'm so tired, Rose, so bloody tired!"

She'd kissed his cheek and held him close for a moment.

"Go to sleep, Harry – let's just be thankful you're home."

When Monday came, Beth clamoured for her dad to meet her from school, and saw with a thrill his tall uniform-clad figure waiting at the railings. She felt six feet high as she walked down the road by his side, shuffling her feet in the brown and gold autumn leaves. Once home, it was milk and biscuits and then, while Rose cooked their dinner, Harry took both children to visit Grandma Sherwin, who also lived in the small district of Minsden. Her terraced house was ten-minutes' walk away in the middle of a poky street backing on to the small railway station. Walking carefully over the slimy moss-covered 'backs' with their lines of washing strung across, they opened the wooden gate, and walked through the backyard into the dark scullery. It was a matter of life and death to Grandma Sherwin that her backyard was kept swilled clean, and her front doorstep polished regularly with red Cardinal. If Beth ever went to visit her and knocked at the front door, then woe betide her if she trod on the step! The tiny house smelt strongly of cabbage and disinfectant, and the children were never allowed to enter the cold parlour, which was only used at Christmas and on special occasions.

Beth was a tiny bit scared of Grandma Sherwin, who made no secret of the fact that she thought children should be seen and not heard. Sitting stiffly on the horsehair sofa with Gordon fidgeting beside her, she prepared herself for the ordeal to come.

"How are you, Elizabeth?"

"Fine, thank you, Grandma. How are you?"

Glorying in an audience, she complained bitterly about her bad knee, her neighbours, the inadequacy of her widow's pension, and the fact that Rose didn't visit her often enough.

"I'm glad to see you've got more sense of duty, Harry," she sniffed. "But I just hope you keep it up when you're demobbed. You don't know what it's like sitting here all alone," she whined.

Beth saw her dad's lips tighten, and wished they could go.

"You're not that old, Mum. Why don't you get out more, get a little job for instance."

"Oh, it's like that, is it? You want me to go out slaving at my age – well, let me tell you . . ."

She's off, Beth thought miserably, and nudged Gordon.

"Dad," he interrupted, "I feel sick!"

"You'd better take him home." The complaining voice stopped in mid-stream and, in an effort to avoid any disgusting mess, she hurriedly ushered them out of the back door.

"That boy's always feeling sick. You ought to get him to the doctor!" she shouted after them, as they picked their way through the flapping washing.

Harry stared at Gordon suspiciously as they walked home and then, his lips twitching, gave them both a threepenny bit. "Ask your mum for some sweet coupons tomorrow."

Ooh, Beth's mouth watered at the thought of a

sherbet dip, and perhaps even a piece of liquorice root.

But much as she looked forward to her dad meeting her in the afternoons, Beth was beginning to dread going to school, not because of the lessons, but because of what was happening in the playground.

"Oh, Beth you're a funny 'un

Got a nose like a pickled onion,

Got a face like a squashed tomato

And legs like matchsticks!" chanted a gang of girls, older and more solidly built than herself.

"Why's your name Beth? Why aren't you called Lizzie or Betty like everyone else? You think you're better than the rest of us!"

It had been Harry who wanted to name his baby daughter after one of the young princesses, and Rose had agreed to Elizabeth but only on condition they could call her Beth.

"It'll get shortened anyway," she'd argued.

Brought up a Methodist, Rose had been given a copy of Louisa M Alcott's *Little Women* as a Sunday school prize, and she'd always liked the name. But Beth wished she'd been called Jean or Mary or anything that wasn't different.

"Sticks and stones may break my bones, but names will never hurt me!" she shouted back.

One of the girls lunged forward and roughly pulled

the ribbons off her plaits, jerking her head painfully. Beth flew at her, trying to grab her tormentor's hair, but the other girl snatched her wrist and with her superior strength brought Beth's arm down to her side. She kicked out futilely, but was forced struggling back against the wall of the lavatories.

"Weakling, weakling!" they chanted.

"Leave her alone, you bullies," shouted two of Beth's friends.

"Oh, you want some, do you!"

The small girls retreated warily before the threat.

It was always the same, every playtime. She just didn't seem to have the strength to fight them off and anyway it was true – her legs were like matchsticks.

Then she came out of school one day to see her dad talking to Father O'Neill, and as they walked home, he said, "I stood watching you in the playground, this afternoon."

Beth flushed. Now her dad would think she couldn't stick up for herself, but she tried, she really did! "I'm not as strong as the others," she defended herself.

"You'll grow out of it – it's 'cos you were premature."

"What's premature?"

Harry explained that a month before Beth was due to be born, Rose had slipped and fallen in an effort to avoid being bitten by the notoriously bad-tempered horse which pulled the milk cart.

"So you see, Beth, you were very tiny when you were born, not even five pounds."

At the weekly mass the next morning, which the whole school attended, Father O'Neill stood on the altar, his golden vestments gleaming in the rays of the morning sun streaming through the windows, his hands tucked inside the sleeves of his surplice.

"Can anyone tell me now, what is the second commandment?"

"Love thy neighbour as thyself," the children chorused.

"Then why don't you do it!" he thundered. "It doesn't just mean the people next door, does it, children?"

"No, Father!" came a hundred and twenty whispered answers.

"It means being kind to everyone, and never willingly hurting anyone, even with words. Shall I tell you the one thing that makes Our Blessed Lord unhappy more than anything else? Children being unkind to each other." He paused dramatically, his eyes roaming along each row of wide-eyed faces.

The atmosphere was electric, each guilty child convinced he could see right into their souls.

"Now I don't think there is any child in this school who knowingly wants to make Our Blessed Lord unhappy, is there?"

"No, Father!"

The thin, bespectacled priest stared sternly at the sea of small faces. “Good! For make no mistake about it, neither I nor Miss Colclough will have bullying in this school. Now if any child wants to come to confession, I’ll be waiting after Mass!”

It was a subdued congregation which filed out to their classrooms after that!

Oh, she liked Father O’Neill, she did, Beth thought happily, as she joined in the skipping at playtime. Now she’d have no more trouble in the playground, and there was no doubt in her mind that her saviour was her dad. Oh, wouldn’t life be wonderful when he was demobbed!

Chapter 2

"But, Dad," Gordon wailed, "Stan Matthews is asking for a transfer – I might not have another chance of seeing him play!"

"I don't care if the King himself is playing, you're not moving out of that bed!" Rose snapped, her forehead creasing with anxiety as she looked at her son's feverish eyes sunk in his pale face. "Typical! You come through one of the worst winters this century with nothing more than a sniffle and as soon as the weather picks up, down you go!"

"You stay put, lad, like your mum says. I'll bring you back a programme."

Beth followed him down the stairs.

"Can I come instead, Dad," she said hopefully.

"Don't be silly, love – girls don't go to football

matches." Tweaking the end of her plait, Harry left, his Stoke City scarf flying in the breeze. It was his proud boast that he'd never missed a home match since his demob in 1946 and, regardless of the weather, every other Saturday afternoon he and Gordon would stand at the Boothen End, cheering on their team. It was a world Beth couldn't share, and she hated being excluded from their male comradeship. Why should being a girl make any difference?

As Gordon was still ill in bed the following morning, Beth took his turn in fetching the weekly oatcakes. She didn't mind. She loved going to the oatcake shop, which was really just an extension built on to one of the end houses further up the road.

As she entered the door, she breathed in the wonderful warm oaty smell, watching with admiration the dexterity with which the large circles of batter were dropped on to the hot griddles and then flipped expertly over. She decided that this was what she'd like to do when she grew up: have her own oatcake shop! Rose had told her that only people in North Staffordshire ate oatcakes like these, but Beth found this difficult to believe. Hurrying home, clutching the warm bag to her chest, she eagerly anticipated the smell of bacon being crisped under the grill.

Sunday in the Sherwin household meant not only bacon, egg and oatcakes, but also going to Mass. They normally attended as a family, Rose having turned Catholic at the time of her marriage, but today as Gordon was so poorly, they took it in turns. Beth elected to go with Harry, the thrill of having her dad home still with her even though he'd been demobbed for the best part of a year now. At least she was the one to get his splinters out, she thought smugly. Harry had returned to his old job of packer on a potbank, packing ware for all over the world in coarse straw which left his hands rough and sore. Beth's job every night, after he'd taken off his overalls outside and shaken the straw off, was to examine his large calloused hands for splinters and then with a needle ease them out of the cracked flesh. His hands were a mass of hard ridges where the sore places had healed, but he didn't seem to mind.

"You'd make a good nurse," he'd tell her good-naturedly. "Not like your mum or Gordon – they're too heavy-handed!"

After Mass came Sunday dinner, and for once Harry didn't go down to the Queen's Head beforehand, instead sitting with Gordon while Rose was busy in the kitchen, for as the day progressed the young boy gradually became worse.

Later that afternoon, Beth watched apprehensively

as Harry carried a shovel of flaming coals upstairs to light a fire in the front bedroom, and Gordon was wrapped in a blanket and transferred from his own room to Rose and Harry's big double bed.

"He's burning up!" she heard Rose say, her voice tight with anxiety.

"Keep Beth away from him. I'm fetching the doctor in."

"But Harry, it's Sunday!"

But Harry was already on his way downstairs calling, "I don't care if it's Christmas Day! That lad needs a doctor!"

Beth followed him into the kitchen as he took his coat from its peg.

"I'll come with you, Dad." she offered.

"No, Beth. I'll be quicker on my own." Standing at the window, she watched him run along the street and turn the corner, her skin prickling with a sense of unease. Gosh, Gordon must be really bad!

Harry was back within fifteen minutes, but an hour and a half later the doctor still hadn't come.

"Where is he?" Rose hurried downstairs carrying a chamber pot and emptied it in the lavatory in the back porch.

"His wife said he was out on a call, but she'd tell him the minute he got in," Harry repeated for the umpteenth time.

"Mum!" Gordon's voice, weak and frightened, called downstairs.

Rose hurried up and then called, "Bring up a basin and cloth. He's been sick again!"

Beth huddled in an armchair having been told to stay out of the way. She attempted to read a comic but even the adventures of Keyhole Kate failed to stop her worrying. Why didn't the doctor come?

Harry came back downstairs and stood peering out of the window.

"He's here now! About bloody time!" Hardly giving the doctor time to get out of his car, Harry opened the front door, an acknowledgement of the status of the visitor.

The doctor went quickly up the stairs, and Beth strained her ears listening to the ominous noises from the bedroom floor overhead. She could hear heavy footsteps moving around the room and the low hum of voices and then, after an agonising wait, the doctor, Rose and Harry came down to the living-room.

"I've put a clean towel and soap by the sink for you, Dr Armstrong," Rose said.

Silently, the tall grey-haired man went to wash his hands, and in the short expectant silence, Beth sat quietly, hardly daring to breathe.

Looking at the three anxious faces, Dr Armstrong wasted no time.

"It's scarlet fever, I'm afraid, Mrs Sherwin."

Rose drew a sharp intake of breath at having her suspicions confirmed.

Dr Armstrong glanced around the cosy, clean living-room and then said, "Now I don't want you to worry – he's got a good constitution, but he's going to need very careful nursing. You can either care for him at home or I can arrange for him to go into hospital."

"I can manage." Rose said proudly. "He'll get no better nursing in hospital than I can give him!"

"Fine, and I'll be in to keep a regular eye on him, but now I'll have a look at this young lady."

Shyly, Beth submitted to his brief examination, breathing a sigh of relief when he pronounced her in the clear.

"It's best if you send her out of the way. It'll give you more time for the boy as well."

Beth's mind whirled. What did the doctor mean, send her out of the way? Her eyes widened. Where would she go? Not to Grandma Sherwin! Oh no, she didn't want to!

She waited in a fever of impatience as the doctor gave Rose some tablets and instructions on caring for her patient.

"Don't you worry, Doctor. I'll look after him." Rose ushered him to the door, her shoulders already squared ready to do battle. Turning, she rattled out instructions. "Harry, nip round Mrs Ward's and see if you can borrow a suitcase. Beth, you go upstairs and start getting your things together, but don't go near Gordon now!"

"But, Mum, where am I going?" Beth wailed.

"You can go and stay with your Granny Platt. It won't matter you missing school for a bit."

Dusk was falling by the time Beth was ready, and Rose stood at the bedroom window until the two figures turned the corner. Beth would be all right, she had no worries on that score and she knew her mother would be only too pleased to have her. Having recently retired from her job as a lithographer she'd complained that time hung heavily on her hands. Well, it wouldn't with Beth around with her constant questions! She was a funny little thing, always reading. Why, she'd even found her trying to read the *Pears Cyclopaedia*, but of course the words were too hard. Gordon now, give him *The Wizard* and *Hotspur* every week and a football annual at Christmas and he was more than happy.

She drew the curtains and turned into the shadowed room, the only light coming from the flickering flames in the small grate. The electric light hurt Gordon's eyes, so she couldn't knit or sew as she sat uncomfortably on a hard chair at the side of the bed. He was sleeping fitfully at last, his face flushed and damp with perspiration.

Unaccustomed to sitting with her hands idle, Rose's mind searched for a problem to unravel. Harry's job, that was it, while she had the time she'd give it some thought. She hadn't liked the bout of bronchitis he'd had just after Christmas and he'd never got rid of that tickly cough. Working in dusty straw didn't help, she was sure of it. He'd often told her he didn't really like the work and had a fancy to work outdoors, so the first job that came up, postman or milkman, she'd get him to apply for it. Her decision made, the matter was as good as settled as far as Rose was concerned – talking Harry round was a minor consideration.

Gordon stirred and Rose placed a handkerchief soaked in eau de Cologne on his forehead, stroking the damp hair which lay in tendrils on the pillow. Hospital indeed!

A fine drizzle was falling as Beth trotted beside Harry, her short legs trying to keep up with his long strides. The rain became heavier, and father and daughter huddled together beneath the large black umbrella as they walked along the wet pavements, Harry carrying the large cardboard suitcase. Granny Platt lived three miles away, but Beth was used to the walk.

"Gordon won't die, will he, Dad?" she asked tremulously.

"Not with your mum looking after him, he won't," Harry reassured her.

Her legs aching, they reached their destination, and the door of the small terraced cottage opened cautiously to Harry's knock and then was flung open, light streaming out on to the tiny front garden.

At Harry's words, "Gordon's got scarlet fever!" they were gathered in like refugees, Granny Platt leading the way through the chilly parlour to the warm kitchen with its cheery fire and appetising smell of baking.

Rose's mother doted on her two grandchildren and, watching the plump comfortable figure bustling to make some tea, Beth hoped to be thoroughly spoiled.

It was while she was staying with Granny Platt that Beth caught her first glimpse of the grown-up female form. She'd never seen Rose in a state of undress; she always entered and left their tiny bathroom fully clothed. Beth, as she'd been taught, always took off her underclothes underneath her nightgown, and she'd never even seen Gordon without his vest and pants on.

Illumination came on the second morning of her

visit, when creeping down the steep stairs, her feet cold on the lino, she lifted the latch to open the door into the kitchen.

Granny Platt was towelling her long grey hair. Having washed it in the cold scullery, she'd come through to the warm fire before putting on her blouse. She stood there in a pair of pink bloomers, her full stomach supported by a boned corset and as Beth watched, a generous sagging breast slipped out of her vest, and hung down like a balloon from which the air had been expelled. The white dimpled flesh with its large brown nipple drew Beth's eyes like a magnet until her granny tucked it away and got dressed. Beth drew back, knowing instinctively that she'd intruded on something personal and private.

The scene was to remain locked in her memory, and at first she cast covert glances at her granny, picturing what lay behind the cross-over floral apron, but she soon pushed it from her mind in the excitement of a proposed trip to the park. Oh, she loved the park with its lakes and boats and ducks to feed. She liked the huge grassy areas, the flower-beds, the aviary and the wishing stone. Most of all she liked the playground with its swings and slides, and the teapot lid. She was sorry Gordon was ill, of course, but this was better than school any day!

The only thing she didn't like at Granny Platt's

was the lavatory. This was situated at the end of the backyard and there was no light, so if she had to go after tea she had to take a torch. Although there was a piece of string to flush it, there wasn't a proper seat, just a long bench with a large round hole to sit over. It was far too big for Beth, and she had nightmare visions of slipping down into this black pit, never to be seen again. The squares of newspaper threaded on to a piece of string and hung on a nail were fixed too high for her to reach and if she forgot to take some in with her, she was really in trouble.

On the whole though, she had a lovely time and when it was judged safe for her to return home, she almost didn't want to leave. But as soon as Harry came through the front door and held out his arms, she ran into them like a homing pigeon.

"Thank you for having me, Granny," she whispered, when they were ready to leave.

"It's been my pleasure, chicken." Granny Platt gave her a suffocating hug and then thrust a bag of sweets into her hand.

"Those are for Gordon now, so no pinching any on the way! Off you go. I'll be coming up to see you soon." She stood at the gate, and Beth turned when they reached the corner to wave goodbye.

"If I hear you say, "Granny let me" once more, Beth,

I'll scream," Rose said in exasperation, removing the half-empty plate of food from the table.

"But Granny did let me have pop with my Sunday dinner!" Beth said mutinously.

"Maybe she did, but it fills you full of gas, and you don't eat enough as it is."

"She used to buy me a shop cake if I ate all my dinner."

Rose raised her eyes to heaven,

"Shop cakes! All the baking that woman does, and she buys rubbishing shop cakes."

"They're not rubbishing. I had one with pink icing on and cream inside," Beth boasted to Gordon, who wasn't a bit interested.

"I think I'll go round to Pete's this afternoon, Mum," said Gordon, "and show him my new stamps."

"So long as you're back for your tea."

Beth glared at Gordon. No one was the slightest bit interested in what had been happening to her while he'd been ill.

"She's been the centre of attention at her granny's, that's the trouble," she heard Rose whisper to Harry.

"Aye, well, things'll soon settle down to normal." Harry was a great believer in a bit of peace and quiet.

"Granny Platt reads four library books a week, all westerns," Beth announced proudly.

Harry looked up from his paper. "I didn't know your mum went to the library," he said to Rose.

"Oh, yes, she always had her nose stuck in a book when we were small. Our Cyril used to creep up and snap the book shut just to annoy her."

Harry thought for a few moments. "I don't know why we didn't think of it before. Tomorrow, Rose, after school, I think you should take Beth to the library and get her a ticket."

"Is she old enough?"

"'Course I am!" Beth answered indignantly. "I could read most of Granny's westerns and I'm in the top group at school."

Beth thought of all those books waiting to be read, and she'd be able to choose any one she liked! Her eyes like stars, she gazed at Harry in gratitude. Who wanted to go to a stupid football match anyway!

"Got one!" Rose announced triumphantly, as the sharp steel comb scraped the tiny bug down Beth's long hair on to the old china plate. She passed it round to Beth, who watched the insect crawl for a few moments and then cracked it with the back of her thumbnail.

"That's five!" she counted.

"Right, I'll give it another do after it's washed. The next time the nit nurse comes, you're going to be clean as a whistle!"

"You mean Nutty Nora the Nit Explorer," Beth grinned.

"Don't be disrespectful. You're a big girl of ten now! And don't go getting your head next to anyone else's, do you hear!"

Beth obediently lowered her head into the kitchen sink and submitted to the foul-smelling shampoo as Rose vigorously massaged her scalp, pummelling and washing the long dark hair until it squeaked.

After a rough towelling she knelt in front of the living-room fire, her thick hair hanging down before her like a curtain. I'll do it now, she thought, then I shan't be able to see their faces when I ask.

She waited until Rose came back into the room and was seated comfortably, a basket of darning by her side. Gordon was out swopping cigarette cards and Harry sat in his usual armchair in the corner, quietly smoking his pipe.

Beth took a deep breath, her face flushed with the heat, her eyes anxious behind the gently steaming hair.

"Miss Colclough wants to put me in for the scholarship!" There, it was said.

"What did you say?" Rose asked.

"Miss Colclough wants to put me in for the scholarship. She says I've to ask you and Dad first if you'll let me go if I pass."

She held her breath, sensing the tension crackling

in the room. She was well aware of the enormity of the question but she did want a chance. She did! She swung around to face them, leaning back against the warmth of the fire.

Harry removed his pipe. "And what happens if we say we won't?"

"Then I won't be put in. She says to tell you the uniform and extras cost a lot of money, added to which I'd have to stay on longer at school."

"But would you want to go to the High School?" Rose asked. "It's a long way – you'd have to catch two buses."

Beth lowered her eyes. "If we can't afford it, it doesn't matter."

"No one said we can't afford it," Harry said sharply.

No one had said it, but Beth knew how tight money was. In the small house with only the one room to live and eat in, there wasn't much she didn't know. A voracious reader, most evenings and weekends found her curled up with a library book, so quiet that Rose and Harry often forgot she was there. She'd heard the arguments about how much Harry turned up out of his wages as a postman, how much he allowed himself for 'spends', namely beer and tobacco, and how Rose struggled to make ends meet.

"There's no point in a man working if he can't have a drink and a smoke," Harry would claim.

"A man works to keep his family, not spend it down at the Queen's Head!" Rose would retort. She not only resented Harry drinking, a habit she blamed on the Army, she begrudged the money.

"Miss Colclough wants to know on Monday." Beth looked warily at them both, knowing that if sacrifices were to be made, they'd have preferred it to be Gordon; but Gordon, now at the secondary modern, had never been in the top group.

"Well, that gives us the weekend to think about it. We'll let you know." Harry's tone was such that Beth knew the subject was closed.

That night as she lay in bed toasting her toes on the stone water-bottle, Beth could hear the voices rising and falling downstairs and knew they were discussing her. In a way she wished it had been Gordon. Everyone said education was wasted on a girl, a view she found difficult to understand. After all, the teachers at school were all women and what if no one wanted to marry her? She doubted if they would. The boys at school only liked the girls with blonde curls, and rounded limbs, particularly the ones who already had a hint of bosoms. She felt her own chest which was still flat as a board wondering if she'd ever put on weight.

On tenterhooks all weekend, Beth had to wait until Monday morning before Rose said,

"You can tell Miss Colclough to put you in."

Beth's eyes lit up, and then clouded. "What about the uniform, Mum? Are you sure we can afford it?"

"We'll cross that bridge when we come to it. You just do your best, and remember, you've lost nothing if you don't pass."

Beth wasn't the only girl in the street who was taking the scholarship. Valerie Tams, a plump, fair-haired girl who lived six doors away, was Church of England and went to a different school, but the two eleven-year-olds were close friends. Like Beth, Valerie was desperately keen to go to High School, and they tested each other every night on their tables and general knowledge. They were thrilled when they both came through the written exam with flying colours. Now there was only the dreaded 'oral' or interview to get through at their chosen school, and eventually the appointed day arrived.

Beth followed the unsmiling nun along the long tiled corridor, feeling very small and insignificant behind the tall black-robed figure. She wondered if it was true that nuns had to cut all their hair off. There was certainly no sign of any beneath the imposing white wings. Hardly daring to look around, she tried to walk quietly, and was ushered into a large book-lined room, with the announcement,

"Elizabeth Mary Sherwin."

Taking a deep breath she forced her trembling legs to move forward.

Rushing home from school and opening the back door, Beth stood inside the tiny kitchen, breathless with excitement. Rose was making pastry – they always had meat and potato pie on Wednesdays.

"Mum! I've passed the Oral!"

Rose turned and stared at her daughter, her face crumpling with pride and love, and then, not caring that her hands were floury, gave her a hug.

"I've got a letter, about the uniform and everything." Beth held out a large brown envelope.

"Put it on the mantelpiece. I'll look at it later. Congratulations, love!"

Her face glowing with happiness, Beth said, "I'll go and see if Valerie's heard."

She hurried along the street and, running up the side path, knocked sharply on the door.

She knew something was wrong when Mrs Tams stood there, her face pale as she jerked her head, indicating that Beth should go in. Apprehensively, Beth went into the living-room. Valerie was lying on the settee, her face so swollen with crying that her eyes were mere red-rimmed slits.

"She didn't get a place," Mrs Tams said in a strangled voice. "How about you, Beth? Did you?"

Beth nodded, tears springing to her eyes, all her joy and excitement draining away. She felt awful . . . why her and not Valerie? She knew for a fact that Valerie's arithmetic was better than hers. It didn't make sense.

That was the sentiment over the dinner-table that night.

"I can't understand it. She's a nice, well-mannered girl, and I know Mrs Tams would turn her out well. After she'd worked so hard to pass the written exam as well," Rose said sadly.

Harry stabbed his fork into a cube of meat and mopped up the last of his gravy.

"I know why! It's because her dad's a miner and her mother works as a cleaner! Two bloody World Wars we've fought and still things haven't changed." He pointed his knife at Beth and Gordon. "Don't you ever let anyone look down on you! You're as good as the next person, and a damn sight better than most!"

Rose had long given up trying to stop Harry swearing, another crime she laid at the Army's door.

"Well, I suppose we'd better open this envelope." She reached over and, taking it off the mantelpiece, inserted her finger under the flap. They all four craned their necks to read the two pages of typescript.

It was worse than they'd ever imagined. The list seemed endless: two of everything – gymslips, blouses, cardigans, a gabardine coat and beret, a blazer and tie, summer dresses, a straw boater, four pairs of navy knickers, all to be purchased from the school's official stockist. Then there was PE kit, a tennis racquet, a hockey stick, and to top it all, dinner money was to be paid termly in advance!

There was a shocked silence and then Gordon said tentatively, "I could try and get a Saturday morning delivery job at the Co-op."

Beth stared at him in gratitude and, seeing her surprised expression, he looked down sheepishly.

"Well, I reckon I owe you something for those tricks I used to play."

"Good lad!" Harry murmured, and Gordon flushed with pleasure. Compliments in the Sherwin household were few and far between, both Harry and Rose believing that praise gave rise to vanity.

Rose said nothing, her expression thoughtful, but when Beth came home from school the next day, the house was empty. Rose had gone down to the Labour Exchange.

Chapter 3

"O Mary, what are you weeping for, what are you
weeping for, what are you weeping for,
O Mary what are you weeping for, on a bright
summer's day?"

Standing inside the school railings, Beth watched a small girl crouching in the centre of the circle place her palms over her face as she sang in a sweet voice,

"I'm weeping for my true love, my true love,
my true love,
I'm weeping for my true love on this bright
summer's day."

"Stand up and face your true love, your true love,
your true love,
Stand up and face your true love on this bright
summer's day."

The chorus of young voices rang clear and true, and Beth felt a lump in her throat. It was her last day and she was leaving all this behind, the girls throwing their balls against the wall in the space between the school windows, the game of skipping, the groups practising little tap-dance routines. There wasn't a playground at the High School. She'd seen tennis and netball courts and a large field, but no playground.

"Come on, Beth!" a voice called, and she ran over to join the circle, weaving in and out of the upstretched arms as she sang for the last time,

"In and out among the bluebells . . ."

"Watch out, here comes Fred, the randy sod!"

Rose, now working at a local potbank, tensed as the warning was passed along the line of workbenches. The portly figure of the decorating manager strolled along, every so often leaning over a woman, ostensibly checking her work, while placing his podgy white hands on her shoulders.

Flo who sat next to her seemed to enjoy laughing at his smutty jokes and sexual innuendoes, but then Flo could match any bloke in language and coarseness. Rose, on the other hand hated what she called 'rough' talk, even though she knew the others thought her straitlaced.

The balding, middle-aged man came nearer and

then paused and leaned against Flo's side, as he picked up a plate and examined the band of gold around the edge.

Rose kept her head down. She could hear his heavy breathing and knew that his face would be flushed and his tongue constantly wetting his lips.

"Enjoying yourself, are you, Fred!" Flo said sarcastically, turning to glare at him.

"What do you mean?" he blustered.

"Aw, bugger off and take that bulge in your trousers with yer, eh girls!" She gave a gust of laughter and some of the other women joined in, one calling,

"What's it like then, Flo?"

"No bigger than a peapod, if you ask me!" she cackled.

Fred, or Mr Mountford as he would have liked to be called, tried to muster his dignity as he stalked off amidst catcalls and whistling, snapping, "Minds like sewers you lot have got! Call yourselves ladies!"

Slimy creep, Rose thought. She flexed her shoulders to relieve the tension in her neck muscles. That was the trouble with this job, sitting in one position all day, but she was proud of the way her skill as a gilder had returned after so many years.

"Well, that's the last lot. I hope they aren't going to keep us bloody waiting," Flo said.

Rose glanced along the long table in the middle of

the decorating shop. It was true, after this teaset there was no more ware waiting to be gilded with best gold. That meant less money, for she was on piecework, and wouldn't get paid for waiting time. She resented the injustice of the system. After all, the girls were there waiting at their benches. It wasn't their fault if there was no work for them to do.

"P'raps it won't be long, Rose," Flo said and then launched with relish into an account of a row she'd had with her Jack the night before.

Rose pretended to listen while she mentally calculated her wages for that week. If she managed to be on time every day, then she'd get her bonus. That would mean that with what Harry turned up, once she'd put out the money for rent, coal, electric, and insurance, bought the milk checks and groceries, then she'd still have two pounds left to go in the tin at the bottom of her dressing-table drawer.

Flo thrust her face near hers, "Isn't it today your Beth starts her new school?"

"Yes." Rose reflected on how smart Beth had looked that morning in her navy gymslip, white blouse and striped tie. She was proud of the way they'd managed to turn her out, postponing buying any summer uniform had helped and then Beth had said she could manage with one gymslip if she changed as soon as she got home.

"I'd rather do that anyway, Mum," she said. "I

wouldn't want to go round to Valerie's in my uniform. It would seem a bit, well, you know . . ."

Rose did know, and not for the first time wondered that a girl so young could be so sensitive. That in itself was becoming a problem. Beth was far too easily 'sneeped', upset at harsh words or raised voices. She was going to have to toughen up, although she'd been a good girl about the uniform, particularly that gabardine coat. Horrified at the cost in the official stockist's shop, they'd trailed around the town until they found a much cheaper one. The colour was blue rather than navy and the material different but Rose felt that was an advantage, as it would do for 'best' as well as for school. She'd known by the expression on Beth's face that she wasn't happy about it, but she hadn't made a fuss.

Unexpectedly, since she made no bones about the fact that she thought educating girls a waste of money, Grandma Sherwin had offered to knit the navy cardigans, as long as Rose paid for the wool. They looked different from the official ones of course, but were much cheaper.

A satchel had been found on a stall in the market, slightly inkstained and scuffed at the corners, but still serviceable, while Granny Platt's contribution had been a new wooden pencil case, with a centre piece which slid out, and a hardly-used geometry set.

"Here it comes," called Flo.

The new ware arrived and Rose concentrated on gilding a gold band around a translucent china plate. Well, she thought, we've given her a good start. I just hope she makes the most of it.

The nun, Sister Mary Teresa by name, was brisk and efficient as she ushered Lower IIIA into their classroom.

"Find a seat quickly now, and settle down."

Beth slid into the nearest empty desk and tried not to look as anxious as she felt, having been separated from the other two girls from her school, who'd been allocated to Lower IIIB. Most of the other girls seemed to know at least one other person, and she soon realised that several of them had moved up from the Convent's private preparatory school. Before the three girls had left the junior school, Miss Colclough had told them that not all the pupils at the Convent were Catholics. As the school had such a high reputation, many parents of other denominations wanted their daughters to attend. The fees were high, but this enabled the school to offer scholarships.

"So remember how lucky you are, and that you are ambassadors for our school," she'd admonished them.

Beth didn't feel much like an ambassador as she sat by herself at the double inkstained desk in the large dusty classroom. She'd found morning assembly intimidating with its regimented blocks of uniformed girls segmented into 'houses' bearing the names of saints. She was in St Joan's as her surname began with 'S' and was allocated a red badge to be worn at all times, with instructions to be conscious of the honour it bestowed. She was only thankful a nun had led the procession of new girls to the classroom or she'd never have found her way in the rambling old building.

"Good morning, girls." Sister Mary Teresa's voice was crisp, the early morning light glinting on her spectacles. "So that we can all get to know each other, I'd like all of you in turn to stand up and say what school you came from."

Beth leaned forward to watch the first girl move out of her desk into the aisle.

"Hilary Cartlidge, from St Mary's in Hanley, Sister."

"And what does your father do, Hilary?"

"He's a solicitor, Sister."

"And does your mother go out to work?"

"No, Sister."

A nod of approval, and then the next girl stood up.

"Ah, Maria, you came up from the junior school, didn't you?"

"Yes, Sister."

"And would you tell the rest of the class what your father does?"

"He's a consultant at the hospital, Sister."

"And, of course, your mother doesn't work?"

"Oh, no, Sister."

And so it went on, Beth's heart racing as the time came nearer to her turn. Doctors, managing directors, headteachers – one girl's father was the Chief Constable. She breathed a sigh of relief when a tall girl stood up and announced that her father was a bus-driver, but then said no, her mother didn't go out to work. A seed of resentment began to grow in Beth's mind. She didn't like telling everyone her business – Rose always said it was wiser to keep your own counsel. Another girl announced that yes, her mother worked, but explained that she was a doctor, so that received a nod of approval.

When her turn came, Beth moved hesitantly out of her desk, and then suddenly remembered Harry's words, 'Don't ever let anyone look down on you. You're as good as the next person, if not better.' She drew a deep breath.

"Elizabeth Sherwin, from St Clare's Junior School, Minsden."

"And your father's job, Elizabeth?"

"Most people call me Beth, Sister, and my father's a postman."

"Ah, and does your mother work?"

"Yes, Sister, she works on a potbank," Beth said clearly, her head held high.

Sister Mary Teresa wrote something in the register and, giving Beth a friendly smile, moved on to the next girl.

Beth sat down, heartened to hear the next girl state that her mother worked in British Home Stores. She calculated that out of thirty-five girls, only six had mothers who worked, and there were several girls whose fathers had been killed in the war.

As the nun began to give out their rough books, with the dire warning that every page would be counted before a new one was issued, a girl across the aisle leaned over and whispered,

"You must live in a council house, then!"

"No, I don't!" retorted Beth, but she knew that everyone would assume she did, as all the buses in the city displayed as their destination "Minsden Council Houses". Although their estate of small houses was similar in design to the council ones, it belonged to a private landlord, which in Rose's eyes gave her family a superior status.

Just before break, Beth was concentrating on copying out her timetable from the blackboard when the door opened and a young nun came in accompanied by a slim fair-haired girl.

"This is Ursula Dawes, Sister. She was put in Lower IIIB by mistake."

After being recorded on the register, Ursula

collected her books and sat at the empty desk next to Beth.

"Have I missed much?" she asked.

"Only having to tell everyone your private business," Beth muttered.

"Nosy old trout!" Ursula whispered, as she began to hurriedly copy from the blackboard.

Beth giggled, then glancing sideways her eyes met a pair of conspiratorial green ones and knew she had found a friend.

"Elocution lessons! Does that mean you'll be talking all lah-de-dah from now on then?" Harry teased twelve months later, as he studied Beth's meticulously ruled-up new timetable. "Seriously though, Beth, I don't want you forgetting your roots now you're at that posh school. Remember you're a Potteries lass, born and bred." His eyes twinkled as he quoted, "Cost kick a bo agen a wo, an yed it till theyn bost it?"

Beth struck a pose, and in a parody of a BBC accent said, "Don't you mean, my man, 'Can you kick a ball, against a wall, and head it until you've burst it'?"

Harry and Gordon burst out laughing, and Harry said, "It'll be a pity if the old Potteries dialect dies out completely."

"You're not teaching these kids Pottery, I hope!" Rose protested, as she came in from the kitchen.

Harry grinned and then began coughing.

"I wish you'd come straight home from work sometimes instead of working on that allotment in all kinds of weather," Rose said worriedly.

"You worry too much. That reminds me, Gordon. I'll mend those shoes of yours after tea."

Beth loved to watch her dad cobbling shoes in the back kitchen and she liked the smell of turpentine which always seemed to linger on Rose's clothes after a day at the potbank.

She was looking forward to the elocution lessons. She was happy at school, and the main reason was her friendship with Ursula. Sworn best friends, the two girls did everything together, even pricking their fingers to become 'blood-sisters'. Next to her family, Ursula had become the most important person in Beth's life.

"Mum, Ursula's having a birthday party at the end of this month. She says please can I go? I can stay overnight!"

Rose looked at Harry, her eyebrows raised.

"Where does she live, this lass? he asked.

Beth named a village just outside Stoke-on-Trent.

"But that's over fifteen miles away, the other end of the city."

"I know, that's why we don't see each other in the school holidays. She says I can get a bus all the way, and she'll meet me. Her parents can bring me back on the Sunday tea-time."

Rose frowned.

"Please, Mum!" she pleaded.

"Well . . ." Rose looked at Harry, who nodded. "All right then."

Beth knew exactly what present she would take. A book, that's what she herself would like more than anything in the world. Every Christmas she asked for a book, but Rose always refused, saying it was a waste of money buying books when you could borrow them free from the public library. So Beth would receive an annual, usually *The Girl's Crystal*, but it wasn't the same. She dreamed of having a bookshelf in her bedroom with her own books on it, books she could hold and stroke and smell, knowing they were hers.

The choice hadn't been easy. *Black Beauty* was a definite contender, as was the *Famous Five* series, or *What Katy Did Next*, but her final decision was Elinor Brent-Dyer's *The School at the Chalet*, and the book was carried home with as much care as if it had been solid gold. Rose drew the line at buying wrapping paper and a gift card, so the present was wrapped in a remnant of green crepe paper left over from the previous Christmas, and Beth wrote carefully on the top, '*Happy birthday to Ursula, the best friend anyone ever had, love Beth*'.

When the great day arrived, she set out in high

spirits. Granny Platt had bought her a new white blouse with a Peter Pan collar, and she was wearing her best grey pleated skirt. With Mrs Ward's smallest case in one hand and her Dorothy bag in the other, she felt ready for anything, and promising to remain downstairs where the bus conductor could see her, waved an excited goodbye to Rose.

Ursula was waiting for her at the other end of her hour-long bus journey and led the way down a wide tree-lined road.

"You're the first to arrive, Beth, so you'll have plenty of time to change before the party – that's if you want to, of course," she added hastily.

"No, I don't need to," Beth told her. Then, as they turned into a driveway, her eyes widened in bewilderment as she saw the huge white detached house fronted by immaculate lawns and flower-beds. Two Georgian pillars flanked the imposing oak front door, and at the side was a tennis court! A private tennis court! But why hadn't Ursula told her they were so rich? How could they have been best friends for so long without her knowing?

Subdued, Beth politely greeted Ursula's mother, feeling overawed by the elegance of her blonde French pleat and pale blue twinset and pearls.

"So this is Beth we've heard do much about," she said coolly, her eyes flickering over Beth's serviceable blue school coat and the battered and shabby suitcase.

"Take your friend upstairs, Ursula, and then you'd better get changed."

Nervously, Beth trudged up the staircase, her feet sinking into the deep-pile red carpet. Ursula casually flung open a door saying, "This is your room, Beth, and I'm just next door."

It was a large pretty room, with flowered wallpaper, a patchwork bedspread, a pink velvety carpet, and to her amazement her own washbasin in one corner.

"The bathroom is across the landing. See you in ten minutes!"

Beth unpacked her pajamas and sponge bag, placing her clean knickers and socks in one of the drawers. Nervously, she used the lavatory in the gleaming white and mahogany bathroom and going over to her washbasin, picked up the white gardenia-scented tablet of soap and cautiously washed her hands and face trying not to splash the carpet. Drying herself on the soft handtowel, she straightened the red ribbons on her plaits and sat on the bed clutching Ursula's birthday present, overwhelmed by the luxury surrounding her.

She tried to recall that first day at school. When Ursula had asked where her father worked, Beth had told her the Post Office. In answer to her own question, Ursula had said her father worked at Beresford's which Beth knew was one of the main potbanks in the city.

Later, when Ursula had mentioned that they had a car, Beth had said jokingly that he must do a lot of overtime, at which Ursula had laughed, and said he didn't work in the factory, silly, but in the office. Well, that had made sense, as Mr Forrester along the street had just bought a car, a small black Morris 8, and he worked in an office. It had just never occurred to her that their backgrounds were so different. She knew Ursula spoke differently, but she came from down South and everyone knew they spoke like the BBC.

Beth glanced at her watch and went next door to Ursula's room, tapping gently on the door.

When Ursula called, "Come in," she entered to gaze in consternation at her friend's red taffeta party dress, white socks and black patent shoes. Ursula's blonde hair, free of its customary ponytail, hung in a shining bob, and she wore a gold locket and chain. She looked like a stranger, and Beth's confidence ebbed away, painfully aware that her own plain clothes which had seemed so smart at home were totally unsuitable.

She offered the present, her spirits lifting hopefully in anticipation of her friend's delight. Ursula merely ripped off the paper, gave the book a cursory glance and tossed it on to the bed. "Thanks."

Beth flushed and looked around the room. By the side of Ursula's bed there was a bookcase crammed full of books, many of them familiar titles. With bitter disappointment she realised that her precious gift meant nothing.

"Come on. There's lots of people coming." Ursula seized Beth's hand and hurried her downstairs.

It was unlike any birthday party she'd ever been to. No pass the parcel, no musical chairs, no pin the tail on the donkey. Instead there were lots of grown ups who stood about drinking something called 'cocktails', and then disappeared when after tea, a thin man with a bushy dark beard arrived and began to perform magic tricks. Although there were a couple of other girls there from school, Beth felt awkward, knowing she looked out of place among the others with their party frocks, and it was with a sense of relief that at half past nine she climbed into the strange bed.

The following morning was much better. She was the only guest staying the night, and after attending Mass at a nearby church she and Ursula took Meg, Ursula's golden Labrador, for a walk in the nearby woods. Their easy camaraderie returned, and Beth asked the question uppermost in her mind.

"What exactly is your father's job?"

"He's the Financial Director of Beresford's. I thought you knew that," Ursula replied.

"Not exactly," Beth said quietly.

They didn't have Sunday 'dinner' at the Dawes house, they had Sunday 'lunch', and to her dismay Beth found herself seated at a formally set table complete with napkins and an array of cutlery. To her further amazement, a woman appeared in a black dress and white apron, and proceeded to serve the meal.

"Who's that?" she whispered to Ursula.

"Oh, that's Mrs Hall, our housekeeper."

Housekeeper! Beth felt a million miles away from Minsden. This was another world, and which spoon did she use for her soup? That was another thing, fancy having soup as well as a dinner! She copied the others, spooning her soup in an away movement, and was beginning to feel proud that she'd acquitted herself well when Mrs Dawes said,

"Ursula tells me your father is with the Post Office, Beth. What exactly is his position there?"

"He's a postman, Mrs Dawes."

There was a small silence and then, as Mr Dawes cleared his throat, Ursula's mother said lightly, her voice tinkling like ice into the silence, "How nice, dear."

After the main course, where Beth had carefully passed the gold and white tureens and gravy-boat, they had something called Queen's pudding. Then Mr Dawes, a quiet balding man, offered to drive her home.

"Daddy prefers to drive himself, so we don't have a chauffeur," Ursula explained.

A long sleek car drew up outside the front entrance, proclaiming itself to be a Daimler, and Beth sank into the soft leather upholstery, inhaling the faint scent of polished wood and tobacco.

"Beth," Mrs Dawes queried from her seat in the front, as the car purred effortlessly along, "have you seen the film, *The Card*, from Arnold Bennett's series, *The Five Towns?*"

"Yes, Mrs Dawes."

"Well, the way the people are portrayed, living in poverty in those back-to-back streets, do people in the Potteries still live like that?"

Reminding herself that the Dawes lived on the outskirts of Stoke-on-Trent and were new to the district, Beth decided to forgive them their ignorance.

"Some people do, Mrs Dawes."

"It was a jolly good film," Ursula said and, agreeing, Beth sat quietly for the rest of the journey, staring out of the window as the car glided along the deserted roads. A fine rain began to fall, adding to the overall impression of gloom and shabbiness as they approached Minsden.

"You can drop me off here, on the corner," she said, suddenly frantic that they shouldn't come in.

Mr Dawes looked around at the narrow street of small identical houses.

"Are you sure? Ursula, you go with Beth and see her safely inside."

"Thank you for having me," Beth said politely, and scrambled out of the car.

"Which one's yours?" Ursula asked as they hurried along the street.

"This one, with the flowered curtains," Beth replied, beginning to feel sick with apprehension. Oh, please let the house be tidy, and Mum not wearing her apron! They went up the side path and through the back door. Entering the living-room, Beth stood motionless, seeing her home through the eyes of a stranger. The cramped, cheaply furnished room, the pink glass light fitting with its sticky fly-paper, the stippled walls, the square table in the middle still cluttered with the remnants of Sunday tea. Rose, comfy in a flowered overall, sat opposite Granny Platt, who was wearing her brown carpet slippers with holes cut in to allow her bunions to breathe. Both women were toasting their legs before the fire, and Rose's face was flushed with the heat. There was no sign of Harry or Gordon.

Granny Platt beamed. "So you're back! Did you have a nice time, luv?"

Beth nodded.

"You must be Ursula we've heard so much about," Rose said with a friendly smile.

Ursula half-moved forward to hold out her hand then dropped it at her side. "I'm very pleased to meet you, Mrs Sherwin." Turning to Beth she whispered, "See you tomorrow," and was gone.

Beth confronted Rose, her chest heaving with stung pride.

"I might have know it would be like this, the tea-table not even cleared!" She spat out the words, glaring at Rose, her eyes angry and hostile.

"Hey, just because you go to a posh school doesn't give you leave to speak to your mother like that!" Granny Platt said sharply.

Beth gave a strangled sob and ran upstairs, ignoring the icy coldness of her bedroom. She flung herself on her bed, her cheeks burning. Visions of the ordered spacious house, with its drawing-room, dining-room, sitting-room and study, floated before her. She looked at her small, bare room, devoid of pictures and books, at the home-made rag rug on the lino at the side of her bed, at the faded curtains, cast-offs of Grandma Sherwin. It wasn't fair!

Granny Platt looked at her daughter's stricken face.

"Now don't you take on, Rose. The lass didn't mean what she said – she's at a funny age. I wouldn't be surprised if she didn't start her monthlies soon."

"Oh, do you think that's all it is?" Rose said with relief.

"I'm sure of it. Leave her to calm down a bit."

It was dark when Beth woke from an uneasy sleep and, as she lay in the chilly room, she remembered with guilty shame her bad-tempered outburst. How could she have been so spiteful! She wasn't stupid. She knew you had to be born into wealth to live like the Dawes. How could she go downstairs and face everyone? They must hate her! She buried her head into the pillow, and then heard Rose call up the stairs.

"Beth! Come on, love. I've made you some cocoa."

Her heart leaping with relief, Beth ran downstairs. She was forgiven!

"Did you enjoy Ursula's party, Beth?" a couple of girls asked on Monday morning, as they jostled through the door of Upper IIIA's form room.

"Yes, it was super," Beth laughed over her shoulder. She was still smiling as she turned to sit in her usual place and then faltered and stopped in confusion. Ursula was already sitting at their double desk, but beside her sat Fiona Hartley, a girl Beth disliked, regarding her as "stuck-up".

She waited for a few seconds, and then as Fiona made no effort to move, said,

"What's going on?"

Fiona remained silent, but Ursula said in a tight voice, "Fiona's going to sit by me in future." Her face was expressionless.

The bald words hit Beth like a shower of icy water, and she felt the colour drain from her face.

"But why, what have I done?" she whispered.

Ursula avoided her eyes, and said in a clipped tone, "Nothing. It's just that Mummy and Daddy want me to be best friends with Fiona from now on. You see, they know her parents socially, and they think it would be more suitable."

At the cruel words, Beth flinched, flushing crimson with embarrassment, aware of the curious stares and whispers of the other girls. Ursula looked away, indicating coldly that the conversation was at an end and, bewildered, Beth stumbled away, sitting at an empty single desk at one side of the room. The rejection made her feel sick, and to her horror she felt her eyes stinging with tears. No one, no one must see that she was upset! She sat straight and tall, her back and neck rigid, her eyes stretched wide, hardly daring to blink in an effort to prevent the hot tears of humiliation from spilling.

The lesson was a nightmare but, mercifully, Miss Johnson didn't ask her a single question, and when at last the bell went, Beth quickly rose from her desk, and her head held high walked out of the classroom, down the stairs to the cloakroom and safely into the private haven of a cubicle. Dropping her satchel on the floor, she sank heavily on to the lavatory seat. At last she let out the tears and they came hot and scalding, gushing from her eyes and nose as she wept, her knuckled fist in her mouth to stifle the noise, the shuddering sobs racking her thin body as she rocked back and forth in an instinctive desire for comfort. She knew she was missing the next lesson but she didn't care. Eventually she mopped her face, listening for sounds of movement. All was quiet, and so she unlocked the door and creeping out lowered her head into a basin and began to splash her face with cold water.

"Beth Sherwin, what are you doing out of class?"

Sister Mary Teresa stood there, her voice sharp and accusing, but as Beth lifted her red and swollen face, it changed to one of concern.

"Merciful heavens, child, you do look ill." She darted forward and felt Beth's forehead.

"You have a temperature. Come along, bring your satchel and you'd better go into sick bay."

Hardly able to believe her good fortune, Beth followed her into the small, clinically white room with its narrow bed, secure in the knowledge that she need attend no more classes that day.

She never told her family what had happened and when Rose said a few weeks later, "I never hear you mention Ursula these days," she said simply, "No, we're not friends any more."

Ursula never spoke to her again, and when at

the end of the year she left the High School to attend an exclusive boarding school in Surrey, Beth reflected bitterly that now her former friend would be safe from contamination by the working classes.

Chapter 4

"Wakey, wakey!" The signature tune of the Billy Cotton Band Show reverberated through the house, as much a part of Sunday dinner time as the smell of roast lamb and the sound of mint being chopped. Singing along with the wireless as she set the table, Beth hoped Harry would be back from the Queen's Head on time, and breathed a sigh of relief as she heard the gate click. Rose still disapproved of 'beer swilling' as she called it, and the atmosphere became distinctly chilly if he was late.

They had almost finished their meal when Beth asked, "Have you ever thought about emigrating, Dad, like Uncle Cyril?"

"What? And leave Stoke City football team behind! Never in a million years," Rose said tartly.

Gordon and Harry grinned at each other, and Harry said, "You don't understand about football, do you, Rose?"

"I understand it's twenty-two grown men kicking a ball around a field in all weathers."

"It's much more than that." Harry leaned forward, his expression earnest. "You can learn all you need to know in a game of football. It not only teaches you about winning, you also learn how to be part of a team, to strive for something, to cope with disappointment. Don't you knock football, Rose. It's a reflection of life – and no, Beth, no matter how good this Assisted Passage Scheme is, I don't reckon it's for us."

"Don't forget your Uncle Cyril's single," Rose reminded her. "Mind you, me and your granny won't half miss him." She got up to fetch a large apple tart fresh from the oven while Beth removed the used plates.

"Dad, instead of me waiting until I'm eighteen to do my National Service, I think I'd like to enlist next year as a regular," Gordon said.

"What's brought this on?" Harry asked.

"Well, I've been talking to Barry Triner, and he says if I go in next year when I'm seventeen for three years instead of the National Service two, I'll get more leave, more money, and most importantly, I'll learn a trade."

There was a short silence, and then Harry said thoughtfully, "You might have a point there."

Rose smiled. He was a good lad, turning up his wages each week from his job in a warehouse, content with the pocket money she doled out. Not like some of these young people, paying board if you please, just as if they were lodgers. She didn't hold with that, not unless they were saving to get married.

She looked at Beth sitting gracefully on her chair sipping her tea. She was growing into a lovely girl, although she seemed totally unaware of it. Gone were the days of the puny pale child – she had gradually blossomed and was now a slim fourteen-year-old, her dark shiny hair confined in a single heavy plait but when loose it hung in a glorious wavy stream to her waist. She was now of average height, with long slim legs and a figure which was at last beginning to show signs of womanhood. Rose sighed. They were both growing up, and look at Harry how he was changing. He'd always been a thinker rather than a talker but lately he was always spouting off about politics and was even talking about joining the Labour Party.

A few days later, Beth was trying to force herself to get up. The thought of the day ahead filled her with gloom. Double Latin, followed by history, and then maths, yawn, yawn!

"Are you up?" shouted Rose.

"Yes, I'm getting dressed," she called back, and heard the back door close as Rose went out to catch her bus.

She hurried downstairs and a few minutes later carefully placed a small newspaper-wrapped package at the back of the fire, pushing it down with a poker. At least as everyone was at work, she didn't have to carry the smelly thing around, spying her opportunity! The secrecy regarding her periods seemed daft to her. Even at school she'd never heard any girl admit to having them, and yet everyone knew they did. When she'd first called Rose upstairs in panic after seeing the trickle of blood in the chamberpot, she'd thought she was bleeding to death of a fatal disease. Rose's embarrassed few words that she was now a woman and could have a baby had terrified her and having only a hazy idea of how this could happen, for several weeks afterwards, every time a man had pushed past her when standing on the bus, she'd frozen in fear, pulling in her buttocks in case he pressed against her and made her pregnant. However, after a session in the public library searching the medical books, she'd gone home enlightened but appalled. How could Rose and Harry do such a disgusting thing? And yet they must have done it at least twice or she and Gordon wouldn't be here. Beth had decided there and then to become either a nun or a spinster.

A few days later, on a fine summer evening, she found herself an unwitting eavesdropper. She'd been along to see Valerie, but had returned when no one answered the door. Harry and Rose were weeding in the tiny back garden and hadn't seen her return. Sitting in her favourite place on the stairs immersed in *Jane Eyre*, Beth heard the rise and fall of their voices when they came in for a break, and hearing her name mentioned, raised her head.

"I'm bitterly disappointed in her, Rose. I don't mind telling you," Harry said, his voice tight with anger.

"I'm sure she's doing her best," Rose said anxiously, trying to placate him.

"No, she's not – you know it and I know it. I wouldn't mind if she was out of her depth at that school, but she's not. That girl's got a brain, we've seen it since she was a nipper, and look how she shone the first year, second out of thirty-five. Now she's slipped to twenty-ninth. She's not trying, Rose. She's not putting the effort in. We are but she isn't."

"Oh, she's at a funny age, Harry."

"Don't make excuses for her! You know, Rose, I really thought that just once, just once a Sherwin had the chance to break through. Look at your dad, spent all his life down the pit and died of pneumoconiosis before he was fifty. Look at my dad, gassed in the trenches in the first World War. You and I never had the opportunity to better ourselves, but Beth has. Education is the key to everything. You've only got to look at the rich and how they've tried to keep it to themselves – it suits them to keep us ignorant. We're the salt of the earth when it comes to producing their wealth, we're born soldiers and patriots when war breaks out, but let one of us try to meet them on an equal social footing and see the drawbridge go up. The only way to fight back is with knowledge and that only comes with education. It's the old 'them and us', Rose, and Beth's letting 'them' win."

Beth heard Harry stump out into the garden, and Rose follow him. She sat there, her face drained of colour, and then went slowly upstairs and, lying on her bed, thought over Harry's words. Miserably, she examined her conscience and knew that he was right. She was letting them down – she even copied her homework on the way to school.

She was pathetic, she could see that now, letting someone like Ursula affect her to such an extent, for her lethargy stemmed from that time. The fact that she hadn't made another best friend was her own fault. She had friends but kept them at a distance, feeling vulnerable and wary of giving her trust.

Her dad's words 'let one of us try to meet them on an equal social footing and up goes the drawbridge' had struck home. She could certainly identify with that. What she hadn't realised was that by opting out she was letting people like the Dawes win.

She thought about how humiliated she felt when Sister Clare seized her arm in the corridor, taking her into her office to drink up any left-over milk. She did this with any scholarship girl, believing they needed building up. She bitterly resented this, knowing she was better fed and turned out than many of the girls from so-called better homes, whose mothers were too busy with their social lives to bother about them.

With a sudden clarity Beth looked down the years ahead and realised her life would be no different from that of her parents and grandparents unless she took her fate into her own hands. Well, she had seen another world, one of beauty and refinement, where anxiety and the worry of everyday bills didn't exist. She thought of Mrs Dawes, with her elegance, her bridge parties, her housekeeper, and then of Rose, working every day from eight until six, even Saturday mornings until one o'clock, and then cleaning, laundering, shopping, and cooking for her family. To spend Wakes week at a boarding house in Rhyl or Blackpool was the height of her ambition and sacrifices had to be made for that.

With an air of finality, Beth closed her library book and going over to the old brown wardrobe which stood in the corner took out a pile of old exercise books.

The first one she found which dated from Ursula's betrayal she opened, and with steely determination began to revise.

Six months later, her head bent against the driving rain, Rose trudged home from work thankful it was Monday and lobby for dinner. Harry would have prepared the vegetables so she would only need to cut up the remains of yesterday's joint.

"You're quiet, Beth," she said later, as they sat spooning the hot tasty stew from earthenware basins.

"No, I'm fine," Beth answered. Not for anything would she tell them that her form were going to see *Julius Caesar* at Stratford-on-Avon, and once again she'd miss out. Rose and Harry were unaware that educational trips were held by the school, sometimes to London, or France, simply because Beth never told them, knowing they would scrimp and save to let her go, and she was having none of it.

A few weeks later she brought home her school report with quiet pride. Gone were the comments 'could do better' and 'lacks concentration', to be replaced by 'an excellent term's work' and 'Beth shows great promise'. Harry passed the white sheet of paper to Rose, his face beaming with pleasure.

"Well done, lass," was all he said, but it was enough for Beth. Her report at the end of the Easter term was glowing, and when at the end-of-year examinations she came 5th in her form, Harry said, "You're not too big for a hug from your old dad, are you?"

"'Course not!" she laughed.

"What are you doing to celebrate?" Rose asked.

"Val and I are going to the Youth Club."

"Val and I, get her!" mimicked Gordon, who was standing in front of the fireplace admiring his Brylcreemed hair in the mirror.

"You'd better shut up," Beth said. "Wait till they get you in the army next week. They'll soon cut you down to size!"

"You'd better go or you'll miss the start," Rose reminded her.

"Gosh, you're right." Beth hurriedly put on her coat. Now that she had a Saturday job in a shoeshop in Minsden, she went with Valerie once a week to the pictures and Doris Day was her favourite.

Walking home after the film, they sang 'Secret Love' and 'The Black Hills of Dakota' without a care in the world. Calling at a fish and chip shop they tucked into hot bags of chips doused in salt and vinegar, and then took turns in singing the parts of Calamity and Katie Brown much to the amusement of passers-by who smiled at their high spirits.

Neither had a boyfriend although Valerie, who was

now working at a dress shop in the town, admitted that she fancied Gordon and was thrilled to hear he was coming home on leave at the weekend.

How he'd wangled a pass was beyond Harry, as the timing was crucial. It was the last game of the season and Stoke City were playing Derby County. It was critical that they won this game if they were to stay in the First Division.

"Well, I don't think you should go, Harry," Rose grumbled. "You've only just got over that last bout of bronchitis and there's a bitterly cold wind."

"Not go! Don't you understand, woman, that if Stoke lose this game, they'll be relegated. Not go, you must be daft!" Harry retorted, winding his red and white scarf firmly around his neck.

"Well, make sure you get a hot drink at half-time," Rose fussed.

When the two supporters returned home, they were frozen both in body and spirit.

"It was 2–1 and then Ken Thompson missed a bloody penalty! Twenty years and it's come to this, relegated to the Second Division!" Harry said bitterly, shivering as he warmed his hands at the fire.

"I just hope you haven't caught a cold, that's all," Rose said crossly. "Here, get that down you." She handed them both a freshly baked Cornish pasty, and they bit into the warm crumbly pastry with relish.

But by the following morning Harry was coughing again, and by Sunday night running a temperature. Rose packed him off to bed, and she and Beth went down to the railway station to see Gordon off.

"I just hope you grow up to have more sense than your father," Rose said as he climbed on the train.

"Oh, don't be too hard on him, Mum! You couldn't expect him to miss such an important match!" he retorted with a grin.

Harry stayed in bed on Monday, with Rose rushing home from work at dinner time to make him a fresh flask of tea and some food, but he said he wasn't hungry.

"I've got this pain in my chest when I breathe," he complained.

"Serves you right. You wouldn't listen," she said, plumping up his pillows, and piling on another eiderdown. "We'll sweat it out of you. Now try and get some sleep. Beth'll be in at five o'clock."

Flinging her satchel on a chair, Beth put the kettle on before going upstairs. Knocking on the bedroom door she peeped in. Harry turned towards her, his face and hair damp with perspiration. She could hear his breathing rasping harshly and before she could speak he broke into a paroxysm of coughing, clutching his chest, his face contorted with pain.

Two bright spots of red burned on his cheekbones as he croaked urgently, "Get the doctor!"

She ran downstairs, out of the house, and along the street, her navy and white school scarf flying behind her. She reached the top of the hill and was halfway down Elm Road before she paused for breath, remembering Harry's advice,

"When you want to get somewhere in a hurry, walk a lamppost and run a lamppost, that way you won't get a stitch."

She did, arriving at Dr Armstrong's in less than fifteen minutes, praying he wouldn't be out on a call.

He wasn't, but was just about to sit down for his tea.

"I'll come along after surgery. It's probably only another bout of bronchitis."

Beth's chin set mutinously. "No, it's not, Dr Armstrong. He's really bad. I think you should come now."

The tall silver-haired man looked at the slim schoolgirl, her blue eyes glaring fiercely at him, and with a sigh put thoughts of his poached egg on toast to one side, and went to fetch his bag.

"Come on then. I'll give you a lift back."

Ten minutes later, Beth stood at the bottom of the stairs, her pulses racing, her eyes moist with emotion. She brushed her hand across them, irritated as always by her ready tears. Please Jesus, Mary and Joseph, please don't let it be anything serious, she prayed.

Dr Armstrong came quickly down the stairs.

"Where's your mother?"

"At work. She'll be home soon," Beth answered, trying to read his expression.

"Well, I want you to pack up some things for your dad – pajamas, sponge bag, that sort of thing. I think he'll be better in hospital. I'll go and phone for an ambulance – you and your mother be ready to go with him."

"What's wrong with him?"

The doctor said one word, "Pneumonia!", and was gone.

Beth ran upstairs and to the front bedroom. Harry lay with his eyes closed, and she darted a frightened look at him before collecting clean underwear and pajamas from a drawer in the tallboy. He seemed to be asleep, so she raced downstairs and into the bathroom. She put his hairbrush, razor, shaving-brush and soap in a pile. Would they have towels in a hospital? Better be sure, so she fetched a towel from the airing cupboard, and then put everything on the table in the living-room.

She checked them over. Slippers and dressing-gown! She ran upstairs and, rifling through a drawer where Rose kept things especially for holidays, found a sponge bag and new flannel.

"Beth? Are you upstairs?" came Rose's voice. "What's all this clutter on the table? How's your dad?"

Beth glanced at Harry, still lying with his eyes closed.

She ran downstairs.

"I had to fetch Dr Armstrong , Mum. He says dad's got to go into hospital. He's got pneumonia!" Her voice wobbled on the last word, and seeing Rose's shocked face she gave her a quick hug. "I'll just go and borrow a case from Mrs Ward. We have to be ready to go with him."

Rose rushed up the stairs and stood motionless just inside the bedroom door. Harry turned his head, his eyes feverish, his voice hoarse as he said weakly, "I'm not asleep."

He held out his hand and Rose grasped it, registering numbly the hot dry skin. "I'm sorry, I should have listened . . ." he whispered weakly.

Rose smoothed his hair. "Don't try to talk. Just rest."

"No!" he clutched at her hand, struggling to speak, "If I don't come out of this . . . promise me . . . you'll see that Beth finishes her education." He lay back exhausted by the effort.

"What are you talking like that for? They can do wonders now for pneumonia. It's not like it used to be!" Her voice rose an octave as the full impact of Harry's words hit her.

"Here's the ambulance!" Beth called upstairs.

Rose moved out of the way as the two ambulancemen came upstairs, gently wrapped Harry in a blanket and lifted him onto a stretcher. Then they carefully lifted him down the stairs and out to the ambulance.

Rose and Beth climbed after him into the ambulance, watched by several silent neighbours and Beth felt her heart lurch as the bell began to ring, and then they sped away from Minsden, along the main roads, through Stoke, and on to the Infirmary. She reached out and took Rose's hand, her heart pounding while she mentally recited the rosary. Silently they sat watching Harry's still form during what seemed an endless journey, until at last they were in bright lights and bustle and they could only stand helplessly as he was wheeled away from them.

"I should have stayed with him. I should never have gone back to work!" Rose burst out.

"Dad's had bouts of bronchitis as long as I can remember! How were you to know it would turn to pneumonia!" Beth tried to console her, but it was no use. Rose was locked in her own private hell of guilt.

Eventually, they were taken along long corridors smelling of polish and disinfectant, through large swing doors, and into a huge ward. Harry, looking ill and frail, was in a high bed halfway down.

"Only five minutes," a nurse warned them.

Leaning over the bed, they each took one of Harry's hands. His eyes were closed, his breathing laboured and shallow.

"He's exhausted," Rose whispered.

The nurse returned and drew screens around the bed, ushering them away.

"It's visiting time soon, but the doctor thinks he's best left alone. Ring at nine o'clock in the morning, and leave a phone number with Sister."

"We could stay overnight," Rose offered.

"No, you're better going home – he needs complete rest and quiet."

They walked back down the ward and paused outside Sister's office.

Rose rummaged in her handbag.

"I've got the number of the top shop somewhere. I had it to give Gordon."

It was raining as they left the hospital and walked down the hill to the bus stop.

"We'd better let your grandma know," Rose said, and half an hour later they were knocking on the door of the tiny terraced cottage. For the first time in her life Beth saw the small ramrod figure crumple.

Rose was nervous of the telephone, so at five to

nine the following morning Beth waited inside the public telephone box in the High Street. At exactly nine o'clock she rang the hospital.

After being put through to the ward she asked, her throat constricting with anxiety, "Could you tell me how Mr Sherwin is, please."

"Are you a relative?"

"Yes, I'm his daughter."

There was a short pause and then came the answer, "I'm afraid his condition worsened during the night, and he's on the critical list. If you'd like to come and see him . . ."

"Yes, of course," Beth said quickly.

She pulled open the heavy door and stepped outside, and then leaned back against it in panic. Critical! That meant . . .

She hurriedly crossed the road, fishing inside her coat pocket for an old letter from Gordon she'd picked up from the mantelpiece, and went into the Post Office.

"I'd like to send a telegram, please," she said shakily, tears welling in her eyes.

The two women and Beth sat by Harry's bed all day as he lay struggling for breath. At seven o'clock Father O'Neill arrived and, placing his purple stole around his neck, whispered that he wished to administer the Last Sacraments.

They stood in fear and despair in the corridor outside the ward, and then suddenly heard the thump of heavy army boots along the corridor and the next minute Rose was enfolded in Gordon's arms. Beth stood by, Grandma Sherwin at her side, her cheeks running with tears. She couldn't believe any of this was happening.

Harry died two minutes before midnight, his family around him. Stunned with shock, the grief-stricken group made their way to the main entrance and stood in the cold night air.

"The last bus will have gone," whispered Rose.

"Wait here." Gordon disappeared inside and returned saying gruffly, "I've ordered a taxi."

A distraught Grandma Sherwin stayed the night, sleeping in Beth's bed, while Beth climbed into the big bed with Rose in the front room. Only then did she grasp the enormity of her loss as she lay in Harry's place and realised that she'd never see her dad or hear his voice again. She was conscious of Rose weeping silently and turning, drew her close, knowing that her mother's bereavement was even greater than her own.

On the morning following the funeral, Beth slipped quietly out of the house before the others were up. It was a bright spring morning, and as she walked through the churchyard, the daffodils stood tall, their golden cups a herald of hope for the summer to come.

She stood for several minutes before the mound of earth bedecked with wreaths and flowers, and remembered. Remembered Harry's philosophy, his ambition for her, his hope that she would make something of her life.

"I promise, Dad," she vowed. "I promise I'll never forget."

Chapter 5

Standing with Valerie watching Joe Loss bounce across the stage to introduce his famous band playing 'In the Mood', Beth savoured the heady atmosphere and the glamour of the large ballroom. She'd been to dances before, of course – not only the Parish Dances, but also ones at the Village Hall, where she'd learned to jive, her tulle petticoats whirling to the trio doing their best to emulate the big band sound – but they couldn't compare with the sophistication of Trentham Gardens. Apart from anything else, here there were young men from all over the city. What did it matter if the unattached ones were lined up at the back, while the girls gossiped in small groups, surreptitiously casting flirtatious glances? Sooner or later they'd have to ask someone to dance!

Not that she stood much chance – in Beth's opinion, she was far too skinny. She envied Valerie her 36-inch bust and blonde curls, just like Marilyn Monroe. Not like me, she thought glumly, disparaging her own looks. No matter how much deep breathing she did, her bra-size was still a measly 32! Granny Platt told her she was a late developer, and she'd be twenty-one before she reached full womanhood.

"Don't envy these other girls! They'll lose their figures by the time they're thirty, while you'll keep yours all your life," the elderly woman consoled her. But at almost seventeen, thirty seemed ancient to Beth. It was now that mattered.

"What about that one with the fair hair?" Valerie nudged her.

"I thought you'd got eyes for no one but Gordon!" Beth teased.

"Well, there's no harm in looking, is there?" Valerie wrote every week to Gordon ever since he'd taken her to the pictures just before being posted to Cyprus. "You know everyone's beginning to call you the Ice Maiden."

"So what!" Beth said more carelessly than she felt. She wished she could be more like the other girls, flirtatious and fun-loving, going out with first one boy and then another. But most of the boys bored her rigid, and she knew they thought she was odd and pulled her leg about always having her nose stuck in a book. Well, she had to, didn't she? If she ever found herself wearying of studying for her 'A' levels, she'd only to remember the day when her 'O' level results were published in *The Sentinel.* Grandma Sherwin had brought it round, seating herself importantly on one of the hard dining-chairs.

She'd read out, 'EM Sherwin (10)'! That's more than anyone else got!"

Beth had already rung the school, so she and Rose knew how well she'd done.

"Well, what do you intend to do?" The small ramrod figure bristled.

"How do you mean?" Rose answered defensively.

"About keeping this girl on at school."

"I thought you didn't approve of girls being educated, Grandma!" Beth said.

"Well, I still think they'll only end up getting married and having babies, but that's not the point. Our Harry was set on you staying on. He told me so before . . ." she faltered, and then looked at them both with moist eyes. "You and Gordon are all I've got left, and I know that with all the will in the world, Rose, you can't afford to keep her on, even with Gordon's allotment, and that won't go on forever. Well, I can! I took out an insurance policy on Harry years ago with the Pru. Anyway, it's not a lot, but they've paid me out, and I can't think of any better use for it, can you?"

At first Beth had stared at her in disbelief. She'd never known her Grandma Sherwin to part with a penny if a ha'penny would do. Then, with a sudden flash of insight she'd known that this was Harry's influence; it was his way of reaching out to help her from beyond the grave.

Well, Beth thought proudly now as she tapped her foot to the music, I'm on my way, Dad. I'm Head Girl now!

"He's coming over," Valerie said, her voice squeaking with excitement.

"Who?"

"The fair-haired one."

They both froze and then looked the other way, putting on a nonchalant air.

"Could I have this dance?" His eyes bypassed Beth, and Valerie inclined her head graciously before being whirled away in a quickstep.

Beth spotted an empty chair and sat down, but before long she was on the floor, waltzing, foxtrotting, doing the samba and jiving, with a succession of partners. Oh, this was wonderful! She couldn't remember ever enjoying herself so much.

At the interval, she and Valerie slaked their thirst

with a bottle of Fanta orange, noticing that several of the young men had disappeared.

"They've had a pass out down to the pub," another girl told them. "Some of the girls have gone as well."

Beth and Valerie exchanged disapproving glances – only the fast ones would go drinking in a public house!

Valerie leaned forward. She'd kept the same partner all evening. "His name's Roger, Beth. He's invited us to a party next Saturday at his house – what do you think?"

"Oh, I don't know," Beth said cautiously. There was something about Roger she didn't like. He had thick lips – she never liked people with thick lips.

"Oh, go on, Beth. You're always saying you want to meet some new people. He says he'll get someone to give us a lift. He's asked lots of people here. There should be loads going!"

Seeing Valerie's pleading face, Beth relented. "OK, then."

They headed for the cloakroom, struggling to peer over the heads of a crowd of girls, all titivating, spraying glitter on their hair, pencilling beauty spots on their cheekbones, and stopping ladders in their stockings with nail varnish. Beth smoothed her pageboy bob and repainted her mouth with lipstick. Thank goodness she had the holiday job at Woolworth's as well as her regular Saturday job in the shoeshop, or she'd never be able to afford evenings out like this, and then look what she'd miss!

Rose glanced at her watch, telling herself she was silly to feel anxious. The late bus picked the girls up right outside the ballroom, and Valerie's dad was walking down to meet them at the bus stop. Shivering as she moved away from the fire, she went into the kitchen and put on a saucepan of milk to warm for cocoa. Thank goodness she still had Beth to look after. She'd have gone barmy otherwise living on her own these last few months. Rose kept her grief to herself. No one knew just how much she missed Harry, how bereft she felt lying in the big double bed alone. It wasn't so much the sex, it was the physical contact, the curling around his body, the sharing of problems, that was what she really missed.

Beth burst in through the back door.

"Oh, it was smashing. Mum, I really enjoyed myself! Oh, and Val got friendly with a boy and he's invited us to a party next Saturday."

"Where?"

Beth named the area several miles away. "We'll be all right. He's fixing up for someone to give us a lift there and back."

"What do you know about him?"

"Not a lot, except he works in the Council offices."

"Hmm." Rose compressed her lips. She knew she mustn't be too protective, the girl had to spread her wings a bit, but it wasn't easy to let the reins go, and the sole responsibility rested heavily on her shoulders.

The following Saturday, Beth wriggled into her roll-on wondering for the umpteenth time why Rose insisted on her wearing the wretched thing – her stomach was as flat as a board. At least she hadn't suggested she went to visit the Spirella lady down the road to be measured for a corset! Grimacing at the thought of being confined in one of the pink whalebone monstrosities Rose wore, she slipped into her black shot-taffeta skirt and white blouse, checked her seams were straight, put on her black patent shoes, and went down to show Rose.

"You look lovely," she said approvingly. "Now remember, don't drink anything alcoholic, and watch carefully any drink a boy brings you. Some of them think it's clever to try and get a girl drunk."

"I know!" Putting on her warm Harris tweed coat, Beth gave Rose a kiss, and was gone.

She could hear the row at Valerie's house as soon as the door opened.

"You're not going, and that's final!" Mrs Tams stood facing the angry girl, her arms akimbo.

"But Mum, someone's coming specially to fetch us!"

"I don't care if the Queen's coming. You're not

going out in this night air with that sore throat and temperature, not to mention swollen glands."

Valerie looked miserably at Beth. "I only started with it this morning."

"You wouldn't enjoy it if you're feeling ill," Beth said, her heart sinking with disappointment. "Never mind, we'll just have to tell them."

"We'll never get invited to anything ever again if we let them down!" Valerie wailed. "You go, Beth!"

"But I don't know anyone!"

"Yes, you do. You know Roger! Oh, please go, Beth! Besides, you never know who you might meet!"

A car horn honked outside and, going to the window, the girls looked out at a blue Ford Zodiac, its engine revving.

"Go on, Beth. They're waiting!" urged Valerie, giving her a push. In a quandary, Beth dithered for a few seconds, then impulsively ran down the path, climbing quickly into the back seat.

"I thought there were two of you?" queried the driver, a spotty youth with spectacles.

"Valerie's ill. She can't come."

"Oh, rotten luck. I'm Barry, this is Pete next to me, and that's Sylvia in the back."

Beth turned to smile at the redhead next to her, feeling dismayed at her dyed hair, heavy make-up and overpowering scent of Evening in Paris.

The car reversed at speed out of the street, and then they were off, Beth's stomach fluttering at the unexpected turn of events. It was one thing to go to a strange party with Valerie, quite another to go on her own.

The house, situated in a quiet street, was an old Victorian terraced villa, with high ceilings, and a large stained-glass window on the landing overlooking the black-and-white-tiled hall. Music blared out from one of the rooms. It was one of Beth's favourites, The Platters singing 'Only You' and her spirits lifted as she placed her coat on top of a pile in one of the bedrooms. Sylvia had hardly spoken on the journey, and flounced off shrieking with delight as she saw someone she knew.

Beth went downstairs and stood inside the large packed room, where the carpet had been rolled back for dancing. The air was full of cigarette smoke and a boy dressed in a Teddy Boy suit suddenly caught her arm and then she was in the middle of a group of dancers, her partner hardly glancing in her direction, his eyes glazed as he bopped away. When the record finished he muttered, "Thanks, babe," and lurched off, leaving Beth standing in the middle of the floor.

"Charming!" she thought, and then saw the makeshift bar in one corner crowded with bottles of whisky and gin, with several crates of beer at one side.

Even though the party was in its early stages a few people were already the worse for drink, and Beth groaned inwardly. Her eyes searched for Nigel. If things got out of hand, she wanted to ask him what time the last bus went, just in case Barry and Pete had too much to drink.

She eventually found him, only to be whirled on the floor and told not to worry.

"I'll see you get home all right," he said, his hand playing with the back of her bra.

"Like hell, you will," she decided, feeling relieved when the music finished. She did meet lots of new people, but soon tired of her partners' beery leers and whisky-laden breath. Was there no one in this room who hadn't been hitting the bottle? The smoky atmosphere and hectic dancing made her thirsty and she went over to a long table at one end of the room where refreshments were laid out. In the middle was a large silver bowl with fruit floating on top of a pale pink liquid.

"What's that?" she asked a girl next to her.

"Fruit punch. It's lovely."

"Does it have alcohol in?" Beth asked suspiciously.

"I wouldn't be drinking it if it had!"

The punchbowl was flanked by mounds of sandwiches, and plates with cheese and pineapple chunks and sausages on sticks. Reassured, Beth took a small cup, filled it and sipped cautiously. Mmm, it was cool and refreshing. This was better. She'd stay down this end of the room.

After that she relaxed and began to enjoy herself. She didn't have to worry about getting home. Barry had told her it wasn't his scene, so he was going to visit a friend nearby.

"Don't worry. I'll be back about half-past eleven."

She danced every dance, twirling in the middle of the crowd of jostling couples, returning thankfully several times for a drink of the refreshing punch, which seemed to be endlessly replenished. As the evening progressed, several of the couples began smooching, and she wandered back to the table suddenly feeling dizzy. She blinked to try to clear her head and, realising that she'd have to spend a penny quickly, headed for the lavatory, finding to her horror that her legs didn't seem to want to obey her and she stumbled as she began to climb the stairs.

"You too! Some idiot spiked the damn punch!" It was the girl she'd spoken to earlier, on her way down the stairs clinging on to the banister, and looking distinctly green. "I'm off home," she muttered thickly. "I only live down the road."

Beth managed to get to the top of the stairs and into the lavatory, sitting sprawled on the seat, her head swimming. She sat there for several minutes, her face in her hands, and then as someone pounded the door, pulled herself up and wobbled out on to the landing. She felt dreadful. All she wanted to do was lie down. There was no way she could go downstairs. Staggering, she turned a handle and found herself inside a cool dark room and like a homing pigeon headed for the bed, collapsing heavily on top of the silken eiderdown. If she could only rest her dizzy and heavy head for a few minutes . . .

But she wasn't to rest for long, for suddenly the house was full of noise and shouting, with heavy feet stomping up the stairs.

"Clear off, you bloody gatecrashers," someone shouted. There was the sound of breaking glass and then, hazily, she was aware of the door opening and three youths swaying in the doorway. For a few seconds she thought she was hallucinating, and then dimly realised they were in fancy dress as masked Lone Rangers.

"What have we here, all ready and waiting!" one slurred. "Didn't he turn up then? Well, we can't disappoint the little lady, can we, chaps!"

Beth peered at them foggily. If only they'd keep still. Struggling, she tried to sit up but one of them leapt on to the bed holding down her shoulders.

"Heigh-ho, Silver!" the other two shouted. "It looks like your lucky night!" They guffawed with laughter.

Beth's head was trying to keep pace with the movement of the ceiling which was dipping and swaying, the face above her blurring and moving. She tried to speak but her tongue clove to the roof of her mouth.

"I think she's drunk! Come on. Let's leave him to it!"

They left, closing the door and leaving Beth in almost total darkness with the masked stranger lying heavily on top of her. A scream gurgled in her throat but he put a sweaty hand over her mouth, pinning her down as he fumbled clumsily with the buttons on her blouse. She struggled and twisted, sour bile rising in her throat. He gave up the struggle with the tiny buttons and lowering his hand roughly lifted her skirt, and to her horror grabbed her knickers and dragged them down to her ankles. She clutched at his face and dragged her nails down his cheek, digging them in as far as she could, but nothing would stop him. Her arms flailed wildly and she beat him on the back, and then pushed hard at his chest, but his suffocating body was solid and felt like a lead weight. Grabbing his hair she yanked it, tears of frustration and despair beginning to rain down her face.

"Get off me!" her mind screamed. His hand still squashed her mouth and she could hardly breathe, feeling sick with fear, and then with pain and her body was splitting in two while in the distance she could hear the plaintive voice of Dickie Valentine. Suddenly the heavily breathing youth sagged and rolled awkwardly off her, and Beth was aware of a sore wetness between her legs. She retched, leaning over the side of the bed, vomiting on the floor, and remained there, her head lolling down, the full horror of what had just occurred overwhelming her. She wasn't aware of her attacker leaving, but when she struggled off the bed he'd gone. The room was empty except for herself and the disgusting mess on the floor.

She stumbled along the landing and into the bathroom, tearing off sheets of lavatory paper and scrubbing at the stickiness between her thighs. Taking a bunch of the paper she returned to the bedroom and, her head spinning as she bent down, cleaned up the mess she'd made, flushing it down the lavatory pan. Rinsing her face and mouth, she leaned against the sink with trembling legs and looked at her watch. It was twenty past eleven. Then the sickening realisation hit her that she had no idea who the youth was; she hadn't even seen his face or heard his voice. He'd never spoken, not once! Oh God, what should she do? Waves of shame and humiliation swept over her, but her head hurt so much she couldn't think straight and her mind began to draw down a curtain.

All she wanted to do was to get back to Minsden without anyone knowing.

True to his word, Barry was there on time, and Beth crept quietly down the stairs, out of the house and into the car.

"The other two are staying the night," he told her. "I hear there was some trouble with a crowd of gatecrashers in fancy dress!"

"Yes, there was," Beth said wearily.

Barry talked all the way home, but she never knew what he said. She thanked him politely, and then, opening the gate, forced her trembling legs to walk slowly up the side path to the sanctuary of home.

Chapter 6

Lying huddled under the blankets Beth stared despondently at her bedroom wall. It was a week since the night of the party, and the burden of her shameful secret pressed heavily upon her. She longed to confide in Rose, she wanted to feel her mother's arms around her, to weep on her shoulder. But the thought of Rose's deep shock and distress deterred her. How could she inflict more misery on her mother after all she'd suffered over recent months, just to relieve her own feelings? What purpose would it serve? Nothing could undo the damage. She'd been tempted to confide in Valerie, but humiliation and pride held her back. Besides, there was always the chance that she'd tell her own mother or even Gordon. Beth couldn't bear the thought of people knowing of the horror of that night. She still felt soiled and dirty. Damaged goods, that's what I am, she thought tearfully, and no one can turn back the clock.

Downstairs, Rose bustled about preparing the Sunday dinner. She'd told Beth to have a lie-in and miss Mass this week. The girl looked so peaky she hoped she hadn't caught tonsillitis from Valerie. She'd make her a nourishing egg custard and give her a call when *Two-Way Family Favourites* came on the wireless.

Perhaps going down to help Granny Platt pack this afternoon would buck her up. Just fancy, going to New Zealand for a visit at her age! When the letter and money for the ticket had arrived from Cyril, Rose hadn't really believed her mother would go. She'd never been further than Blackpool in her life, but she seemed to have taken on a new lease of life with the excitement of it all, and tomorrow was the big day.

"Are you all right, lass?" Granny Platt's shrewd old eyes swept over Beth's pale face as she helped to strap down the suitcases.

Beth hesitated. If there was one person she could have told it would have been Granny, but not as things were. This was a once-in-a-lifetime opportunity and how could she spoil her trip?

"I'm fine. I just think I'm coming down with a cold."

Wandering into the tiny scullery, Beth lifted the kettle on to the gas hob. It was chilly and dark. Her gran still clung to the old-fashioned green and brown paint, while the uneven stone floor cheaply covered with cracked lino did nothing to provide warmth. The only comfort was an offcut of shabby carpet before the brown chipped sink. There wasn't even a bathroom, just the tin bath hanging out in the yard. She thought of the American dream kitchens she saw at the pictures with refrigerators and gleaming fitments, and wondered whether Uncle Cyril lived anywhere like that in New Zealand. Gazing out of the tiny window at the grey slated roofs wet with rain, Beth only knew that she wanted more out of life, and as her dad had said, the only way was through education. At least when she got back to school tomorrow and became immersed in her books, it might stop her from dwelling on her ordeal. If she didn't stop thinking about it she'd go mad!

Things seemed very flat once Granny Platt had gone, but somehow Rose and Beth got through that first Christmas. The house was quiet and empty, just themselves and Grandma Sherwin. They went to Midnight Mass, finding some comfort in the simple beauty of the crib and the sound of familiar carols, voices lifting with joy at the celebration of Christ's birth. As they walked home along the frosty pavements, each was preoccupied with her own thoughts, Rose thinking of the previous year when her hand had been tucked cosily into Harry's arm, and Beth wretchedly conscious that her period was three weeks late.

When she still hadn't 'come on' for the third time, she went to the library, sick with worry. The only information she'd been able to glean from *The Woman's Home Doctor* which Rose kept in the bureau, had said that sometimes periods could cease for a while after shock but she needed to be sure. She consoled herself that she hadn't been sick in the mornings, apparently the other major symptom of pregnancy, and surely it couldn't happen after just one time?

Sitting huddled in a corner poring over diagrams and detailed descriptions of the reproductive cycle and gynaecological problems, her heart sank when she saw that morning sickness only affected a certain percentage of women. Then, in the next paragraph she read of breast changes which occurred and, crouching forwards, surreptitiously slid her hand into her coat, undoing the buttons on her blouse and gingerly feeling the area around the nipple. It was hard, exactly as was described. Certainly her breasts were fuller, although she'd hoped that was normal development, but lately they were tender and tingly just as it said on the page. Oh, please God, no, don't let it be true. She couldn't be going to have a baby, she just couldn't! Panic rose in her throat, and in a daze she gathered up the books and returned them to the counter.

It was snowing when she went outside, and she trudged home thankful she was wearing her bootees. The wind whipped around her face stinging it with icy flakes but she hardly felt the pain. What on earth was she going to do?

It was not until a month later that she and Valerie saw Nigel again. They'd gone to Trentham Gardens on Saturday night as usual, Valerie blissfully unaware of the trauma in Beth's life.

"Hi, Nigel, long time no see!" called Valerie.

"No, I've been away on a course. I haven't seen you since the party, Beth. Did you enjoy it?"

"Yes, until the gatecrashers arrived!" Beth said shortly.

"You didn't tell me there were gatecrashers?" complained Valerie.

"Yeah, boozed up to the eyeballs, all dressed as Lone Rangers. Smashed our front window they did – my parents went wild."

Beth stared at him.

"How many gatecrashers were there?"

"Search me! Funny fancy dress I call it – you'd have thought there'd have been at least a few Roy Rogers or something."

"Well, how many Lone Rangers did you see?" Beth persisted.

"How do I know? Five or six. They came in two cars, glory knows where from. I'd like to know how they heard about it – they ruined the whole party."

"You mean you still don't know who they were?"

"I was too busy booting them out to ask for introductions. Why?"

"Oh, no particular reason," she said tightly.

Nigel asked Valerie to dance, and Beth sank down into a chair. It was even worse than she'd thought. It would be futile to try and trace him. After all, he was hardly going to own up to raping her and she couldn't identify him. It was hopeless. The whole thing was a complete mess.

By the beginning of the summer term, Beth was still in a quandary. She was now in her sixth month and she knew she wouldn't be able to keep her condition secret much longer. At school, her hated gymslip had proved a boon. Simply by loosening the belt she could disguise her thickening waist. Fashion too had smiled upon her: Sloppy Joe's were all the rage, so wearing Gordon's old sweaters hadn't caused any comment. She laundered her own underwear at certain times of the month, and had continued to write sanitary towels on the shopping list, so Rose was completely without suspicion. Beth knew however, that now the warm weather was coming she wouldn't be able to hide her rapidly growing bulge. She needed advice and soon, and frantically searched her mind for someone to help her. There was Mrs Ward – she knew the plump and kindly widow would prove a staunch friend, but to confide in a neighbour and not her own mother would be disloyal to Rose. No, that wouldn't do at all – besides she was too ashamed. Night after night she lay awake clammy with anxiety and fear for the future, and then one morning awoke calm and determined. There was only one answer.

"Father, forgive me for I have sinned." Beth knelt in the dim confessional, her eyes gazing steadfastly at the mesh grill. "It is six months since my last confession, and I accuse myself of these sins."

She listed her usual ones of forgetting her morning and evening prayers, of selfishness, of allowing her attention to wander during Mass, and . . .

"Yes, my child?"

Beth faltered, and then, "I'm going to have a baby, Father, and I'm not married," she whispered.

The relief of having spoken the fateful words was overwhelming, and she found her eyes filling with tears. She brushed them away and waited.

"How long have you been having this relationship?"

"I haven't. I mean . . ." Mortified with embarrassment,

Beth haltingly confessed the whole sorry tale, finishing with, "I was so stupid, Father."

"Well, you're not the first, Beth."

Hearing her sharp intake of breath, he said, "Now you don't suppose after listening to your confession all these years that I don't know your voice? As I see it, child, you're more sinned against than the sinner. Tell me, are you the last for confession?"

"Yes, Father."

"Right. Well, it's me housekeeper's day off, so why don't you come to the presbytery and we'll have a little talk? Make a good act of contrition now."

Beth bent her head and prayed earnestly, receiving the priest's absolution and blessing, and with it a sense of release.

"Have you told your mother?" Father O'Neill asked, as he settled Beth into an armchair in the book-lined study.

"No, Father, and I don't want her to know," Beth said sharply.

"Rose is a good woman. She'd stand by you!" he said quietly.

"I know that, but how could I do it to her? She'd never get over the shame, and look how many sacrifices she's made for me. You know how much she values her self-respect, Father – it's all she's got left. Then there's Grandma Sherwin. She's supported me at school, you know, and now she's got a weak heart. No one knows only you, and I told you in confession so –" her voice rose hysterically.

"Now calm down," he soothed her. "You know I can never betray the sanctity of the confessional. Have you thought about when the baby's born?"

"I've thought of nothing else!" she said miserably. "Even if I did tell Mum, what sort of life could I give it, illegitimate, with no father and a mother still at school? Where would the money come from to keep it, and even though it wouldn't be the child's fault, it would carry my shame – you know how cruel people can be! No, it's best if it's adopted, but oh, I don't know what to do!"

"Hmm." The elderly priest removed his spectacles, polished them, and then perching them on the end of his nose leaned forward, patting Beth's hand. "You go on home now. Leave it with me and I'll see what I can come up with. No promises mind, but two heads are better than one."

Beth stood up to go.

"And Beth, don't let yourself get burdened down with guilt. Don't let this ruin your life. As I said, you're more sinned against than sinner. Your only mistake was lack of judgement. Life serves us all hard knocks at times and it's how we cope with them that's important. God bless now, and try not to worry."

Beth walked home feeling better than she had for months. Undoubtedly there were difficult days ahead, but she was determined to protect Rose at all costs. It was her problem and with God's grace she'd cope with it alone.

A week later, Rose was on her knees cleaning the oven when a sharp knock came at the back door and Father O'Neill entered.

"Say one for me while you're at it, Rose," he joked.

Flustered, she jumped up, wiping her hands on her apron.

"Father! Come on in. Would you like a cup of tea?"

"Now how did you know that's what I came for?" he smiled, and going through to the tiny living-room greeted Beth, who was polishing the brass ornaments and ruefully held up her blackened fingers.

"Carry on with the good work. I'll not be keeping you long," he said, with a reassuring smile.

Beth continued her task with downcast eyes, anxiously wondering what was coming next.

"Ah, thank you, Rose! You'll be joining me now? I'd like a word."

Rose brought in tea for herself and Beth, and sat down apprehensively, raking her mind for any missed Masses or neglect of her Easter duties.

She waited.

"It's like this, Rose. I'd like you to do me a favour. I know it's a lot to ask but do you think you could spare Beth for the summer?"

At her look of surprise and consternation, he held up a hand.

"Let me explain, now. There's an old priest friend of mine in Westbourne, on the south coast, and he's not too well. He's been told he's to have a few months' complete rest. Now how can a man rest with nothing to occupy him? He's a great man for literature, do you see, and his eyesight's failing. Well, I thought of our scholar, Beth here!" He paused and Rose looked at him warily.

Father O'Neill glanced at Beth who was sitting tensely on the edge of her chair.

"Now, as I see it, if you could spare her to go down for the summer, the trip could benefit them both. Beth could read to him. He's got a vast collection of books and a fine brain – it would help develop her mind. A bit of sea air wouldn't go amiss either – she's been looking a bit peaky recently."

"Too much studying," Rose said defensively.

She looked at Beth, whose eyes were shining with enthusiasm.

"When would you want her to go?"

"As soon as she can, next week if possible."

"But what about school?" she objected.

"Oh, we're only doing private study now. It's so

near the end of term – I can just as easily do it there," Beth said eagerly.

Rose looked at her. "Do you want to go, Beth?"

Beth knew she'd have to tread carefully. She didn't want Rose to feel she was anxious to get away.

"It seems such an opportunity, what with the books and everything, but what about you, would you be all right on your own?"

"Oh, don't worry about me. I'm sure I'll survive!"

Beth felt helpless. She knew Rose would miss her dreadfully – she wouldn't even have Granny Platt for company. The initial visit of three months to New Zealand had stretched to six, and there was still no word of her coming home.

"What about your job at Woolworth's? You'll miss the money?" Rose said anxiously.

"Come on now, Rose. You don't suppose I'd be asking the girl to do this for nothing!" Father O'Neill protested. "Sure, it won't be a fortune, but she'll have her bed and board, and a bit besides."

Beth looked at him with grateful relief.

"But there's your Saturday job at the shoeshop – you can't expect them to keep that for you!"

"I'm not bothered. I wanted a change anyway."

Rose looked at them both and sighed. Funny how things came out of the blue. It would be a long empty summer, but Beth was right. It was a good opportunity.

It'd broaden her outlook as well. Harry would have been all for it, she knew that.

"Well, if you want to go, Beth, it's fine with me!"

"Oh, thanks, Mum!" Beth jumped up and hugged her, then turned to the priest and said,

"What do I do now?"

"Come back to the presbytery with me and we'll finalise the details. Thank you for the tea, Rose, and don't worry about her. She'll be well looked after."

As they walked up the hill to the church, Beth mentally gave thanks for what she saw as her deliverance. Father O'Neill told her that arrangements had been made for her to enter a mother and baby home when she went into labour.

"In the meantime, Beth, it's exactly as I said. My old friend is in need of someone to act as, well, a companion, shall we say? He's been very down since his last operation, and I see this visit as beneficial to both of you."

"I can't tell you how grateful I am, Father."

"Yes, well, I can't say I enjoyed withholding the truth from your mother, but as you told me your problem in the confessional, me lips are sealed. It's not always an easy life, being a priest, you know!"

"No, Father."

The next days were busily spent in preparation and at last Beth closed Mrs Ward's shabby case.

"I don't know why we don't save up and buy a case!" she said.

"What with?" Rose replied. "You know what I say, why buy when you can borrow!"

"Yes, but if everyone did that, no one would have anything to lend!"

Rose bristled.

"Now you can get off your high horse, lady. Who does Mrs Ward come to when she wants to borrow a stepladder and wallpaper brush? Tell me that!"

The prospect of Beth having to change trains in London of all places worried Rose.

"It's a good job it's not winter or you wouldn't have gone! Just remember 4,000 people died down there in that smog a couple of years ago."

"Well, there won't be any smog in May, Mum. Anyway they're bringing in a Clean Air Act next year."

"Aye, I'll believe it when I see it!" Rose, like all women in the Potteries, fought a daily battle against smuts of soot, watching which way the wind blew before daring to hang out white washing. The combination of smoke from domestic coal fires and bottle kilns made housework doubly hard.

"How will you cope with that Underground?" she asked anxiously.

"I've got a map and a tongue in my head. Honestly,

Mum I'll be eighteen next year. Don't worry. I'll be perfectly all right."

"Well, make sure you sit in a carriage where there are other women, and don't talk to any men!" Rose warned.

The damage is already done, if only you knew! Beth thought miserably.

Chapter 7

The day she left was warm and sunny, and Beth stood alone on the platform at Stoke station feeling relieved but apprehensive. She wished Rose had been able to come to see her off, but it would have meant losing her bonus, and money was much too tight to risk that. Her train fare had been provided, and the priest's housekeeper was going to meet her at the other end.

Arriving at Euston, she stood for a few moments bewildered in the middle of the bustling crowds, and then purposefully set out to negotiate the Underground, soon finding the Victoria Line, where she felt at first alarm and then exhilaration as the tube train hurtled along beneath the capital.

She caught her connection without any problem and, arriving punctually at Westbourne station, stood by the clock scanning the platform. A small thin woman wearing a brown felt hat hurried towards her.

"Mrs Flanagan?" she queried.

"I am that, and you must be Beth. Well, come along now. There's a bus due any minute."

She almost ran out of the station, and Beth followed, awkwardly carrying the suitcase. They just managed to clamber on the bus as it drew away.

"Did you have a good journey?" Mrs Flanagan asked.

"Yes, thank you." Beth felt shy, wondering just how much the housekeeper knew about her.

The older woman looked at her curiously. "When's the baby due? Don't look so startled – if you're going to be part of the household you'll have to get used to my plain speaking."

"The middle of August," Beth replied, her cheeks hot with embarrassment.

"And you're keeping well, lass?" Her tone, though brisk, was kindly.

"Yes, I am, thank you."

"Well, I understand you haven't seen a doctor yet, so we'll have you checked over at the Home once you've settled in. I'll have you know that if you can keep that ould devil in good humour, you'll be most welcome."

Beth's look of shock at the irreverent reference to Father Murphy brought a peal of laughter.

"He's a good man but a saint he is not, and he's driving me up the wall so he is, lying there with nothing to do but complain. 'Tis only his books keep him civil so now you're here I'm hoping it's a bit of peace I'll be getting. Here's our stop now. Let me give you a hand with that case."

Beth found herself warming to the small Irishwoman with her tightly permed greying hair and twinkling blue eyes. The torrent of words which tripped off her tongue had a lilt and music which robbed them of any sting and, weary after her journey, she began to hope that she'd found an ally.

The presbytery was a pre-war detached house with two large bay windows overlooking the busy main road. The Catholic church was adjacent, a small modern building fronted by a green lawn.

Mrs Flanagan led the way into the kitchen.

"You'll be needing a cup of tea, I don't doubt. Sit yourself down now."

"Er, could you tell me . . ."

"Aren't I the stupid one! In your condition it'll be the first thing you'll need. Along the corridor, first on the left."

When Beth returned she was grateful to find a generous piece of slab cake waiting for her, and after a refreshing cup of tea she asked, "When do I meet Father Murphy?"

"Oh, let him wait till you've unpacked and got yourself sorted out. Once that man has your nose in a book there'll be no holding him!"

Her room was plain but airy and clean, with a green candlewick bedspread and green patterned curtains. There was a utility chest of drawers topped by a small mirror to double as a dressing-table, and a square of brown mottled carpet on the cream linoleum. Crossing to the window, Beth looked out on the view which would greet her each morning until after the baby was born, and was delighted to see a beautiful weeping willow in the centre of a lawn, surrounded by rosebeds. Unpacking, she hung up her few clothes in the single wardrobe, placed the rest of her things in one of the drawers, and pushed the case under the bed.

She and Father Murphy took to each other like the kindred spirits they were. He asked her no questions, nor did he sit in judgement, simply informing her when they first met that she was to rest assured that she would be cared for when her time came.

He was a small rotund man, his white hair springing like a halo around his pink head. She soon learned that he was much loved by his parishioners, whom he referred to as his 'flock'. His assistant, Father Cotton, was in his early thirties, a tall, bespectacled, serious man, who treated Beth with distant courtesy.

A week after her arrival Beth attended her first appointment at the Home. She found the medical examination intensely embarrassing and uncomfortable.

"Just relax!" the doctor said impatiently.

Relax, she thought, with some stranger poking and probing you in unmentionable places! I'd like to see you relax!

"You're lucky. Everything is proceeding normally, but you really should have seen a doctor before this!" he reprimanded her, as he helped her off the bed.

"Sorry," she muttered.

"Right, well we'll check you over in a month's time. Next!"

Relieved to have the ordeal over, Beth wandered back along the seafront. Westbourne was a quiet little town, and she was unlikely to bump into anyone from home even when Wakes week arrived. If people ventured as far as the south coast, they usually chose one of the larger resorts such as Bournemouth or Eastbourne, and there was no chance of Rose visiting. The fare alone would be prohibitive and then there would be the expense of accommodation. Coming across a market she browsed around the stalls and bought two flowered maternity smocks and some white baby wool. Mrs Flanagan had told her that she'd be able to put together a layette from jumble donated to the church, but she wanted the baby to have at least one brand new matinee jacket.

As her pregnancy progressed she found it difficult to maintain her careful detachment from the child she was carrying. The baby constantly reminded her of its presence, its vigorous kicking often startling her as she sat in the quiet study reading to Father Murphy as he lay covered with a tartan rug on the old leather sofa.

The hours she spent with the priest were a revelation. She'd thought she was fairly well read, but soon became aware of the paucity of her education as he introduced her to *Pilgrim's Progress*, and authors such as Teilhard de Chardin, whose revolutionary theories on Catholicism they would debate together. The priest had a fine brain and told her he saw her mind as virgin soil, and proud he was to have the honour of planting a few seeds. They immersed themselves in Hardy, Thackeray, Galsworthy and Voltaire, and read poetry together in the long summer evenings. It was a time for Beth not only of intellectual stimulation but also one of quiet preparation for the inevitable emotional upheaval ahead.

It was the beginning of August, while she was writing her weekly letter to Rose, that Beth became aware of the dull pain low in her back. The first sign? It couldn't be – she wasn't due for another week. Several minutes later she felt it again, and then was suddenly bent double as a pain in her abdomen pierced like a knife. Swiftly, she packed her few belongings and then went out to the landing and called, “Mrs Flanagan, Mrs Flanagan!”

“What is it?”

“I think the baby’s starting.”

“Merciful heavens!” Calling to Father Cotton to get the car out, Mrs Flanagan came running up the stairs.

Beth stood facing her, already dressed in her coat, outwardly calm but inside feeling like a frightened child. She was sad also, to leave this ordered household where she’d been so happy.

“Now then, lass, you’ll be fine. Give me your case now, and I’ll come along with you.”

“No, Mrs Flanagan, I’ll manage. You wouldn’t want to show favouritism now. would you?” Beth knew the church had close connections with the Home. “I’ll let you know how I go on.” Her eyes wet, she hugged the kindly housekeeper and walking slowly down the stairs met Father Murphy, who’d struggled into the hall with the aid of his walking-stick.

“God bless you, child,” he said, his rheumy eyes shining with warmth.

Six hours later, Beth lay in the high bed, waves of excruciating pain sweeping over her body, feeling more lonely than she’d ever felt in her life. One hint that she could contact Rose and her resolve might have faltered. But fortunately that hint never came, and she put all her energies into delivering both the child and herself from the nightmare of the past nine months.

"Come on now. You've been a very brave girl. We're nearly there. I can see the head! Now push!" encouraged the nurse, and Beth pushed until she thought the veins in her head would burst. "And again, good girl, a big push now!"

Just when she thought she couldn't bear any more, there was a heavy slither and the baby was out.

Beth lay back exhausted, her eyes closed against her weak tears.

"You have a daughter, Beth."

The nurse placed the warm bundle in her arms, saying softly, "She's a fine healthy baby, seven and a half pound."

Beth looked down at the scrap of humanity nestling against her and then the baby opened her eyes and from that moment she was lost in wonder. She tentatively put her finger against the tiny fist which opened and grasped her tightly, the blue eyes meeting hers and Beth felt a surge of overwhelming love and tenderness. Gently, she opened the blanket, marvelling at the perfection of the small rounded limbs, pearly nails and pretty shell-like ears.

"She's beautiful," she breathed.

"What are you going to call her?"

"Rosemary. Rosemary Elizabeth." Beth gently kissed her daughter's downy head. "Rose for your grandmother," she whispered, "Mary to place you in Our Lady's care, and Elizabeth for me. It's all I can give you."

Chapter 8

"I can't understand how anyone with any sense can vote Tory," argued Rose as she bustled around the kitchen.

"They can and they will at the next election if all these strikes continue. People are becoming afraid that the unions are getting too powerful," Beth retorted.

"And where would we be without the unions!" said Rose angrily, wiping down the kitchen table. "I'll tell you where, at the mercy of the bosses, that's where. If it wasn't for the unions do you think they'd pay a fair day's wage for a fair day's work? Not them, they'd still be paying us in company tokens if they could get away with it!"

"Well, with a few exceptions, I don't think pottery workers are paid a fair wage," Beth said. "I was reading only the other day about the high wages some factory workers in other parts of the country earn. Their work can't be any more skilled than some that's done on the potbanks, but from what I've seen very few reap the rewards."

"No, but the Master Potters do!" Rose said darkly. "You should see how they live! Did I ever tell you about a schoolfriend of mine, Jenny Wilson? Fourteen she was, and never very strong. The doctor said she was only to do part-time light work. Anyway, the wife of one of the Master Potters in a big house near the Park took her on. Light work! She told me on the first day she had to carry in coal, scrub stone floors and steep cellar steps, scour all the kitchen cupboards out, and goodness knows what else."

"No, you never told me," Beth said.

"Well, it's true, and all the time she was working she could smell roast beef being cooked for the family's dinner, mouthwatering she said it was, and afore she went home do you know what they gave her? A piece of bread and marge and a cup of water! She said the house was furnished fit for a queen, and that particular potbank paid the lowest wages they could get away with. God bless the unions, that's what I say. The Tories only look after their own, you mark my words!"

Hanging the damp tea towel over the door of the oven to dry, Beth nodded in agreement.

"Anyway, I'm glad to see you're looking better," Rose said. "When you got back from Westbourne you worried me, I can't help telling you. You must be the only girl who can spend three months at the seaside and come back paler then when you went. Got your head buried in books all the time, I suppose." Rose looked keenly at her daughter who was busily drying the dishes.

"Yes, I expect so." Beth's expression changed, and she looked away for a moment, her eyes shadowed, before saying, "But you should have seen Father Murphy, Mum. Honestly, I learned such a lot from him. I've never met anyone like that. Debating with him was so intellectually stimulating it was an education in itself."

"Hmm. Well, you sound to me as though you've swallowed a dictionary since you've come back," Rose laughed, secretly proud, although she hoped Beth wouldn't use all these long words among the neighbours – they'd only think she was getting above herself. She sighed – it was funny really how some people resented anyone getting on.

"Mum," Beth said quietly, "I'm coming under pressure at school to apply for either Oxford or Cambridge."

Rose went through to the living-room and sat down heavily in the shabby armchair. Beth followed her.

"I just thought you'd like to know, that's all. I've no intention of going."

"I don't see how we could afford it, Beth," Rose whispered.

"I know. Grandma told me last week that her insurance money's nearly all gone. No, I'll get my 'A' levels and then I'll get a job. Don't worry. I'll explain things to Sister Mary Veronica." Beth spoke with more confidence than she felt.

The Headmistress was horrified.

"Don't tell me a brain like yours is going to be wasted, after all your hard work too. It's a criminal waste!"

"It doesn't have to be, Sister," Beth urged. "Just because I can't follow an academic career, it doesn't mean I can't achieve anything. I've been thinking about working in the pottery industry!"

"On a potbank?" The nun's eyes widened in dismay.

"Why not? Oh, I don't mean as a lithographer or a flower-maker, I don't think I'd be any good anyway, but in management. Surely there are training opportunities? I've been doing some reading at the library and Marketing seems to be the concept of the future. I can't see any reason why a woman shouldn't do a job like that."

Sister Mary Veronica gazed reflectively at the slim attractive girl before her. Beth's quiet demeanor and fragile beauty were deceptive. She'd frequently displayed a surprising strength of character when carrying out her duties as Head Girl.

"You're sure you haven't a vocation? You'd make an excellent nun," she said hopefully.

Beth smiled. "I'm positive, Sister."

"Well, there's time yet. God works in mysterious ways."

Disappointed, not only for Beth, but at losing the credit to the school an Oxbridge scholar would have brought, the Headmistress watched Beth quietly leave the room, and then sat back in her chair, a speculative gleam in her eyes.

Over the next few months Beth plunged into her studies, using the concentration as a therapy to alleviate her despair and guilt over the loss of her child. Memories of her baby's periwinkle-blue eyes, her downy head, of the bonding between them during that first six weeks haunted her. If only she could have confided in someone, shared her grief, but Father O'Neill, who might have been able to help, had been transferred to another parish miles away. The only way she could find peace of mind was to plunge into an academic marathon.

Her reward was that her 'A' level results were outstanding and, unable to dissuade her from her chosen career, Sister Mary Veronica used her not inconsiderable local influence.

As a result, a week later, Beth waited nervously to be interviewed in the Works Manager's office of a large china-manufacturing company.

Mr Walters, a balding, middle-aged man with a gruff no-nonsense manner, flung open the door and, sitting impatiently in his chair, took off his horn-rimmed spectacles and glared at her over the expanse of his large untidy desk.

"So you're the girl with the brains, who can't afford to go to university! Well, I don't know what gun your Sister's held to the gaffer's head, but I'm supposed to give you a chance. I don't suppose you can do shorthand and typing?" he said hopefully.

Beth shook her head warily.

"Bookkeeping then?"

At her negative reply, he said resignedly, "Well, what can you do?"

Beth looked at him hopefully.

"Mr Walters, rather than an office job, I want to have a career in Marketing. As I need to gain experience of materials used in the industry, I was wondering whether there are any openings in the Purchasing Department."

"Why Marketing?" He raised his eyebrows.

"Because over the next few years I see it emerging as a separate discipline rather than part of Sales, and I think it's a field full of opportunity."

The Works Manager looked at the determined blue eyes gazing at him, with speculation.

"You seem to have done your homework! How old are you, eighteen?"

"Yes, and able to start almost immediately."

"Hold on a minute, young lady. Mr Robert said to give you an interview – I make up my own mind about whom I employ. Suppose you tell me why you think we should give you a job."

Beth took a deep breath and then spoke incisively. "Because I'm the sort of person the industry needs. My qualifications are ten 'O' levels and three excellent 'A' levels including Italian and French, which would be useful to you as I know you have a thriving export market. I possess both initiative and common sense and am not afraid of hard work. Also, all of my family have worked on potbanks, and I can identify with both the product and the people."

"Tell me more about your family and how they've been involved in the pottery industry."

He listened carefully as Beth gave details of the various potbanks where her grandparents, Rose, Harry and Gordon had been employed.

The Works Manager looked searchingly at her as he ruminated, stroking his bushy moustache, and then said, "I think we may have an opening in our Purchasing Department. I'll arrange for you to see the Purchasing

Manager and have a chat with him, and then dependent upon the outcome I'll see you again next week."

A few days later, she met Mr Turner, the Purchasing Manager, a small, wiry man, with a perpetually harassed expression.

"Let me show you around the office and introduce you to everyone," he smiled, and shaking his hand before she left, Beth felt fairly optimistic that she'd made a good impression.

Then she received a letter asking her to attend for a further interview with the Works Manager.

Mr Walters came directly to the point.

"Well, Beth, I've had a word with Mr Robert, and we're prepared to offer you a job. We'll take you on initially as a Purchasing Assistant, and a note has been made of your interest in Marketing." He went on to give details of her hours of work, salary and holiday entitlement.

Happily, she left his office and began to walk down the corridor, adrenaline coursing through her veins. She'd show them – she intended eventually to be the best Marketing Manager in the industry. She was just about to descend the creaky, wooden stairs when she heard a voice which took her back five years.

"Let me have those figures back before the end of the day."

"Yes, Mr Dawes." A bespectacled young man hurried out of an office, while Beth stood frozen on the spot. Ursula's father? She read the name on the door, Mr A Dawes, Financial Director. He must have left Beresford's to join Rushton's.

At that moment, Mr Walters walked briskly along the corridor and at the same time Ursula's father came out of his office.

"Still here?" The Works Manager paused in surprise. "Mr Dawes, let me introduce you to our new Purchasing Assistant."

"How do you do? Welcome to Rushton's." There was no sign of recognition but then, Beth rationalised, she hardly looked like that twelve-year-old schoolgirl.

"I'm pleased to meet you. I'm Beth Sherwin," she said clearly, emphasising her name and watching his eyes for any sign of reaction.

He nodded without interest, the name obviously meaning nothing to him. Good, Beth thought, she preferred it that way.

Two months after she began working, the news arrived that Gordon was, at last, coming home on leave. He'd also decided to remain in the Army.

Overjoyed at the prospect of seeing her son, but worried and apprehensive about the implications of the Suez crisis, Rose was slightly miffed that Valerie had heard first. Ever since he'd been posted to Cyprus, the young couple had written copious letters, and over the two years' separation, romance had blossomed. Now a pretty, blonde nineteen year-old, Valerie was adamant.

"We know what we want," she confided in Beth. "We want to get married, as soon as possible."

"But you only went out with him a couple of times before he went away – how do you know you'll both feel the same?" Beth protested, looking anxiously at her best friend. "He'll have changed and so will you."

But Valerie was supremely confident. "Just you wait and see!" she said airily.

Gordon arrived, tanned, muscular and every inch a self-possessed young man. Rose couldn't take her eyes off him as he stood before the fireplace, his presence dominating the tiny living-room.

"Gosh, Mum, it's freezing! I'd forgotten how cold it can get here!" He rubbed his hands together. "How about a decent cup of tea, and then you can tell me all the news."

But after a couple of hours, he was restlessly pacing up and down.

"I've told you, Valerie doesn't get home from work until six o'clock," Rose said, her fingers tracing with pleasure the hand-embroidery and lace on his gift of a linen tablecloth.

Gordon grinned sheepishly, but at half past five he put on his khaki greatcoat and went down to wait at the bus stop.

Rose stood at the side of the window, hidden by the curtain, remembering Granny Platt's words: "They're very young. Just keep your fingers crossed no one's heart gets broken."

She crossed them, and then saw the young couple turn the corner. One look at their shining faces was enough and she felt an enormous sense of relief and gratitude. Please God, she prayed, let these young people have a chance. Don't let there be another war!

Gordon's leave was overshadowed by anxiety over the invasion of Egypt by British, French and Israeli forces, with its resultant international condemnation. Terrified that Gordon would become involved, Rose prayed daily to Our Lady until the crisis in the Suez gradually eased.

"I think Eden will have to resign over the Government's handling of the whole business," Beth forecast correctly.

By the time Gordon returned to his barracks at Lichfield, he and Valerie were engaged and planning to marry as soon as possible.

"I want you to stop your pay allotment," Rose told him. "I've been more than grateful for it ever since your dad died, but now that Beth's working, we can manage."

The wedding took place the following Easter, with Beth a proud bridesmaid in peach taffeta. Waving the happy couple off at the railway station prior to their honeymoon in Blackpool, she envied their uncomplicated happiness. Not for them the burden of an untold shameful secret. She turned away sadly, aware that without Valerie she was going to feel even more alone.

Chapter 9

Over the next few years, Beth immersed herself in her career, and sponsored by Rushton's attended a sandwich course at the North Staffs Technical College where she gained the extra qualifications she needed. She also underwent an intensive practical training on the potbank, spending time in the various shops observing the different processes, knowing that she needed both to understand and be knowledgeable about the technical aspects of china manufacture. It was at these times that Beth really felt part of the creativity and bustle of the potbank, and in some ways she felt she belonged. Working in the Decorating shops, the pungent smell of turpentine was a familiar one, as Rose usually still wore her flowered wrap-around overall when she came home from work.

Then there was the Packing house. As she watched the two men packing ware into large crates, their hands swiftly interleaving the protective coarse straw, her nostrils would wrinkle at the rank odour which she remembered lingering on Harry's brown overalls. If she closed her eyes, she could almost hear Rose's voice saying sharply, "Take those overalls off and shake out the straw, before you come into the house!"

Looking at the calloused hands of the packers Beth remembered how she used to ease straw splinters from her dad's sore hands. The two men sitting on their wooden stools were brothers working together, and never used their Christian names, always referring to each other as 'our youth'. It was quite usual to find members of the same family employed on a potbank, just as in previous generations.

She also studied designs and shapes, worked for several weeks in every office, and just before her twenty-fourth birthday was appointed Assistant in the Marketing Department.

A part of her job she particularly enjoyed was conducting visitors around the factory, and one cold day in October found her giving a guided tour to a group of Americans.

"The history of pottery goes back 10,000 years when man found that clay could be moulded, dried and hardened, and about 6,000 years ago small vessels were glazed from a recipe of sand, seaweed and chalk," she explained as the small group gathered around a thrower, watching in admiration the dexterity of his hands shaping the clay on his wheel.

Her voice tailed off, feeling that someone was watching her and she glanced up to meet the eyes of a tall young man standing in the doorway. Immaculately dressed in a plain grey suit, he indicated with a wave of his hand that she should continue the tour.

Beth frowned, irritated by what she saw as an arrogant gesture from the stranger. Then deciding that perhaps he was a latecomer to the group, she was about to go over to him when she became aware of covert glances and sly nudges among some of the workers.

"It's Mr Michael!" The word was swiftly passed around and a buzz of conversation erupted. For a split second Beth was puzzled, and then illumination struck her. So, the son and heir had returned at last! Well, that would please Mr Robert. Most of the potbanks were family businesses, the owners known as Master Potters, and Rushton's was no exception. It was the female employees' considered opinion that Mr Michael, the eldest son, was a 'bobby-dazzler," but Beth had never seen him, his infrequent visits to the potbank having always coincided with her days at the

Technical College. 'Bobby-dazzler' was a fair description, she thought reluctantly, though he was probably conceited. In her experience handsome men always were. Over the past few years, he'd spent much of his time in Milan and Frankfurt setting up distribution networks but now that these were running successfully under his younger brother, James, there had been rumours that he was about to return to the parent company.

Flushing, acutely aware of his scrutiny, Beth continued.

"With flatware, the shaping is made easier by a plaster mould on which iron templates called jiggers are guided by hands, pressing out the plates and saucers on the flat mould, although this process is changing as mechanisation is introduced."

She ushered the group of businessmen along to the Casting Shop, answering fluently their technical questions, and introducing them to one of the cup handlers who was a long-service employee. She felt uncomfortably conscious that she was being assessed, as the owner's son tagged along with the group, always standing a little to one side and listening intently to her well-practised explanations.

For once she watched with relief as the coach taking the visitors to the railway station drew away, and turning found her onlooker waiting patiently.

"I'm Michael Rushton. I thought you must be the remarkable Miss Sherwin!" he said, glancing at the badge on her lapel. "Father has told me about you."

"I don't know about the remarkable bit!" Beth smiled, shaking his proffered hand.

"I thought you handled the whole tour most commendably. How long have you been with us?"

They fell into a companionable walk back through the potbank, Beth explaining her role in the firm and the experience she'd gained.

The owner's son left her at the door to her office, and she watched him go, feeling absurdly pleased at his praise. He was undeniably attractive, with an intelligent angular face, dark curly hair, and slim yet muscular build. Assured and confident, his blue eyes keen and observant, he was a typical product of his middle-class background, she thought wryly. She judged him to be about thirty years of age and felt a faint and unfamiliar stirring of interest.

The sensation disturbed her – it was so long since she'd been even remotely attracted to anyone. Oh, she'd tried. After she'd reached twenty-one without showing any interest in the opposite sex, Rose had begun to show concern. More to placate her mother than anything else, Beth had begun to accept invitations to the pictures, or dancing, or sometimes to an orchestral concert at the Victoria Hall.

She'd even gone out with Brian, whom she'd met at the Tec, for as long as two months, but although she liked him, the moment he wanted more than a goodnight kiss and one night began to indulge in a heavy necking session, she recoiled.

"Come on, sweetheart," he coaxed, moving his hand down to her thigh. "I won't make you do anything you don't want to."

But that was the problem. She didn't want to do anything at all. She didn't want him even to touch her. As his kisses became more and more insistent, and he tried to force open her mouth, her throat closed in panic, his rapid breathing and heavy body pressing against her reminiscent of that fateful night of the party all those years ago. Cringing beneath his caresses, she shuddered and when he began to fumble with the buttons on her blouse she pushed him away violently, snapping, "Leave me alone, Brian. Just leave me alone, damn you!"

Furious, he accused her of being a tease and leading him on, but she hadn't meant to. Aware that the rape had left her deeply disturbed, she always hoped that with time, the psychological wounds would heal. The revulsion and fear that Brian's sexual advances aroused convinced her that she was frigid and, afraid of a similar situation arising, since that time Beth had avoided male company altogether.

She preferred to go out with old schoolfriends, although as they gradually married or moved away, these opportunities were dwindling. Missing Valerie's company, she had begun to retreat into herself, finding her pleasure, as always, in books.

Now, as the days went by she found her thoughts returning to the morning of the tour, and dwelling on glimpses of the tall figure striding briskly around the potbank.

You're a fool even to think about him, she told herself. He's hardly going to be interested in a girl from your background. In any case what would be the point, the way things are? Beth thought with bitterness of the shameful incident which had scarred her life. Why couldn't her life have been straightforward, like Valerie's? But then, it was pointless expecting life to be fair or just, it never had been – anyone with a knowledge of history knew that.

But her mind wouldn't be controlled.

"Did I tell you Mr Michael's back?" she said casually to Rose, one Saturday evening.

"Yes, at least three times!" Rose remarked wryly, looking quizzically at her.

"Oh!" Beth said, gazing into the distance. "I think I'll buy a new cocktail frock for the firm's Annual Dance."

"About time," Rose reproved her. "You've worn

the same one the last two years. It's not right for someone in your position!" Rose was very proud of Beth's status, referring constantly to 'my daughter, the Assistant Manager in Marketing at Rushton's', even though Beth told her she wasn't at all important.

But Beth was miles away, wondering whether Michael would attend the Dance. She had heard on the grapevine that he was back for good, so it was a fair assumption that he would be there. She always attended the function, which was held just before Christmas, seeing it as an important cementing of industrial relations, and she knew the workers greatly enjoyed it. For many of the women the event was their only social outing, and it was looked forward to for weeks with much planning and discussion of what to wear and who to go with. Held at the local Town Hall, with a live band, streamers and balloons, it was a jolly affair and the senior staff and directors often condescended to dance with the workers, causing much gratification, embarrassment, or derision, dependent upon the individual's reaction.

Not that the Dawes lowered themselves to any such mingling. The Financial Director and his wife sat stiffly on the specially reserved table always situated halfway down the room so as not to be too near the band.

Beth thought back to the first time she'd met Mrs Dawes again. Apprehensively, she'd watched the elegant, fair-haired figure expensively dressed in black crêpe de Chine, nod and smile patronisingly to employees as she glided to her seat, where she sat for the duration of the dance, obviously considering their mere presence was honour enough.

Seeing Ursula's mother again had rewakened those feelings of hurt and betrayal she had thought long buried, but Beth was older and wiser now, and instead of allowing her emotions to gain supremacy, she channelled them into controlled dignity.

"Good evening, Mrs Dawes," she said crisply, upon being introduced by the Works Manager.

The well-remembered prominent blue eyes appraised her coolly. There was not a flicker of recognition on the flawlessly made-up face.

"Good evening. Welcome to Rushton's."

Beth was dismissed with an inclination of the head, and she breathed a sigh of relief, not unmixed with a feeling of resentment that an episode which at the time had been devastating for her hadn't caused the slightest ripple in the Dawes's household.

"We could take a trip to Manchester on the train," Rose was saying now, her fingers busy with knitting for her first grandchild due in January. "You'd have plenty of choice of frocks there. We could have a look in C&A. Oh, put the telly on, love. It's nearly time for *Dixon of Dock Green*."

Beth complied, then settled herself in an armchair in readiness for their favourite programme. She looked wistfully at the tiny garment taking shape beneath Rose's skilful fingers, remembering her own clumsy efforts before Rosemary was born. She would be six now and already at school. She wondered for the millionth time whether she was well looked after. Was she healthy, bright – above all was she happy? Beth, as always, tried to console herself that any couple whose spirit was generous enough to adopt a child would be unlikely to neglect it but the guilt and sense of loss never left her.

But all thoughts of a shopping trip to Manchester were forgotten, when at six o'clock the following morning there came a rat-a-tat at the still rarely used front door. Beth and Rose collided on the tiny landing in alarm and Rose hurried downstairs. This could only mean bad news!

It was.

"Are you Mrs Sherwin?" the young lad asked.

"I am," Rose answered apprehensively.

"Old Mrs Sherwin's bin took bad. Can yer come?"

Rose took a sharp intake of breath and then said, "Tell her we'll be there as soon as we can!" She and Beth dressed quickly and hurried through the foggy, wet streets.

"I've been expecting this!" Rose said breathlessly.

"She's never been the same since that last heart attack. I wanted her to come to stay with us but no, you know what she's like."

But it was obvious that the old lady's stubborn independence was coming to an end, as she raised her head weakly from the pillow.

"I know my time has come," she whispered. "Our Lord's been calling me these last few days, and I'll not be sorry to go. I just wanted to say something to you both. I misjudged you, Rose, when my Harry first brought you home. You've been as good, if not better, than any daughter to me and I want to thank you."

"I want to thank you, Grandma, for all you've done for me," Beth whispered, close to tears.

"Nay, you've done well, lass. Your dad would be proud." She paused, fighting for her breath.

"There's one thing I want you to have," she said weakly, clutching at Beth's hand. "In that right-hand drawer, there's a little box."

Beth went to fetch it and brought it to her.

"Go on. Open it!"

Beth gingerly opened the tiny box to find an exquisite tiny gold locket and chain.

"It's beautiful!" she breathed in bewilderment. She'd never seen Grandma Sherwin wear any jewellery.

"Aye, it is," said her grandmother, speaking slowly and with difficulty. "It was my twenty-first birthday present. I've always been too scared of losing it to wear it, but I want you to wear it, and perhaps think of me sometimes."

"Oh, I will, Grandma," Beth said brokenly.

"Don't talk, Mother. You'll only tire yourself," Rose chided, her face pale with worry.

"I shan't last the day, and I know it, so I may as well speak while I can. Now there's enough insurance to bury me and perhaps a bit left over. I want you to give that to Gordon, and anything you get for my few sticks of furniture. Promise me, mind!"

"I promise," Rose said, her throat constricting. Since Harry's death, his mother had softened and over recent years the two women had reached an understanding, the link between them being the man they had both loved. With his mother gone, Harry would seem even further away, she thought sadly.

As she'd foreseen, Grandma Sherwin died peacefully that same evening, and after the simple funeral, Rose and Beth cleared out the poky terraced house in readiness for the next tenant. There was little of any value, but they managed to get a few pounds for the few pieces of heavy old-fashioned furniture, and they found a drawer full of bedlinen, neatly folded and scented with lavender. Her well-worn cheap clothes smelt strongly of mothballs and, apart from a couple of drab felt hats which Granny Platt wanted, everything else went for jumble.

"Not much to show, for seventy-five years," Beth remarked sadly.

"Her generation had it tough," Rose said. "What with the slump and two World Wars, life was just a constant struggle for most people."

Taking a lingering last look at the house before she locked the door, Rose walked sombrely home beside Beth, both sheltering from the rain beneath an ancient black umbrella. As they turned the corner of their own street she said, "Didn't Valerie look well? It's a pity they couldn't have stayed longer."

"She did!" Beth agreed with a pang, remembering her friend's pride in her condition. Not for her the guilty concealment of a bulge! She carried all before her like a ship in full sail. Gordon had amused them both with his protectiveness.

"I'd begun to think we couldn't have a family – we've been trying for the last two years" Valerie had confessed to Beth, as they enjoyed a good gossip while Gordon and Rose went down to visit Granny Platt. "What about you, Beth? Is there still no man in your life?" Valerie had looked curiously at the quiet, attractive young woman sitting with her legs curled beneath her in the big armchair.

"Oh, Mr Right will come along in his own good time," Beth said lightly. "I'm much too interested in work to be bothered with men." She swiftly changed the subject. "How do you feel about the possibility of a posting to Germany?

"Fine, as long as it's after the baby's born. My dad seems to think that if it's born in Germany it'll come out wearing a moustache like Hitler. You should have heard him this morning! 'I'm having no grandchild of mine born a bloody Jerry!'" She gave a good impersonation of the small, bristly miner and Beth laughed.

"I know all Gordon's worried about is, if it's a boy, would he be able to play football for England. Honestly – men!" she exclaimed.

Rose and Beth were damp and cold when they let themselves into the house, only to find to their dismay that the fire had gone out.

"Let's call it a day and have an early night," Rose suggested, as she filled the kettle. "I'll put the hot-water bottles in the beds while you make some cocoa."

Clutching her steaming mug, Beth climbed the cold staircase to her bedroom, relieved to see that Rose had switched on the small single-bar electric fire. She quickly undressed, snuggling into her warm candlewick dressing-gown and was about to slip into bed with her cocoa, when she suddenly remembered the locket, placed carefully in her dressing-table drawer the night Grandma Sherwin died.

Sitting on the bed she took it out of the tiny box. It really was lovely. She ran her fingernail carefully around the edge, wondering whether it opened, and had regretfully decided that it didn't when she found a tiny catch and it suddenly sprang into two halves. Beth sat for a moment, her pulses racing. It was ideal, just what she needed. Going to her wardrobe, she felt under the lining paper at the back of one of the shelves, and withdrew a tiny folded piece of tissue paper.

Carefully, she took out the tiny curl of silvery baby hair and inserted it into the locket, closing the catch firmly. Placing it in readiness on the dressing-table, she got into bed and thoughtfully sipped the strong, sweet cocoa. Now she could keep the precious memento close to her, in the perfect hiding-place.

Rose noticed the locket immediately at breakfast the next morning. "That looks lovely. Does it open?"

Beth looked steadily at her, and said quietly, "No, it's just ornamental."

"Oh, that's a pity. You're looking very smart this morning. Is there something special on at work?" Rose asked, admiring Beth's tailored grey suit and emerald green blouse.

"Just a meeting," Beth answered offhandedly, not mentioning that she'd seen a memo saying that Mr Michael wished to attend.

"What are you doing today?" she asked Rose as she

put on her coat and gloves, ready to catch the 8.15 bus.

"I'm going to do that upstairs," Rose said. "I've got all behind what with the funeral and everything."

One of Beth's most prized achievements had been to persuade Rose to reduce her working hours to three days a week.

"After all," she argued, "I know I don't earn a fortune, far from it, but we could manage and you know how tired you get."

Rose, who although she wouldn't admit it was going through the 'change', knew she was right and three days it was. I know what she really needs, thought Beth, as she walked down the road to the bus stop. A twin-tub washing machine so she doesn't have to pile the washing in the shopping trolley and trail it down to the launderette in all weathers. I'll buy her one for Christmas on HP. She'll never know, and if I'm careful I can just about afford the repayments.

The meeting began promptly at ten o'clock, and taking her seat at the large table, Beth found herself directly opposite the man who had figured so largely in her thoughts. He sat impatiently tapping a pencil on his notepad, and she felt her colour rise as their eyes met briefly and he smiled in acknowledgement.

By the end of the meeting, Beth was aware that the owner's son was no fool. His mind was razor sharp, quickly recognising flaws in any argument, his comments shrewd and knowledgeable. Surprising a look of admiration in his eyes as she looked up from her notes, her pulses quickened. He's probably an inveterate flirt, she thought gloomily. In any case, she didn't know why she was wasting her time even thinking of him. You need to take care, my girl, she told herself grimly. We all know what goes on between bosses and workers and it doesn't end in marriage! One fall from grace was bad enough; two would be the height of lunacy!

Her logic, however, didn't prevent her from wanting a new dress for the Dance although she felt guilty at the thought of going out and treating herself so soon after the funeral.

"Nonsense!" Rose said briskly. "Life has to go on. Besides you've got your young life to live," and the following Saturday they returned in triumph from Manchester.

It was midnight blue with a full swirling calf-length skirt. The mandarin collar was in the height of fashion, and the shantung silk bodice accentuated the soft swell of Beth's high breasts and slim waist as though the dress was made for her. On the night of the Dance, wearing slender high-heeled silver sandals, she stood before Rose's triple mirror and knew that she had never looked better. Her dark glossy hair obediently fell in a softly curling style to her shoulders and her large blue eyes fringed by dark lashes were enhanced by the depth of colour in the rich fabric. The tiny gold locket added the perfect touch, and she felt a glow of quiet satisfaction.

That early December evening the weather was bitterly cold and several days of snowfall had left the roads and pavements icy. Beth put on her warm winter coat, grateful for the warmth of the astrakhan collar, zipped up her bootees, and carrying her dancing sandals in a string bag, gingerly made her way down the side path, along the street, and down the hill to the bus stop.

Chapter 10

Rose stood at the window, holding the curtain to one side as she watched Beth go. With a sigh she let the curtain fall back into place and going to the mantelpiece picked up a framed photograph of Harry, resplendent in his Stoke City football scarf.

"You'd have been proud of her tonight, love," she said. "She really did look like a princess, just like you used to call her." She often talked to the photo when she was alone in the house, and although she wasn't a fanciful woman, sometimes, just sometimes, she could have sworn she felt a light touch on her shoulder.

Sitting down, she took up her knitting, her spectacles halfway down her nose as she checked the pattern, knit one, purl one, slip one, pass slipped stitch over. Frowning in concentration she finished the shaping, and then as the needles clicked automatically along the rows of stocking stitch, her thoughts began, as always, to reflect upon her family.

Fortunately, Granny Platt kept in good health, still sprightly despite a touch of arthritis and she managed to come up for Sunday dinner each week. She was even planning another trip to New Zealand to see Cyril when he'd saved enough for the ticket. Tremendously proud of Beth and thrilled at the thought of being a great-grandmother, she gave Rose little cause for concern.

Gordon and Valerie were happy enough, looking forward to the next posting, and Valerie's pregnancy was proceeding normally. No, the only one Rose felt anxious about was her daughter.

Most people would think you mad to worry, she chided herself. She's got a good job, what more do you want? But the fact that Rose lacked education didn't mean she wasn't perceptive. She wasn't blind to the sadness she often detected lurking deep behind Beth's open blue eyes. The girl had never been the same since the trip to Westbourne, and Rose just couldn't put her finger on it. It was as though she went away a young schoolgirl and came home a woman. She'd been short-tempered too, which wasn't like her. She'd always had an even disposition, so long as no one 'sneeped' her, then it had been the Niagara Falls every time. She seemed to have her emotions more under control now, but still showed no sign of being interested in marrying and settling down. It just didn't seem natural. Rose sighed as she began another row. You never stopped worrying about your children no matter how old they were.

Beth joined the crowds going into the Town Hall and made her way to the Ladies' Cloakroom where she queued to leave her belongings with an attendant. The noise level was deafening as the women exclaimed over each other's outfits, already shrieking with laughter and high spirits at the thought of the evening ahead. The atmosphere was infectious and Beth felt a flutter of nervous anticipation as she joined the rest of her department at their table in the already crowded ballroom.

"*Que será, será*," the voice of the blonde female vocalist belted out the number and a chorus of voices accompanied her as couples danced around the floor. Beth smiled, humming to herself. It was good to see everyone enjoying themselves. She loved the first couple of hours of the annual 'do', before people began to let their hair down. Some of the raucous and boisterous behaviour which took place as the night wore on embarrassed her, and she usually slipped away before midnight. Beth wished sometimes that she could enjoy the earthy humour and smutty jokes which she heard daily in the factory, instead of having to conceal her innate distaste. After all, it was her choice to work on a potbank. Not that she regretted it; she found her fellow workers generous of spirit, good-humoured and fiercely loyal. Well, most of them, she thought grimly, her heart sinking as one of the warehousemen she particularly disliked came over to ask her to dance.

To refuse would give offence, so Beth stood up with the straw-headed perspiring young man facing her, his ill-fitting brown suit straining over his plump body. He smiled triumphantly, giving the thumbs-up sign to a group of his mates lounging against the wall, and clumsily steered her into the throng of dancers.

It would be a quickstep, Beth thought irritably. Ernie had the proverbial two left feet and constantly trod on her toes, vulnerable in their open-toe sandals.

"Ouch!" she exclaimed as she felt her big toenail stub against his heavy leather shoe.

Damn, I bet he's laddered my stockings, she fumed. Ernie was oblivious, being far more interested in trying to pull Beth's rigidly resisting body ever closer.

"Cut it out, Ernie!" she snapped.

He grinned. "The nobs have arrived!" he muttered, jerking his head towards the directors' table with its white cloth, flowers and bottles of spirits and mixers.

Beth's eyes searched the familiar faces, and then saw Michael. Yes, he was there, talking to . . .

She'd only caught a glimpse of his companion but the colour drained from her face in shock.

Thankful when the dance finished, she walked apprehensively back to her seat and stared intently across the room at the directors' table. The young blonde chatting animatedly to Michael was stunningly dressed in red. Her poise and confidence, the way she threw her head when she laughed! The intervening years slipped away, and Beth was transported back to the High School on that first day. There was no mistake. It was Ursula!

Well, it's not surprising, she reasoned as she danced foxtrots, waltzes and the barn dance with a succession of partners. After all, with her father a director in the firm, the family were bound to mix socially.

"Hey, Beth!" bawled Ivy, one of the spongers. "Come over 'ere. Can yer solve this bet?" One of the other women nudged her saying, "Shhh, you'll embarrass the lass."

"Aw, 'course I won't, Vera. Yer worry ter much!" grinned Ivy, taking a gulp of her gin and orange.

"Go on, then," Beth said, smiling.

"Is it true, the reason yer never bring a partner, is 'cos you're knockin off a married man?"

Beth stared at her and then began to laugh, "You what?"

"See, I told you, Ivy, you with yer big mouth!" someone said.

"Well, is it?" persisted Ivy.

Beth took a stance, holding up her right hand. "I swear, on my honour, that this is the truth, the whole truth and nothing but the truth: no, I'm not."

"Right, Ivy, I'll have a gin and lime – no, make it a double. Serves yer right. You always did have a dirty mind," chortled Vera.

"Shhh, 'ere comes Mr Michael." Ivy sat up straight, her face creasing in a grin.

"Now then, girls, I hope you're behaving yourselves," Michael teased, as he paused by their table.

"We are. How about you?" Ivy challenged impudently. "Hey, Mr Michael, why don't yer ask Beth to dance. She's just as good-lookin as that blonde you're with!"

"Ivy!" Vera said, in a shocked voice.

Beth looked sympathetically at Michael – everyone knew what Ivy was like, a rough diamond if ever there was one.

"You must be a mind-reader, Ivy," Michael bantered. "I was just about to suggest the same thing." Taking Beth's elbow, he escorted her swiftly on to the dance floor to the accompaniment of suggestive cheers.

"You don't have to," Beth protested. "Ivy put you in an awkward position."

"No, she didn't. I spoke the truth, I had come over to ask you to dance."

The band struck up and Michael groaned as the male vocalist began to belt out 'Livin' Doll'.

"Can you do this sort of thing?"

"Just watch me!" Beth laughed, her feet already moving to the rhythm. "Don't you like jive?"

"Yes, I do, but I don't know that I'm much good at it," he said, as they twisted and turned.

"Yes, you are. You're too modest. I like Cliff Richard. Do you?"

He nodded as the music reached a crescendo, making further conversation impossible. When it stopped, he made no effort to return her to her seat but said, "Mind you, I was in Liverpool a couple of weeks ago, and heard a group of four lads play their own songs in a place called The Cavern. Their first single, 'Love Me Do', got into the hit parade. Did you hear it?"

"Yes, I did. I thought it was great. I can't remember what they were called, though."

"The Beatles."

Beth laughed. "Yes, that was it."

"They spell it b-e-a-t, clever isn't it? Anyway, I reckon Cliff will have to watch out – they're going to be really big."

The next number was a waltz, the gentle music a complete contrast. Beth felt acutely conscious of Michael's hand against her waist as he held her firmly, their steps in perfect unison. She didn't want the dance to end, enjoying the unusual feeling of complete relaxation in his arms, but the music stopped and they drew to a halt in front of the directors' table.

"Thank you," she said politely, and began to turn away.

"Come and join us for a drink?" he insisted.

"Well . . ." she hesitated, but he was already moving towards the table.

"What would you like? Something alcoholic, or there's the fruit punch. That's very refreshing."

Beth eyed the jug suspiciously, and unbidden came the sickening memory of that night so many years ago.

"Honestly," he assured her. "There's no alcohol in it. Look at Mrs Bennett. She's drinking it and you know what a staunch Methodist she is!"

Beth laughed, and accepted a glass, gratefully appreciating its coolness.

"I think you know everyone, oh, except Ursula, Mr Dawes's daughter," Michael said, turning to the blonde young woman who was staring curiously at Beth.

"Oh, Ursula and I went to school together. You remember me, don't you, Ursula? Beth Sherwin?" The old resentment flared, her eyes challenging those of her former best friend.

Ursula hesitated. "Yes, of course. How are you, Beth?"

"I'm fine, and you?" Beth asked coolly.

"I'm OK, thanks. I had no idea you worked at Rushton's." Ursula spoke slowly, her tone thoughtful as her gaze swept calculatingly over Beth's face and figure. "What are you, a typist or something? Surely you don't work in the factory?"

Stung by the disdainful and patronising tone, Beth retorted sharply, "Oh, they wouldn't have someone like me. No, I clean the lavatories!"

Michael shot a surprised glance at her and said hurriedly, "Actually, she's one of our management assistants, and one with a lot of potential too. We see a great future for Beth."

"Oh, I see. In that case, if you're so clever, I don't know why you didn't go to university!" Ursula's voice was mocking, as she placed a cigarette between her crimsoned lips, inclining her head gracefully towards Michael's proffered lighter.

"I could have done, either Oxford or Cambridge but I couldn't afford it, as I'm sure you'll remember!" Beth countered. "I don't suppose you had that problem though?"

Ursula looked at her with raised eyebrows. "No, of

course not, but as it happened I chose to go to Teacher Training College instead."

Which no doubt means, thought Beth, you couldn't get into university. One up for me!

Michael cleared his throat. "Well, I hate to split you two up, but your father's trying to attract your attention, Ursula."

With some reluctance Ursula joined her father on the dance floor.

"It was getting a bit chilly there for a moment – I take it you two weren't bosom pals?" Michael commented, an amused look in his eyes.

"No," Beth answered shortly.

"Are you all right?" he asked. "Would you like to go back to your seat, or would you care to dance again? I promise not to tread on your toes, unlike one of your previous partners!" He looked pointedly at her bloodstained toe and laddered stocking.

Beth smiled. "I'd love to dance, but not if you're doing it out of duty. You've already fulfilled that role once."

"Who said anything about duty?" he murmured as they took the floor to the haunting strains of 'A String of Pearls'. Conversation didn't seem necessary as their bodies moved in perfect unison to the music. He was an excellent dancer, and Beth was aware of not a few admiring and curious glances as they circled the floor. After the dance ended, Michael escorted Beth back to his table, as though it was the most natural thing in the world for her to join his group. Beth glanced over to her own departmental table – she'd come in for some ribbing over this!

Mr Robert leaned over. "Did I hear you say you were at the same school as Ursula? I remember now – you were Head Girl, weren't you?"

Michael held up his hand in mock horror. "I can see I'll have to watch my p's and q's! I didn't know I was in such exalted company."

Beth smiled, aware of Ursula's baleful glare from the other end of the table, where she was listening with a look of utter boredom to the wife of one of the managers.

"Why don't you invite this young lady along to the New Year's party, Michael? We usually have a good evening, my dear, I'm sure you'd enjoy it."

"What a good idea, Father! How about it, Beth? Would you like to come?"

Beth floundered. She didn't really like parties. Anyway, she wouldn't know anyone there! Then her eyes met those of Michael, warm and friendly as he awaited her reply, and suddenly she knew she wanted to go.

"Thank you, yes, I'd love to," she said quietly, and then glanced at her watch, remembering that she had a taxi ordered for eleven thirty. "I must be going," she apologised. 'I've a taxi due in five minutes." She flashed a quick smile at Michael, and hurried along the edge of the dance floor back to her own table.

Picking up her bag, she bade everyone goodnight. But they weren't going to let her escape as easily as that.

"Thought you'd be too stuck up to speak to the likes of us, now you're mixing with the bosses!" and "Watch your step, Beth. Mr Michael eats little girls like you for breakfast!"

Beth laughed and calling, "Don't do anything I wouldn't do! See you on Monday!" hurried to the cloakroom. There she changed into her bootees and coat and made her way out of the Town Hall to the waiting taxi.

What she hadn't anticipated was her mother's reaction to Mr Robert's invitation.

"I don't think it's a good idea at all."

"Why on earth not?" Beth protested.

"It just doesn't do to try and mix outside your station, that's why!" Rose's lips tightened.

"I don't believe I'm hearing this. For heaven's sake, Mum, it'll be 1963 next year, not 1912! Those days have gone."

"Leopards don't change their spots! They'll

patronise you and give you lip service, but accept you, never! It's a closed shop their world, always has been and always will be."

"Are you trying to say I'm not good enough for them?"

"Good enough! You're a damn sight better than they'll ever be. What do the likes of them know about life, cushioned as they are from the moment they're born! No, lass, I'm worried as how you could get hurt, and that's the truth."

"Oh, Mum. What was the point of educating me, and my having all those elocution lessons, if I can't hold my own. In any case, it's only a party, probably a one-off – I'm not intending to move in, you know!"

"Well, just you remember what I've said, that's all."

Chapter 11

Christmas passed quietly that year. It seemed strange without Grandma Sherwin, even Granny Platt grudgingly admitting she missed her old sparring partner as they raised their glasses in a toast to 'absent friends' after their Christmas dinner. Gordon and Valerie stayed in Lichfield, just in case the baby came early, and were hoping the event would be over well before they left for Germany in the middle of January.

At work, Beth didn't see Michael until the morning of the party, when he paused in the corridor saying, "You're still coming tonight, I hope?"

"Of course." Beth smiled.

"You know the address?"

She nodded, everyone knew where the Rushtons lived. She'd never seen the house herself but, according to factory gossip, it was a cross between Buckingham Palace and the Taj Mahal!

"About eight then." Michael walked swiftly away, and she watched his tall figure turn the corner. She'd have to take two buses to get there, but that was no problem, although she begrudged the expense of a taxi home, but there was no alternative if she wanted to go.

The question of what to wear had been easy. She couldn't afford another new dress, and obviously she couldn't wear the same one she'd worn for the dance. That left her only other cocktail dress, which fortunately Michael had never seen. It was black chiffon, with a sweetheart neckline and long transparent sleeves. The skirt fell gracefully into swirling pleats, and Beth had always liked it – she felt feminine and attractive when wearing it, and was rewarded by Rose's smile of approval when she presented herself for inspection.

"Just let them find fault with that!" she declared.

Fortunately, the snow had all cleared away and the weather was dry, so Beth was saved the ignominy of arriving in sensible bootees. Poised and confident in her black patent high heels and sheer seamed nylons, she walked quickly from the bus stop along the quiet residential road and then, as she turned the corner, caught her breath in admiration at the sheer size and beauty of the house. Lights streamed from the ivy-covered windows and the long tree-lined drive was crowded with cars. It was definitely the Rushtons': 'Linden Lodge' was proclaimed clearly on the white pillars at the entrance. Her resolve faltered for a few seconds, and then she resolutely walked up to the imposing oak front door, and rang the bell.

As the door opened, a blast of warm air and noise engulfed her.

"Come on in, the more the merrier!" a fair-haired young man in his mid-twenties greeted her.

"Gosh, you're a new face! I'm Guy Hatton from next door. You're er . . ."

"Her name's Beth Sherwin, and she's definitely too good for you, old man," Michael interrupted as he suddenly appeared in the large oak-panelled hall. "Welcome, Beth. Let me take your coat."

She swiftly unbuttoned her coat. He took it and passed it on to a middle-aged woman in a black dress and apron.

"Come on through and I'll introduce you to everyone, although several you already know."

"I say, Michael, you're a dark horse," grumbled Guy as he followed them into the huge drawing-room.

Beth looked around the crowded well-proportioned room, her eyes drawn immediately to the tall Christmas tree that stood before a large bay window. Festooned and richly decorated with colourful baubles, its twinkling lights created a fairytale background to the party.

The guests were many and of various ages, although all, she suspected, from the same background. Most of the men wore dinner jackets, the women were quietly elegant or fussily dressed and bejewelled according to their taste, but all expensively so, and for the first time she understood why diamonds and rubies were coveted as the light reflected their brilliance. The scene was the epitome of affluence and security as Beth stood hesitantly by Michael's side in her three-year-old dress. She congratulated herself on her wisdom in choosing something without frills and flounces. A simple black dress was difficult to place a price tag on, although she could already see some of the women looking her over with speculation. Why do people do that, she thought with anger, as if having the money to buy expensive clothes makes you worth knowing!

"Father, you know Beth, of course," Michael exclaimed as Mr Robert came over accompanied by his wife.

"Indeed I do," he said jovially.

Michael's mother looked slightly puzzled, and then her brow cleared as she said, "Of course, you were at school with Ursula, weren't you?"

"Head Girl at the convent, no less!" Michael said.

"Ah well, Sister Mary Veronica was always an excellent judge of character. You're most welcome, my dear." She smiled, an unexpectedly sweet smile, relieving her carefully composed features.

Beth watched the silver-haired dignified woman move on to greet the next guests, and asked Michael, "How does your mother know Sister Mary Veronica?"

"Oh, they were at boarding-school together down in Sussex," he replied. "Look, I'll go and get you a drink – white wine OK?"

"Lovely." So that was how the headmistress had arranged her interview with such speed.

She glanced around the room but apart from the people who had been at the directors' table at the dance, there were no familiar faces. Ursula was there, of course, exquisitely dressed in gold lamé and seated on a burgundy leather chesterfield. She gave a low throaty laugh at the man sitting next to her and then, glancing up, saw Michael returning with Beth's drink. She rose and came over to join them.

"Hi, Beth. I'd like a drink too, Michael, if you don't mind," she said, placing her hand possessively on his arm.

"Of course. Vodka and tonic, isn't it?"

"You should know, darling."

Beth surveyed her thoughtfully over the rim of

her glass. So that was how the wind blew, or was it just that Ursula wanted to give her that impression? Anyway, the fact that Michael was being so attentive meant nothing – these people prided themselves on their good manners and social graces.

"Have you met everyone yet?" Ursula asked in a patronising tone.

"No, I've only just arrived."

Michael returned and, as Ursula took her glass, she said, "I'll take Beth and introduce her around. She doesn't want to be stuck with you all night, Michael!"

"I'm sure she doesn't," he said and, with her elbow held firmly by Ursula, Beth had no option but to embark on a round of introductions.

An hour later, wearied of apologising for her lack of knowledge of bridge and golf, of explaining that no, she hadn't any plans to ski this year, Beth began to wonder what on earth had possessed her to come. She didn't have anything in common with these people.

Then, alone for a moment, her eyes met and held those of Michael who was talking to a group of men a short distance away. He smiled, excused himself and began to make his way over to where she stood. She watched him approach. He was more attractive than ever in his well-cut dinner jacket and with sudden insight Beth knew it was no use fooling herself. For the first time in her life she was falling in love and with a man out of her class, and of whose character she knew very little. So much for her analytical brain!

"Have you had any refreshments?" he asked.

She shook her head.

"Come on, then." He led her into the spacious dining-room, where an elaborate cold buffet was attended by a fresh-faced maid and a young wine waiter.

Seeing Beth's eyes widen, Michael winked and whispered, "Hired for the evening."

She laughed, and then deciding to enjoy herself, took small portions of almost everything, only to find Michael looking at her in amusement.

"Don't they feed you at home?" he teased.

"Only on Sundays," she laughed and then tensed as Guy called them over to join himself and Ursula at a small circular table in one corner.

"Great spread, Michael, but then it always is," he said, nibbling on a chicken drumstick. "How's it going, Beth?"

"Fine." she replied, curiously tasting a smoked salmon sandwich.

"I suppose this is a bit different from your usual New Year's Eve bash," Ursula said.

"Not really," Beth answered. "It's all the same idea – out with the old and in with the new."

"I never thought to ask if there was someone you wanted to bring," Michael said. "You weren't with anyone at the dance, so I just assumed . . ."

"No, no one," Beth assured him.

"What about you, Guy? I hear you met someone on holiday?" Michael said, leaning back and sipping his wine.

"News travels fast! Yes, I'm going up to Chester tomorrow to see her, I just hope she's got my letter. Is it normal post at the moment, do you know?"

"Why don't you ask Beth?" Ursula said. "After all, her father's a postman!"

Into the silence that fell, Beth said, quietly, "My father died nine years ago."

"Oh, I'm so sorry," Michael said with concern.

Beth looked at him, seeing only warmth and friendliness, and her tension drained away. She held his gaze for a moment, and then said, "I'm sure you'll have nothing to worry about, Guy. The post goes on as usual except for New Year's Day."

There was a minute's silence and then Michael's father appeared at the door of the room.

"There's dancing in the sitting-room, but remember we want everyone in the drawing-room by five to twelve."

"Come on." Ursula seized Michael's hand, and Guy and Beth followed.

How many more rooms are there? Beth wondered, as they took the floor to the music of Glen Miller.

"*Chatanooga choo choo*," sang Guy, as he and Beth circled the floor.

"Why aren't you spending New Year's Eve with the girl in Chester?" she asked.

"Because, Beth, I've yet to convince her how fascinating I am – but it's just a question of time!" He grinned at her and she laughed.

The music stopped and, while someone went to the radiogram to change the records, he whispered, "Don't you worry about Ursula – she's been after Michael for years!"

"And what makes you think I'm interested?" Beth said.

"It's the way you look at him, my pet. Anyway, leave this to me!"

Was she really so transparent? Warily, she watched him walk across the room where, with a whisper to Michael, he took Ursula's arm and dragged her out of the room.

Michael came over laughing.

"What's going on?" she asked.

"Oh, it's just Guy up to his old tricks. He wants

Ursula to help him dress up as Old Father Time."

He held out his arms and Beth melted into them to the plaintive melody of 'Stranger on the Shore'. Neither spoke, but the electricity between them was so tangible that she could hardly breathe, and gradually Michael drew her close and rested his cheek against her hair as they slowly swayed to the music and danced together until everyone was hustled into the drawing-room to await the magic hour of midnight.

"Michael, come and get this darned wireless tuned in properly!" called his father, and Michael gave her hand a quick squeeze before hurrying across.

People crowded in and Beth found herself hemmed in a corner as the sound of Big Ben began to boom and everyone chanted the strokes to twelve. There was a cheer when Guy entered in a long white sheet and cotton-wool beard, only to slink out of the French windows, and then everyone was kissing everyone else, and suddenly, she was face to face with Michael.

They stood for a few seconds in silence, an island among the high-spirited crowd, before eyes searching hers, he gently lifted her chin and said,

"Happy New Year, Beth."

"Happy New Year, Michael."

His lips came down to meet hers, warm and firm,

and steeling herself to submit to the physical contact Beth closed her eyes, only to find to her joy that she was responding, and for the first time in her life she felt a faint and delicious stirring of desire. As they drew slowly apart, she quickly lowered her eyes feeling suddenly shy, but before they could speak, Ursula pushed her way through the throng and flung her arms around Michael.

"There you are, darling! Happy New Year," she breathed and, twining herself around him, pulled his head down to hers. Beth turned away, feeling a lurch of pain at the intimate scene, and then Guy seized her and laughingly swung her off her feet in a bear-hug.

"Happy New Year, Beth!"

She had no time to collect her incoherent thoughts as a clear tenor voice began to sing "*Should old acquaintance be forgot,*" and crossing her arms she joined everyone else in a large circle to the sentimental refrain of 'Auld Lang Syne'.

As they finished, trays of coffee and mince pies were brought in and, half an hour later, feeling tired and replete, Beth glanced at her watch.

"Don't tell me, you have a taxi coming," laughed Michael. "She's like Cinderella, Guy. She disappears near the stroke of midnight – only not by a fairy coach, by its modern equivalent."

"You'll be taking me home as usual, won't you, Michael?" Ursula flashed a triumphant glance at Beth as he nodded.

"I must get my coat," Beth said. "I'll just go and thank your parents."

"You've enjoyed it, then?" Michael's eyes sought hers and held them.

She smiled. "I've had a lovely time."

Chapter 12

Rose spat on the iron and watched with satisfaction as the bubble of saliva hissed. That was better – the dratted thing was so temperamental. She'd really like one of these new steam irons but they were too expensive. Carefully placing a damp tea towel over Beth's navy serge skirt, she pressed in the pleats and then, hanging the skirt on its hanger over the picture rail surveyed her handiwork with pride. Beth had protested, saying she could get her own clothes ready, but Rose had refused her offer. The girl had enough to do with brushing up her Italian. In any case, if her daughter was going abroad then she wanted to make sure she was well turned out.

"You're back then!" It was a statement rather than a question, as Beth burst through the back door and came into the living-room.

'Slow down, lass. You'll be ready on time. Did Father Daly sign your passport photo?"

"Yes, no problem," Beth sat down to get her breath back. "Someone's driving me to the Passport office tomorrow."

"So, what's next then?"

"I'm going to have to buy a suitcase. I can't possibly take Mrs Ward's, not this time. It's far too shabby. Anyway, don't you think it's time we had a couple of cases of our own?"

"Well, we could buy one for you to take, I suppose," Rose agreed, "but I don't need one. Mrs Ward's is good enough for where I'm likely to go."

"Oh, Mum, you don't change, do you?"

"No, and it's a good job I don't, or our money wouldn't go half so far." Rose switched off the iron, and stretched. "Pop the grill on, Beth, and do me some cheese on oatcakes – I fetched half a dozen this morning."

"OK." Then she called from the kitchen, "Do you want pickle on?"

"Yes, please," Rose replied, raising her voice. "How do you feel about flying?"

"A bit apprehensive naturally, but I'm not too nervous, at least not while I'm standing on the ground," Beth laughed.

When Michael had sent for her at the beginning of

January to discuss the Milan outlet's major publicity event, she'd thought it was merely to confirm administrative arrangements. Barbara Hartley, one of their top decorators, was to demonstrate flower painting in the china department of a major department store and Beth had already arranged her flight and accommodation. The suggestion that she should accompany her had come as a complete surprise. She was to provide liaison with the general public, her understanding of technical terminology, coupled with marketing and linguistic skills, making her the ideal candidate.

"After all," Michael had commented, "it's in the company's interests to use your potential to the full. James will be there, of course, but I shall be over myself halfway through the week, so I'll pop in to see how things are going. Don't worry. You'll enjoy it!"

Checking on the oatcakes bubbling with melted cheese, Beth reached for the jar of Branston pickle.

She remembered seeing Michael's younger brother a few times when he'd come over to the factory from Milan. Not at all like Michael in appearance, he was of a much stockier build, his open freckled face and fair hair more suited to the country than to city life. He'd been abroad now for over two years and from all accounts, had no desire to return to the Potteries particularly since his recent marriage to an Italian girl.

Discussion of the proposed visit had been the only contact between Beth and Michael since the night of the party and she'd begun to upbraid herself for reading far too much into what was after all, only a few dances and a kiss. Now, in Milan, who knew what might happen!

"Hoping to get his leg over, is he?" jeered Les Cartwright, one of the sales reps, when news of Beth's opportunity became known.

"Well, if he is, which I very much doubt, it'll be more than you've ever managed!" She hated him, with his suggestive winks and wandering hands.

"Aw, leave the girl alone, Les, for heaven's sake! You're only jealous!" Gladys, the senior typist, had snapped.

It was a good job no one knew she'd been invited to the party on New Year's Eve, Beth thought wryly as she carried in the tray to Rose.

"I've always wanted to travel," Rose said, her tone wistful.

Beth stared at her in surprise. Strangely, she had never thought of Rose having dreams and ambitions. She'd just always been there, a provider of love, meals, clean clothes and comfort. How shallow of me, she thought, all these years and I've never seen Mum as a person, an individual with her own life to live. She took a dispassionate look at the middle-aged woman seated opposite, neatly dressed in a beige jumper and blue crimplene pinafore dress. Rose was plump, but it suited her, and she had retained her good looks despite refusing to use any cosmetics apart from Pond's Vanishing Cream and a touch of lipstick. She toned down any grey hairs with cold tea, and apart from a furrow on her forehead and a few lines around her eyes, she wore her age well.

"I never knew that," she said.

"Oh, aye, I'd like to see other countries, and how foreign folk live. It always amazes me how there are so many different languages in the world. You'd have thought, wouldn't you, that we'd all have learnt to speak the same. Why should living in a different part of the world make any difference? Did you make any tea?"

"Yes." Beth went into the tiny kitchen and fetched the teapot.

"You never know, Mum, we might be able to go abroad sometime now they're bringing out these package holidays. They're supposed to be really cheap."

"Not cheap enough," Rose called, "unless me Premium Bond comes up!"

The next few days were hectic, Beth spending most of her time in the Marketing Manager's office as he gave her directives, facts, figures and some fatherly advice about avoiding bottom-pinching! Her evenings were spent reading aloud from her Italian books, relieved to find that she hadn't forgotten too much.

The morning of her departure found her ready at least half an hour before the works car was to pick her up. She'd been far too excited to sleep properly, and Rose clucked around her offering aspirins and cups of tea.

"I'll light a candle for a safe journey, before I go into work," she promised, and Beth gave her a goodbye hug.

"Thanks, Mum, but there's no need to worry. I'll be fine."

Barbara, her greying hair tightly permed especially for the trip, was already sitting primly on the back seat, her gloved hands folded on her lap.

At Heathrow they had a welcome cup of tea and then waited in the departure lounge, where Beth indulged in people-watching, fascinated to see a majestic Nigerian resplendent in traditional robes. He was the first black person she'd seen, apart from on the films.

Barbara fell asleep during the flight, leaving her free to absorb every experience, from the patchwork fields below to the wondrous clouds, and the constant bustle of the stewardesses. Her nervousness evaporated after the take-off and by the time they touched down at Linate Airport, her mood was one of keen anticipation.

The hotel they were staying at was modest, but had the advantage of being convenient for the city centre and the department store where they were to work each day. Peering out of her bedroom window, Beth could just perceive the gold Madonna on top of *Il Duomo*, and made an instant resolve to visit the famous cathedral as soon as she could, to find out the times of Masses.

She unpacked, curiously fingering the feather eiderdown on the mahogany bed, and wondering why there were no blankets – after all it was quite chilly. She later discovered with pleasure that the continental quilt was astonishingly warm. To her delight she had the luxury of her own bathroom and shower, and even a bidet! I bet they've never seen one of these in Minsden, she grinned, and they'd use it as a footbath!

Later that evening, after their first Italian meal of *risotto alla milanese*, they went for a short stroll, too tired to go far, contenting themselves with watching the hundreds of pigeons fluttering around *Il Duomo*, before turning in for an early night.

The elegant store was light and airy, with gleaming marble floors and glittering chandeliers. In an atmosphere redolent of affluence and good taste, Barbara's artistry gave rise to much admiring interest, and Beth found her translation skills very much in demand. Initially the effort of converting technical terms into Italian and constantly conversing in a foreign language proved exhausting, leaving little energy for sightseeing. Barbara wasn't interested anyway, content in the evenings to knit the pullover she was trying to finish for her nephew's birthday.

But by the time Wednesday came, the day Michael was due to arrive, Beth found she was coping with her busy day much more easily, and was restless, sensing the exciting pulse of the busy cosmopolitan city and eager to experience some of its nightlife. She had no intention of returning to Minsden having seen no more of Milan than the inside of a department store, and a few hundred yards around the perimeter of the hotel. Perhaps it was being so far away from home, or the excitement of a different culture, but suddenly Beth wanted fun. She felt a desire to be someone different, not the rather serious, hardworking young woman her life had shaped.

At last, about four o'clock, she saw Michael approach, immaculate in a dark business suit. He was accompanied by James.

Smiling a greeting, Michael asked whether they thought the project was successful, nodding in affirmation at their positive comments. "Yes, we've already received several large orders. You make a good team. You know my brother, of course, who has sadly neglected you both." He smiled.

"Yes," James said, "I must apologise that I haven't been in to see you before, but I was called out of town on some urgent business."

He shook hands with them both.

"If you haven't arranged anything for this evening," he said, "would you both like to join us for a meal? Perhaps we could show you a little of Milan."

Barbara hesitated. "Thank you very much, Mr James, but to be honest by the time I've finished here I'm too tired to go gadding about. Beth now, that's a different matter – she's just dying to spread her wings."

"What do you think? Would you like to?" Michael asked her.

"Yes, I'd love to. Are you sure you don't want to come, Barbara?"

"Positive."

"Right, we'll pick you up about eight, then." Michael smiled, and seeing the expression in his eyes, Beth's pulses raced in anticipation.

Chapter 13

Beth was ready and waiting in the small lobby by ten to eight. The decision of what to wear had occupied most of her thoughts since the two men had left, being painfully aware that compared with the fashion-conscious Italians, her wardrobe was woefully inadequate. It had been a source of amazement to her to see so many women wearing fur coats and ostentatious jewellery, even during the day while shopping. Clothes were obviously of the utmost importance here, and from snippets of conversation she'd gleaned that a designer label was a must. Well, she thought, looking disparagingly at her camel skirt and cream angora sweater, I don't think St Michael falls into that category, but it's all I've got.

When the car drew up, she walked out in her

sensible tweed coat, to see James seated next to an extremely glamorous Italian girl, complete with a tiny fur jacket which looked suspiciously like mink.

"Hop in. There's plenty of room," he invited. "This is my wife, Giovanna."

"I am 'appy to meet you," Giovanna said hesitantly.

"Giovanna wants to improve her English, so tonight will be good for her," James said.

Michael closed the door as Beth squeezed in, and then sat by the driver, telling him to drive to *Il Naviglio*.

"*Il Naviglio*, the canal?" queried Beth.

"Yes, it's much more glamorous than it sounds, not at all like the canal in Stoke," Michael laughed. "There are lots of bars and restaurants along it, and there's usually a good atmosphere. Unfortunately, it's too cold at this time of the year, but in the summer people eat outside. Whole families come out for the evening. The Italians are great family people, and love children. Did you know that on a bus or on the Metro, adults are expected to give up their seat to a child, a complete reversal of the custom in England?"

Beth listened, fascinated. It was one thing to learn Italian at school, but another to actually be here, to see how the people lived, to learn their customs and way of life. No wonder people like to travel. What was it the rich used to do when they reached a certain age?

Ah yes, the Grand Tour. What a life they led while the working classes slaved away in factories or on the land, often under appalling conditions. My socialist conscience raising its head again, she thought with amusement. At last now the opportunity to travel abroad was extending to a wider section of the population.

Giovanna was charming and friendly, exquisitely dressed in a pink silk suit which in Minsden would be considered suitable only for a wedding but, on Giovanna and in this environment, it looked perfect. Beth felt dowdy and provincial in her best skirt and sweater, particularly when she looked around the smart restaurant. She could have kicked herself for not bringing a cocktail dress, but had never expected to dine in such sophisticated surroundings.

To her surprise and gratification, Giovanna was looking at her with undisguised admiration.

"Your clothes, they are belle, so English," she said, her eyes coveting Beth's pearls.

They're not real, Beth was about to say, and then stopped. Why tell everyone they came from the Great Universal Stores catalogue!

"How long have you and James been married, Giovanna?"

"Ah, one year soon," she replied, looking fondly at her husband.

Beth studied him, as she sipped her Campari and

soda. He hardly looked old enough to be married, pleasant enough yes, but her impression was one of weakness rather than strength. Next to Michael, he seemed a callow youth, and she noticed the difference in their hands as they studied the menus. Michael's fingers were long and sensitive, while James had short stubby fingers, rather like a schoolboy's. There was no comparison . . . Turning, she found Giovanna looking at her quizzically.

"You like him? Michael?" she whispered.

"I'm only an employee," Beth said, feeling embarrassed.

"It will be our – how you say – our secret." Giovanna's soft brown eyes crinkled at the corners, and Beth smiled, liking the slender, dark-haired Italian girl, who she judged to be about her own age.

The meal was a merry one. Michael and James were obviously good friends and as the wine flowed, their mood became ever more relaxed. Her senses heightened by Michael's presence at her side, Beth thought she'd never been so happy. She loved Italian food with its rich sauces, and each day had experimented with a new dish, although she avoided spaghetti as the technique of transferring it from the plate to her mouth seemed to be beyond her! Tonight, she tasted veal for the first time, appreciating its delicate flavour.

And then it happened, that one moment of

reminiscence which was to have such startling implications. They'd finished eating and were enjoying their espresso coffee when James laughed.

"We had some fun though, in our youth, didn't we, Michael?"

Michael sipped his coffee.

"We sure did. You should have known him then, Giovanna, wild as they come."

"There were rumours in the factory that you were the restless one, James," Beth smiled.

"He spent one year working on a sheep farm in Australia, believe it or not. When would that be, James, 1956 to 57?" Michael said.

"Yes, about then."

"What did he do, this wild one?" laughed Giovanna.

"Ah, that would be telling!" Michael teased.

"Do you remember that time we all dressed up as Lone Rangers?" James hooted with laughter, leaning elbows on the table, his face flushed with wine, his pale blue eyes bright. "We went to a fancy dress party, Beth, all dressed the same to confuse the girls, and then got pissed and gatecrashed another party we'd heard about at some bloke's house." He grinned at Giovanna, who was smiling indulgently.

Beth sat in stunned silence, staring at the two men in profound shock. It couldn't be true! For a few seconds she felt as though she was a spectator at a play. Nothing seemed real: the lavish tables, the other diners, the soft romantic music. Then the food she'd eaten turned sour in her stomach, and she felt suddenly sick, as the full meaning of what she had just heard became clear. Michael? No, please God, her mind screamed, not Michael! James? Those drunken uncaring youths with their coarse jibes? The horror of that heavy body ramming painfully into her, the choking sensation of that sweaty hand suffocating her face surfaced from her subconscious. Oh, Our Lady, please don't let this be happening. It can't have been Michael, it can't!

Michael suddenly leaned over, touching her hand. "Are you all right, Beth?"

"I'm fine." She listened to her calm voice in amazement. Couldn't they see, didn't they know that for her this lovely, exciting evening, was turning into a nightmare? She took a ragged breath and then, her eyes fixed despairingly upon Michael's face, said,

"I can't imagine you dressed up as a Lone Ranger."

"Oh, don't let him fool you, Beth, with that serious manner! He's become an old sobersides lately, but I can remember a different Michael! He was a right tearaway."

Michael frowned sharply, his eyes glinting with annoyance. "Hold on, James. I was never in your league. A bit of fun, yes, like most young people, but nothing I'm ashamed of." He was clearly irritated at the turn the conversation had taken.

"I don't call getting drunk and gatecrashing someone else's party a particularly responsible thing to do," Beth said through clenched teeth, anger burning inside her. How dare they sit there and joke about it! She felt unutterably weary and disillusioned as she waited tensely for Michael's reaction. All her dreams, this wonderful warm feeling she had for him, all to crumble to dust, for even if her rape hadn't been performed by him, his very presence in that group made him an accessory, and she'd never be able to erase that from her mind, never!

Michael looked at her strangely, his blue eyes puzzled. This intelligent, graceful girl, who so intrigued him, was looking at him as though he were the devil incarnate.

"James," he said slowly, his eyes holding Beth's, "I remember the Lone Ranger outfits, and I remember the fancy dress party out at Ursula's house, but I don't remember gatecrashing any party."

"Oh, of course you didn't, did you! Not your style at all. I remember now, you left Ursula's early for some reason."

"Wasn't it the night before I left for my National Service?" Michael remembered.

"Yes, that was it," James said, finishing his coffee with a flourish.

Beth was euphoric. The relief, the glorious wonderful relief of those words. It was like coming up from a dark pit into the sunlight, and she smiled into Michael's eyes, her face alight with joy.

Michael's pulses quickened as he stared at the radiant girl opposite him. He'd never seen her look so lovely.

Beth quickly recovered herself. She mustn't let this moment pass without discovering as much as she could. 'We,' James had said. Who were the others? Could she find out who Rosemary's father was? She took a deep breath.

"If Michael wasn't one of the gatecrashers, who else was with you, James?"

Taken aback at her blunt question, James struggled to remember. "Well, there was John Forrester, Alan Slater, um Peter Harris, me, Tony Morrison, oh, and of course Guy, Michael's next-door neighbour." He seemed uneasy, or was it her imagination?

Guy! That likeable, friendly chap she'd met at the party? He seemed a million miles away from how she remembered those youths. So did James, sitting here enjoying a pleasant evening out with his wife, patiently translating any words she didn't understand. Perhaps it's me, thought Beth, being narrow-minded – I know people think I'm a bit of a square. Oh I don't mean about the rape, but despising the drunkeness and loutish behaviour. James doesn't seem to think any worse of himself for it. She felt bewildered, unable to reconcile Guy and James with the monstrous images she had carried for so long in her mind.

Beth stood up, and picked up her bag. "I think I'll just powder my nose."

"I'll come too." Giovanna accompanied her, but Beth closed her mind to the other girl's pleasantries. Her mind was already whirling, yet nothing must distract her. She needed to keep those names in her mind. Once inside the cubicle, she quickly opened her handbag and, her hand shaking with excitement, scribbled them down in her diary. How strange that she'd had to come to Italy to find the information she needed. Somehow, sometime, no matter what it takes, I'm determined to find out the truth, she vowed.

Back at the table, she struggled to push the conversation to the back of her mind. There was nothing more she could do at the moment. But the time would come. Meanwhile, she was determined to enjoy the rest of the evening.

Michael watched her, admiring her poise and charm as she conversed patiently with Giovanna. She had spirit too, as she'd shown when for some reason James's comments had upset her. He'd observed her moving around the factory, noticing her easy camaraderie with the workers while never losing her natural dignity. She was certainly an unusual young woman. Her personnel file showed a brilliant scholastic record. He found her immensely attractive, but could tell that she wasn't a girl for a casual 'bit of fun'. There was a reserve there, yet she had such an engaging enthusiasm for life. Look at how thrilled she was with this evening out, so different from dining with Ursula whose blasé attitude to life he found rather shallow.

James asked for the bill, and on an impulse Michael touched Beth's arm.

"Tomorrow's my last night, and James and Giovanna are tied up. Would you like to see more of Milan?"

She nodded, her eyes shining.

"What would you like to do?"

"Could we just wander around? I'd love to be able to mingle with the Italian people on their evening stroll – what do they call it? A *passagiata*?"

"OK, I'll pick you up after dinner, say about nine? You don't think Barbara will want to come, do you?"

"I shouldn't think so for a minute!"

They exchanged glances, his relieved, hers full of anticipation. Oh, she loved Italy, she loved the warmth of the people, their unashamed display of emotion, she loved the way she felt inside. Free, that was it, free from inhibition, like a seedling transplanted and suddenly blossoming. One day, she promised herself, I'll come when the sun shines, I'll visit the Italian Lakes and Rome, and Florence, and perhaps even Venice. Suddenly her future stretched before her, full of opportunity, and turning to Michael she whispered, "Thanks!"

"For what?"

"Just, thanks!"

Bemused, he followed her out of the restaurant, and as they dropped her off at her hotel, watched her run quickly up the steps to the lobby.

"Lovely girl," James commented.

"Isn't she!"

By the time he returned to England, Michael knew that this was no ordinary attraction; the evening they'd spent together had shown him that. He'd never met anyone like her. Her delight in simple things entranced him. He remembered with amusement how they had been walking through La Galleria, that so elegant shopping arcade with the mosaic picture of a bull on the floor. When he'd told her of the Italians' custom of spinning around on one foot on its testicles to bring good luck, Beth's shocked face had caused him to crease with laughter. Then she'd daringly followed suit, her cheeks crimsoning when she'd caught a couple watching. It was a scene he'd never forget. She'd looked captivating, her dark hair framing that lovely face, her blue eyes shining with devilment. How he'd stopped himself from kissing her he'd never know, but before he'd left his hotel that evening, he'd decided to keep his distance. This was a business trip, and he was well aware that Beth would have to cope with innuendo on her return. There must be no possibility of misinterpretation. However, of one thing he was certain, he intended to see a lot more of her when they got home.

Chapter 14

"You'rc not going out with him again?" The consternation in Rose's voice caused Beth's lips to compress as she shrugged on her coat.

"And why shouldn't I?" she asked, keeping her tone reasonably calm. "It's not a crime, is it?"

Rose bit her lip. She and Beth never used to snipe at each other like this. Ever since she'd returned from Italy she seemed so restless, no longer content with the steady rhythm of their lives. Reaching for the moon, that's what she's doing, thought Rose.

"No good will come of it," she muttered. "We're not his sort. I've told you."

"He's not like that – you don't know him!"

"And whose fault is that?" Rose demanded.

Beth avoided the question.

"Mum, why can't you be pleased for me?" she pleaded. "I've waited so long to meet someone special – don't spoil things."

Rose stared at her in shocked silence. Spoil things, that was the last thing she wanted to do. Didn't the girl realise she was only thinking of her good? She sat down, feeling subdued. Perhaps she had been going on a bit, but it worried her, it really did, Beth seeing so much of Michael Rushton. He hadn't even had the decency to come and meet her family, so what did that tell you?

"Look, I'll have to go or we'll miss the start of the film," Beth said. "I'll see you later."

She walked quickly to the end of the street, where Michael's car was waiting. He was always punctual, always reliable, and she liked that. Since the Milan trip they'd seen each other at least twice a week – going to the pictures, dancing, or out to a country pub. They'd been to concerts at the Victoria Hall, once to listen to the Halle orchestra, another time to see Chris Barber's jazz band which was a favourite of Michael's. Weather permitting, they often walked across the downs at Barlaston enjoying the beautiful scenery, talking endlessly, finding mutual delight in each other's company. She had never been so happy.

Michael watched her as she approached the red 'E' type Jaguar, and leaning over, opened the door. "Hi."

"Hi yourself." Beth gave him a quick kiss, and putting the car into gear he pulled away from the kerb.

"You OK?" he asked, noticing the strain in her eyes.

"Yes, fine," she answered. She hated arguing with Rose – although she was right. It was time Michael met her family. Beth knew that he was waiting for her to invite him in for coffee when he took her home after a date, but she kept avoiding it. She knew why she was so reluctant and despised herself for it. It was ridiculous to allow herself to be affected by Ursula's rejection of her background all those years ago, but she just couldn't help it. Her fear was illogical too – after all Michael knew where she lived so what difference did it make?

Michael drove competently along the dark roads, unusually silent. Reaching the cinema, he parked the car and, switching off the engine, sat drumming his fingers on the steering wheel. Then he turned towards Beth and said, "Penny for them? You're very quiet."

"So are you."

He hesitated, and then ran one finger gently down her cheek. "Do we have to see this film? I'd much rather be alone with you."

His eyes held hers, his meaning unmistakeable, and she swallowed nervously.

"Yes, but where?"

"We could drive out into the country?"

So at last the moment had arrived, as she'd known it must. But it was one thing indulging in long goodnight kisses in a parked car at the end of the street, and another to be alone with a man in a field miles from anywhere. Beth was terrified of how she'd react if he took their lovemaking further. Shakily she realised that she couldn't keep putting it off. If she didn't face this fear of frigidity and overcome it, she could forget any hope of a future with Michael. And if she couldn't have a physical relationship with someone she loved so much, then there was no hope for her.

Michael waited impatiently for her answer. God, she was lovely, but it had been nearly three months now. Sensing her reserve he'd managed to hold himself in check, never touching her intimately except for a gentle cupping of her breast. Her kisses had shown that she was capable of passion, but the only time his hand had strayed down to her thigh he'd felt her recoil. The rejection had hurt and he'd almost called it a day, but he was crazy about her. Until now he'd been careful, sensing that she was sexually unawakened, but a man could only wait so long.

"Let's do that – it's probably a lousy film anyway," she said, giving him a nervous smile.

"You're sure?"

She nodded.

Michael turned the key in the ignition and swung out of the car park. He switched on the radio to the romantic strains of Frank Sinatra, and the car purred along the busy roads and out into the countryside.

"Are you warm enough?" he asked.

"Yes, fine."

Beth didn't want to talk and sat silently, full of apprehension. The atmosphere between them was charged with sexual tension as Michael drove slowly along country lanes looking for a likely spot to park.

He found it, an open gate, and turning in drew the car to a halt beneath the shelter of a huge oak tree. He switched off the engine and they sat for a few moments in the darkness, the only sound the rustling of the wet branches overhead.

An hour later, they sat quietly in each other's arms, Beth's head on Michael's shoulder, her eyelashes wet with tears. It was going to be all right. If she could feel desire like this then surely she couldn't be frigid?

Michael gently stroked her back, marvelling at the silkiness of her skin. At last he said,

"You'd better get dressed, darling, before you catch cold."

While Beth covered herself, Michael lit a cigarette, winding down the car window to let the smoke escape. His breathing was still uneven – it had taken an enormous effort to restrain himself a few moments ago. But she was like a frightened fawn – he could swear she'd been afraid when he'd first turned to take her in his arms. Eventually, he'd managed to coax her to relax, and then had gentled her until her passion had begun to match his own.

Staring out into the inky darkness, Michael frowned. He wondered why she was so uptight about sex. It was probably that religion of hers – he'd heard about the Catholic guilt complex. It didn't matter. He was confident they could overcome it. Tonight had proved that.

Beth was everything a man could ask for: loving, beautiful, intelligent, sensitive, with an appreciation of literature and the finer things of life. A little serious perhaps, but he liked that – it showed depth and strength of character. In any case, she was already more relaxed and lighthearted when with him. Oh, what the hell, he was old enough to know what he wanted, and he wanted to spend the rest of his life with her. He'd never felt like this about anyone before.

"I love you, Beth," he said, taking her hand.

She turned and faced him, her eyes luminous in the moonlight.

"I love you, Michael."

He reached over and stroked her hair.

"It's too early to take you home. Let's go for a drink. We need to talk."

The small country pub was full and noisy, and Michael grimaced as he fought his way through to the bar.

"Jim, you don't have a quiet spot anywhere?" he asked. He knew the burly landlord from his years working in the Despatch Department at Rushton's before he and his wife took on the tenancy of the village pub.

Jim's eyes flickered as he saw Beth trying unsuccessfully to find an empty table.

"It's certainly busy tonight. Look, there's the front parlour we use for lodgers. There's no one in there at the moment – you could use that."

"Thanks. Could you bring us a couple of gin and tonics?"

"Sure."

Michael beckoned Beth, and she squeezed through the crowd to join him, and they left the bustle behind and found the tiny parlour, thankful of the cosy coal fire in the grate.

Jim arrived, bringing the drinks and a dish of crisps and peanuts, and after greeting Beth with a knowing smile, left them to it.

"It'll be all over the potbank before long," Beth commented.

"So what? It'll give someone else a rest. To us!" He raised his glass in a toast.

"To us!" she said softly.

Michael put down his glass. "Right, so what's next."

"How do you mean?"

"Well, I'm right, am I not, Beth? We are going to get married?"

"Is that a proposal?" she asked, her heart pounding.

"Well, I could go down on one knee if you insist, but I'd feel a bit ridiculous!" he responded, grinning.

"I do appreciate the great honour you have bestowed upon me, sir," she began and then, seeing the uncertainty in his eyes, abandoned her play-acting and said, "You're the only person in the world I could marry, Michael." Her eyes filled with tears and impatiently she brushed them away.

"Hey, this is supposed to be a happy occasion!"

"I know," she said shakily. "I am happy. Oh, we'll have a lovely life, Michael. I know we will!"

"I'll drink to that! So, when am I going to meet my future mother-in-law?"

Beth hesitated. It was best to get it over with. "How about coming for tea on Sunday? You can meet Mum and Gran at the same time."

"Fine. Of course, your brother's serving in Germany isn't he?"

"Yes, you'll like Gordon, and as I told you Valerie's my closest friend. We're dying to see their little boy – he's three months old now."

Michael saw the tender look in her eyes and said softly, "I'd like children, Beth. How about you?"

"But of course." She was surprised he would even query it. After all wasn't that what marriage was all about?

"I warn you. I shall expect my own football team!" he teased.

She laughed.

"Come on. We'd better go. It's getting late," Michael said, downing his drink.

Giving Jim a generous tip for the use of the parlour, he drove Beth home, kissed her tenderly goodnight, and prepared himself for the row which would undoubtedly erupt when he told his parents he planned to marry one of their employees.

In the privacy of her bedroom, alone at last to give rein to her chaotic thoughts and emotions, Beth gazed at her glowing reflection in the dressing-table mirror. I've done it, I've done it, she whispered. Oh, not 'it', of course, Michael respects me too much for that, but everything but! Her cheeks grew hot at the memory of their shared intimacy. It had just seemed so natural to let Michael love her, to let him touch and stroke her.

The wonder of it was that she had wanted the closeness, had wanted to give him pleasure, and to her delight had responded in a way that only a few months ago she would have thought impossible. Oh, she'd been terribly tense at first, but Michael had been wonderful, so tender and patient, giving her the reassurance she needed, just as though he understood her fears. She was so lucky to have found someone like him, someone with his sensitivity.

Perhaps he would even understand . . .? No, she pushed the idea from her mind, she wouldn't think of that, not tonight. Nothing must spoil her happiness, her joy in what she saw as her rebirth as a woman. Above all, she basked in the exhilaration of knowing that Michael wanted to marry her, that she could look forward to a normal future, and perhaps one day a family of her own.

Chapter 15

"Mum, for heaven's sake, he's only coming for tea, not a four-course banquet!" Beth knew she was wasting her breath. Not content with spending the last few days polishing and cleaning everything in sight, Rose was now planning the following day's visit with the thoroughness of a general.

"I don't want him thinking I don't know how to keep a good table. Now, I've made a big fruit cake, and a Victoria sponge, some maids of honour, a sherry trifle, and I've got some nice boiled ham for sandwiches. Do you think we'll need anything else?"

"He's coming to meet you and Gran, not to put on half a stone in weight!"

"Don't try to kid me, Beth. I know you want to make a good impression – why else have you been out and got a new hearthrug? And as for that white tablecloth and napkins you've bought, I warn you your Gran'll probably tuck hers under her chin!"

Beth laughed. "She'll be surprised, won't she? You don't think we ought to let her know Michael's coming?"

"No, she always puts on her best frock when she comes up."

"You'll both like him, I promise you."

Rose looked searchingly at her. "You've not said anything, but it's serious isn't it, Beth?"

"Yes, Mum, it is." She hesitated, and then said, "I might as well tell you. He's asked me to marry him and I've said yes."

Rose looked bewildered. "But how could it have gone this far without my even meeting him?"

"It wasn't deliberate, Mum. The time just seemed to go on. If it's any consolation to you, his parents haven't met me either, at least not as Michael's girlfriend. He's telling them tonight."

"Well, it's a funny way of carrying on if you ask me," Rose complained. "Besides, you haven't known him that long – don't you think you're rushing things a bit?"

She began to wash the floral china tea-set Grandma Sherwin had given her as a wedding present. Shouldn't Michael have asked her permission first, or had those days gone? Harry would have had something to say, that was for sure. He'd been a great one for tradition, and when all was said and done there was a proper way to go about things. She felt disappointed, yes that was it, disappointed, and excluded too, although having voiced her opposition from the start, she could hardly blame Beth for keeping things to herself.

"We're both old enough to know what we're doing," Beth said defensively.

"That's as may be. Anyway, what do you know about him? Is he a Catholic?"

"No, Church of England."

"I suppose that means Easter and Christmas."

"Well, I don't think he goes every week."

"Not many of them do!" retorted Rose drily. "And what about his politics?" she suddenly demanded as Beth picked up a tea towel. "I bet he's not Labour."

"No, he's not, but that doesn't mean I can't vote Labour," Beth said.

"Ha, you've got a lot to learn about marriage, lady!"

"Mum, will you live in the modern world for heaven's sake! Where does it say you have to vote the same as your husband?"

"Look, Beth, you do need to have things in common for a marriage to work," Rose said with a worried expression. "You're from different backgrounds, have different faiths, and don't even have the same politics. It'll all lead to friction, you mark my words."

"We never argue!"

"Not now, no. You're looking at the world through rose-coloured glasses, but as time goes on, these differences could cause problems, that's all I'm saying. I am pleased for you, Beth, I really am. It's just that . . . Oh, perhaps I'll feel better about it after I've met him." Picking up the washing-up bowl and emptying the soapy water down the sink, Rose fervently hoped so.

That same evening, Michael angrily faced his father who was standing before the mahogany fireplace in the drawing-room, his chin thrust forward belligerently.

"You're being a snob, you know that, don't you, Father?"

"Maybe I am, but for you to have the gall to tell me you want to marry one of the factory girls – well, what do you expect me to do, hang out the flags?" Robert Rushton snapped.

"She's not exactly one of the factory girls, dear. She works in the Marketing Department," Sylvia Rushton anxiously tried to defuse the situation, but her conciliatory remark only served to inflame her husband further.

"Oh, just like you to stick up for him! You've

always been the same – your precious son can do no wrong in your eyes!"

"I don't need anyone to stick up for me. I can fight my own battles," Michael said in a curt tone. "OK, if it's not snobbery, what exactly have you got against Beth? You don't even know her except as an employee, and you were quite happy to invite her here at New Year."

"Yes, and that was obviously a mistake!"

"You still haven't answered my question, because you can't."

Robert's tone was bitter as he confronted his son. "I don't mind telling you, Michael, I'm disappointed in you. You could have had your pick of anyone in the country. In fact, your mother and I always thought you and Ursula might make a match of it. I know her parents did. This will come as a shock to them. I hope you realise that!"

"Ursula and I have never been anything other than good friends."

"I don't think she sees it like that," Sylvia said quietly.

Michael flushed. He was well aware that Ursula had been holding a torch for him for years. Because of their parents' friendship, they'd been thrown together from an early age. Oh, she was attractive enough and at one time he'd quite fancied her, but apart from the odd bit of necking after parties, he'd never given her cause to think he was serious.

Sylvia attempted to ease the situation. "Why don't you bring Beth to dinner on Tuesday, so that we can get to know her properly?" she suggested.

"Thanks, Mother, I will." Michael hesitated and then said, "I know I've rather sprung it on you, but it's all happened so quickly."

"She's not in the family way, is she?" Robert demanded.

"No, Father, and I take exception to that remark. You wouldn't have made it if I'd said it was Ursula I was marrying!"

"No, well, Ursula has –"

"Breeding?" Michael interrupted, contemptuously finishing the sentence for him. He turned on his heel and left the room, slamming the heavy door behind him.

"Did you have to say that?" Sylvia demanded.

"Well . . ."

"Never mind 'well' – she's his choice, Robert, and I'll expect you to treat her with respect when she comes on Tuesday. This house will feel empty enough when Michael gets married – we don't want to lose him completely."

"He's not married yet. He could change his mind. They haven't known each other five minutes."

"I think you're fooling yourself. You know what he's like when he's made a decision. He's in love, Robert. Don't you think we should be happy for him?"

"Look, I didn't pay for him to attend public school so that he could go and marry a girl off the potbank," Robert said grimly.

"Maybe, but you can't choose his wife for him. Look," Sylvia sighed, "tomorrow afternoon I'll go and see Sister Veronica, and see what I can find out about her. Michael won't be in for tea – he's going to meet Beth's family."

Sunday afternoon found the Sherwin household in a state of expectation.

"I hope you didn't pay much for that skirt. There's nobbut a yard of material in it. I bet the manufacturers are laughing all the way to the bank with this mini-skirt craze!" Granny Platt looked disapprovingly at Beth's long slim legs, comparing them with her own, decently covered up in 30 denier stockings. It was a wonder these young girls didn't all catch their death of cold!

Beth didn't answer. She was anxiously watching the clock. Five past four, he was five minutes late! She went into the kitchen and turning stood in the doorway looking at the scene which would meet Michael's eyes when he arrived.

The small living-room was much as it had been ever since she was a child. The only difference was Rose's pride and joy, a fitted carpet. Her longing for one had eventually surpassed her stubborn resistance to buying on hire-purchase. The woodwork was now painted magnolia, but the cuckoo clock still hung in the same place, and a wedding photograph of Gordon and Valerie, with a snap of little Paul were displayed proudly on the radiogram.

Rose's brass ornaments were gleaming bright, and she'd splashed out on a bunch of pink and white carnations which adorned the windowsill. Granny Platt was even wearing her uncomfortable leather shoes and, with a tut of exasperation, Beth swooped and picked up her discarded carpet slippers, bundling them out of sight in the bureau.

"He's here!" Rose exclaimed. She turned from the window for a final satisfied look at her table, standing square in the centre of the room with the china tea service and her own magnificent spread, set off by the white cloth and napkins. Smoothing down her best coffee and cream Courtelle dress, she lifted her chin, and waited.

Beth went quickly down the side path to the car. She'd decided against using the stiff front door and led Michael to enter the house in the usual way, through the kitchen.

"Mum, Gran, this is Michael," she said with pride.

Michael moved forward, holding out his hand to Rose. "I'm very pleased to meet you, Mrs Sherwin."

"I'm pleased to met you, Michael."

"Let's have a look at you then," interrupted Granny Platt.

"Gran!" protested Beth.

Michael turned to face the grey-haired plump figure sitting by the fire. The old woman was as shrewd as ever, and her gaze swept over him critically, approving his blazer and flannels and polished shoes.

"Sit yourself down at the table, Michael, and I'll make a pot of tea," Rose said briskly.

"This all looks very nice, Mrs Sherwin. I hope you didn't go to all this trouble on my account."

"Oh, no, not at all."

Beth caught Michael's eye, and he grinned.

"How did you guess I've a weakness for trifle?"

"I've yet to meet a man who hasn't, and there's a good drop of sherry in it."

"Great!"

To Rose's gratification, Michael ate with enjoyment, complimenting her on her baking, and the atmosphere around the table gradually became more informal, as he chatted to them all in a friendly manner.

"I'm looking forward to meeting Gordon and his family, Mrs Sherwin. I believe he's a Stoke fan."

"From the age of two, would you believe!"

"Well, when he next comes on leave, tell him I've got a season ticket and he's welcome to use it any time."

"Eh, he'd like that," said Granny Platt, giving a satisfied nod.

"Your dad always wanted a season ticket, but we could never afford it," Rose said wistfully.

Michael glanced at the photo on the mantelpiece. "He looks a fine man, Mrs Sherwin. I know Beth thought the world of him."

"He was a good husband and father," she answered. "Look, why don't you two young people go off for an hour or two on your own? Gran and I can wash up."

"Are you sure, Mum?"

"'Course I am. You don't want to be cooped up here with us. Bring Michael back later, and I'll make him a nice cheese and onion sandwich for his supper."

"Mrs Sherwin, you're an angel," Michael said, "and thank you for a delicious tea. By the way, don't worry about getting home, Mrs Platt. I can easily drop you off later. I promise not to be too late."

The two women exchanged pleased glances, and then as soon as they heard the car draw away, Rose said, "Well, what do you think?"

Granny Platt sighed with relief as she eased off the tight-fitting shoes and wriggled her toes.

"Just pass those slippers, Rose. What do I think?

Well, it just shows why people pay out all that money for public school and all that. Did you ever see such lovely manners, and the way he talks!"

"Yes, I can see why Beth finds him attractive. There didn't seem to be any side on him, though, did there?" Rose said, feeling more relaxed now the ordeal was over.

"No, in fact he seemed a nice young man to me. You know, Rose, I don't know what you're so worried about. You can't send the girl to a posh school and then expect her to settle for anyone round 'ere."

"No," Rose said slowly, "but I hoped she'd find someone from a similar background. You know as well as I do that it doesn't do to try and move out of your class. It never works."

"Well, I think you're wrong. You're not giving our Beth enough credit. She's a smart lass. She'll know what's what." Granny Platt got stiffly out of her chair and began to clear the table. "Come on. Let's get these dishes done, then we can settle down and watch telly."

Despite her delight at the success of Michael's visit, Beth felt increasingly nervous about her invitation to dinner at the Rushtons'. When on Monday morning, she unexpectedly came face to face with Michael's father in one of the corridors, her tentative smile was dismissed with a cold nod, as he continued on his way.

There was no doubt it was a deliberate snub, and she began to dread Tuesday evening. It was obvious that his parents were opposed to the match, but then wasn't that what she'd expected?

When Tuesday came, the atmosphere in the drawing-room at Linden Lodge was fraught with tension. Sylvia sipped a dry sherry as she watched Robert impatiently pace up and down.

"Oh, for heaven's sake, Robert, they'll be here in a minute."

"They're late!" he said through gritted teeth.

"It's probably the traffic. And I don't think that's a good idea," she added sharply as he crossed over to the decanter to refill his glass.

"And that's all she said?"

"Who?"

"Sister Veronica!"

"She just said that Beth was one of the finest pupils she'd ever had. To be honest, Robert, I felt a bit embarrassed – she obviously thought we were prejudiced because the girl's working class."

"Well, she is. How can I tell people from the Golf Club that my son's marrying someone from Minsden – it's nearly all council houses for a start." He slumped into an armchair, to stare despondently into the fire.

"Michael tells me she doesn't live in a council house – her home is privately rented."

"There you are, rented! What else did he tell you."

"I've told you! Her mother's a widow, and she has one brother, who's married and in the Army. Ah, here they are now."

Michael took Beth's coat and hung it in the hall closet, then squeezing her hand whispered,

"Are you ready to go into the lions' den?"

She nodded.

He opened the door and ushered her in.

"Sorry we're a bit late. I'm sure you both remember Beth?"

Sylvia moved forward.

"Yes, indeed, you're most welcome, my dear." Her eyes swept over Beth's quiet grey skirt and crisp lace-trimmed white blouse with relief. No flashy jewellery, no heavy make-up, and lovely hair. She'd had only a vague recollection of Beth's appearance at the party, and found herself agreeably surprised.

Beth smiled and thanked her, and then turning to Michael's father her smile faltered as she saw the blatant hostility in his eyes.

He shook her hand.

"Lot of traffic, was there?" he asked Michael.

"A fair bit."

"Would you like a sherry, Beth?" Sylvia indicated for her to sit down.

"Thank you."

Robert stood before the fire, his hands in his pockets, his legs straddled, a stance Beth was familiar with from the factory. He was a tall, heavily built man, and his florid face wore an expression which usually forebode trouble.

The conversation was stilted, with Sylvia making an effort to deflect attention from Robert's cold attitude.

"When are we eating, Mother? I'm starving," said Michael.

"You always are," she said drily. "Give Beth time to finish her drink, and then I'll ask Mrs Hammond to serve."

An awkward silence fell, and Beth quickly finished her drink.

"Shall we go into the dining-room then," Sylvia suggested. "We're having lamb as the main course, Beth. I hope you like it?"

"Yes, very much."

The splendid antique table was beautifully laid with fresh flowers and sparkling crystal shown to advantage on a white damask cloth. Robert and Sylvia sat at each end with Beth and Michael facing each other. Beth looked at the array of silver cutlery and glancing up caught a look of expectant malice in Robert's eyes. If you think I'm going to show myself up, you're going to be disappointed, she determined.

Summoning all the social skills she'd developed during her trip to Milan and over the past few months dining out with Michael, she set out to be the perfect dinner guest.

Two hours later as the door closed behind the young couple, Sylvia said, "She's perfectly charming, Robert – in fact, I was pleasantly surprised."

"I have to admit she conducted herself well," he said grudgingly, "but that doesn't mean I'm happy about it. How do we know she's not just after his money?"

Sylvia looked at him with exasperation. "We don't know, and there's no way of finding out. All I know is that he's happy and set on marrying her. We have no alternative but to accept it with good grace. I want no unpleasantness, Robert. It won't achieve anything."

Robert merely grunted, pouring himself another whisky as he stared moodily into the fire.

Chapter 16

Michael drove away from the tree-lined residential area and on to the main road.

"I thought that went very well – you seemed to get on with my mother."

"She's nice, but your father doesn't like me," Beth said.

"It's not you. It's just that he wanted me to marry some horsey type with a voice like cut glass, or better still, Ursula," Michael said bitterly.

"Your parents wanted you to marry Ursula?"

"Both sets of parents. They've been trying to manoeuvre it for years."

"I didn't realise it was serious between you," Beth said in a flat tone.

"It wasn't and before you ask, nothing happened

between us either. You needn't worry. There's no skeleton in the cupboard there." Michael removed his hand from the steering wheel and gave her knee a quick squeeze. "You're the only girl I've ever loved."

But that night she found it impossible to sleep, remembering Michael's words. He'd assured her before that she was the only person he'd ever wanted to marry, saying that although he'd had other girlfriends, the past wasn't important. At the time she'd accepted his statement with relief, but later that night she lay tossing and turning, unable to forget that phrase 'skeleton in the cupboard'. She had a skeleton in the cupboard, a living one, a daughter now aged seven and although she had no idea where Rosemary was, her existence was an unalterable fact.

With all the euphoria of the past few weeks she'd managed to postpone examining her conscience, but she'd known that sooner or later she'd have to face up to the fact that she had some serious thinking to do. She was terrified of losing Michael, but had she any choice other than to tell him the truth? Oh, she should never have let things get this far without confessing her past, but she'd been unable to face the inevitable look of disillusionment and disgust in his eyes. To hear that the girl he planned to marry had been raped at 17, become pregnant and given her baby girl up for adoption, was enough to destroy any man's love.

Beth turned over, plumping up the pillows, and curling up in the foetal position wrestled with her dilemma. What if he couldn't find out, and she didn't tell him? That would mean taking her marriage vows and entering into their life together dishonestly, for surely to keep such a secret would be wrong. But would telling him be selfish, easing her conscience only to inflict unhappiness on him? He was so happy, they both were, with all their lives before them – had she any right to risk ruining their future?

There was another complication. If she did tell Michael, he'd be sure to question her about how and where the rape occurred, and after the conversation in Milan he'd be under no misapprehension as to the identity of the group of youths at the party. He'd insist on confronting them and the whole shameful episode would become common knowledge. Her skin burned with embarrassment at the thought of her privacy invaded, her guilty secret laid bare, of Rose's horror on learning that she'd given away her baby for adoption.

The thoughts circled round and round in her mind until eventually, in the early hours, she drifted into a shallow, fitful sleep, waking unrefreshed and no nearer a solution.

Rose looked at her with critical eyes the following

morning. "You don't look as though you've slept a wink."

"No," Beth said, as she hurriedly gulped a cup of tea. "Excitement, I suppose. I'll have to rush, Mum, or I'll miss the bus."

"What about your breakfast?" Rose protested.

"I haven't got time. I'll get a bacon cob off the trolley!"

Knowing that her colleagues were completely unaware of her relationship with Michael, she began to wonder whether their attitude towards her would change when she became Mrs Rushton, and in an effort to take her mind off her problem, mentioned it to Michael that evening when they went out for a drink.

"I've been meaning to talk to you about that," he said. "Look, I don't know how you feel Beth, but I don't see any reason for us to have a long engagement. After all, we're both sure of our feelings. We could start looking for a house now and perhaps get married in September."

September?" So soon? Her thoughts whirling, Beth could only nod in agreement.

"So, we'll need to get engaged officially," Michael continued, "and well, both Father and I think it would be better if you resigned now. You'll have plenty to do before the wedding, and that would save any embarrassment for you at the works."

Astounded, Beth retorted, "Hang on a minute! What do you mean, you and your father think it would be better if I resigned?"

"Surely you didn't intend to carry on working after we're married? I mean, I can support us both, you know!"

"I know that," Beth tried to remain calm. "You just don't get it, do you? I'm not some puppet your family can manipulate!"

"There's no need to take it like that, Beth. Surely you realise that I can't possibly have my wife working on the potbank." Michael stared at her in bewilderment.

"Oh, and my feelings don't come into it, I suppose. I've worked damn hard to achieve what I have, Michael. We weren't all born with a silver spoon in our mouths, you know!"

"That's a bit unfair." Michael's mouth tightened. "What the hell's the matter with you, Beth?"

"The matter with me, as you put it, is that I'd like to be consulted about my life, if you don't mind."

Michael sighed with exasperation. "Okay! Next time, I'll talk to you first. But that doesn't change the issue. Much as I love you, I'm not prepared to argue about this."

"I didn't realise you were such a snob!" Beth flung at him.

"Snobbery doesn't come into it – it's good business sense."

"And what would I live on over the next few months? Have you and your father thought of that?"

"I'll make you an allowance, of course."

To Beth's surprise, Rose took Michael's side.

"He's quite right. It would never do. It wouldn't be fair on the others either, having to watch everything they said for fear it'd get back to the bosses."

"I wouldn't –"

"That's as maybe, but you could be put in a very awkward position. No, Michael's right, Beth, and they've said they'll carry on paying your wages until the wedding. Anyway, you'll have plenty to do once the babies come along. I take it he knows the Church forbids birth control?" Rose flushed. She still found it difficult to talk of anything to do with sex.

"We've never talked about it, but I suppose he does. After all, he knows we're Catholics."

"There you are then." Rose looked at her shrewdly. "What's the matter? Are you thinking 'all that education and I'm going to end up a housewife like every other woman'?"

"No," Beth said. "I don't agree with the old-fashioned view that education's wasted on a woman, because she'll only get married and have a family. Education isn't only about earning a living. What I do object to is being told what to do. I'd have preferred to make my own decision about whether I carried on working or not."

"You'd probably have come to the same conclusion," Rose commented.

"That's not the point," Beth retorted.

The following evening Michael suggested to her that they become officially engaged on his 30th birthday, in two weeks' time.

"My parents would like to hold a party and announce the engagement then, and we could put the notice in *The Sentinel* that weekend," he suggested.

Beth started to panic. Events were beginning to overtake her. She had to decide what she was going to do before things got out of hand. If she was to tell Michael about Rosemary, then it must be before any official announcement.

"What do you say, darling? Shall we go and get the ring next week? Then you can give in your notice at work and leave before the announcement is made. Luckily, you didn't transfer to the monthly payroll."

"I couldn't afford to," Beth said, her mind frantically striving to find an answer to her dilemma.

"Well, that's one problem you won't have in the future," Michael assured her. He was looking forward to spoiling Beth a little – she'd obviously never had many of the luxuries of life. "You still haven't answered me – don't you want to go shopping for an engagement ring?"

"I just can't believe it's all happening." Beth looked at him with pride – he was so handsome in his sports jacket and flannels. She loved him so much. How could she risk losing him?

That night, she struggled again with her problem in the privacy of her bedroom, and this time before she drifted into an exhausted sleep, at last came to a decision. The logical step was to find out whether she really had a choice whether to tell him or not – and for that she needed medical advice and anonymously. But where?

As before, in her life's crises, Beth found her answer at the public library.

"I've a day's holiday due to me, Mum," she said casually at the weekend. "I thought I'd take it on Tuesday and go to Manchester for the day."

"Oh, what a pity, lass! I'm working or I'd have come with you."

"Yes, I know, but I can't take it any other day," Beth lied, for once in her life grateful that Rose went out to work.

It was a pity she had to go all the way to Manchester, but she didn't dare risk it in any of the six towns of the Potteries. There were one or two Family Planning Clinics, but what if she was seen going in, particularly by someone from the parish out shopping for the day? Apart from that, the Rushtons mixed socially with the professional classes, and her feverish imagination showed her a scenario where she sat down to dinner opposite the doctor she'd consulted. No, in Manchester she would be safe from detection.

It was raining when the crowded train arrived at Victoria Station, and going immediately to a telephone box Beth looked in the directory. She ran her finger down the page. Yes, there it was. Glancing at her watch she realised that if they held a morning surgery, she needed to hurry – it was already nine forty-five. Hurrying out of the station, she hailed a taxi, and ten minutes later was standing in a small side street outside an ugly brick building. A small noticeboard on the wall proclaimed its function.

Apprehensively, she pushed open one of the double glass doors and approached a middle-aged, motherly-looking woman behind the reception desk.

"Good morning, would it be possible for me to see the doctor, please?"

Glancing up, the receptionist frowned. "Have you an appointment? We're very busy this morning, Mrs . . ." She looked doubtfully at Beth's ringless left hand. "You're not married?"

"No, but I'm getting married soon. I didn't realise I had to make an appointment. I've come to

Manchester specially for the day," Beth pleaded. "It's just that I need some medical advice, and I don't want to go to my own doctor."

"Oh, I see. You do understand we don't prescribe contraceptives to single women, not unless you can provide proof you're getting married?"

Beth nodded.

"Well, I suppose an appointment's not strictly necessary, and as you've come so far . . ." She ran her finger down the list of appointments and then said, "If you don't mind waiting, I'll see if she can fit you in at the end of surgery."

"Thank you." With a sense of relief Beth went to the back of the shabby waiting-room and sat on one of the hard wooden chairs. So, it was a lady doctor! She glanced around at the other women waiting. No one spoke, although one woman smiled at her as she flicked through a dilapidated copy of *Woman's Own*. Most appeared to be in their late twenties or early thirties, and sat with an air of weary resignation, their faces as drab as the grey walls. Beth looked at them, wondering whether they had a brood of kids at home and were desperate to avoid adding to their number. This new contraceptive pill, once it became easily available, would free many women from a life of drudgery. Her own church's ruling on contraception Beth considered ambivalent. She found difficulty in understanding its arguments. Surely the concept of whether it was right to avoid pregnancy was the important dogma? Once the Church accepted that it was not wrong to do so, as it had by approving 'natural birth control' or the 'safe period', then the method used ceased to be relevant. The principle was either right or wrong; anything else was superfluous. Beth only knew that if she were in a marriage where pregnancy was an annual event causing hardship, then she would be sorely tempted to follow the example of the other women in the room, and do something about it.

"Could you fill in this form, please?"

Beth looked up to see the receptionist holding out a white form.

"Yes, of course."

She read the printed boxes in panic. They seemed to want to know an awful lot about her.

"I can assure you that we maintain complete confidentiality." The receptionist smiled in encouragement, and Beth swallowed nervously, then began to fill in her details.

She waited with increasing trepidation as the other women were seen, rehearsing what she would say when she saw the doctor. She didn't even know if she could get the words out. She dreaded having to dredge up the whole hated, shameful episode. How did you sit in a room in broad daylight and confess you'd been the victim of rape? Fiercely she blanked out threatening images of that long-ago scene of fear and horror. And then, what would she do if the doctor couldn't reassure her? She'd be forced into making a decision, a decision so fraught with danger that her mind shied away from it. Her whole life, her chance of love and happiness, depended on the doctor's verdict.

Then at last her name was called and, taking a deep breath, she walked along the narrow corridor and paused outside a teak door bearing the nameplate, Dr A Seymour.

"Come in," came the reply to Beth's tentative knock, and she found herself facing a thin, grey-haired woman, her brisk manner and clinical white coat tempered by kindly blue eyes. She finished writing on a notepad, put down her pen and sat back.

"What can I do for you, my dear?"

"It's a little difficult to explain," Beth began.

"Just take your time and start at the beginning." She waited.

Beth looked at a point behind her, moistened her suddenly dry mouth, and launched into her explanation. "When I was seventeen, I was raped and became pregnant. I never told anyone, and went to a different part of the country to have the baby, which was adopted."

"Yes?"

Beth felt the colour rise to her cheeks, and forced herself to meet the doctor's eyes.

"Since that time I've never bothered much with men, but now I've met someone and we want to get married. I haven't told him anything so far, and I want to know if I have any choice about telling him," she said desperately. "What I mean is, would he be able to tell anyway?"

Dr Seymour looked at her searchingly. "Have you had sexual intercourse since the rape?"

"No."

"Well, I'd better have a look at you. Slip off your pants and stockings behind that screen, get on the bed, and I'll be with you in a minute."

Beth undressed, placing her clothes on a chair, and stepping on to a small stool, climbed on to the high, narrow bed with its fresh paper sheet. She lay flat on her back, trying to control her nerves as she awaited what she knew would be an embarrassing and uncomfortable ordeal. Nervous apprehension was almost choking her, and she turned her head to one side, saying a silent prayer.

The doctor was deft and professional, her examination gentle and thorough, and then removing her plastic gloves she told Beth to get dressed and come through as soon as she was ready.

The two women faced each other across the large, cluttered desk.

"You're very lucky," Dr Seymour said slowly. "Giving birth at such an early age you've escaped the normal stretch marks I would have expected to find. Quite honestly, I don't think your future husband would detect anything untoward. A doctor would know, of course, by an internal examination, but certainly it wouldn't be apparent during normal marital relations."

"But would he know I wasn't a virgin?" asked Beth anxiously.

"No more so than in the case of any other modern young woman. Oh, it might have been true at one time, all those tales of blood on the sheets. Nowadays young girls lead such active lives, taking part in sports and wearing internal sanitary protection, that their hymens often tear naturally. No, I don't think you have anything to worry about – you'll be quite tight anyway, if as you say you've never had sex since that time."

Beth's overwhelming relief must have shown as, through blurred tears of joy, she saw the doctor lean forward with compassion.

"Look, I know it's a difficult situation, but in my professional experience rape is a subject few people can handle. Coupled with an illegitimate child, don't you think you're asking a lot of this young man? What happened was in the past long before you met him. Take my advice and leave it there."

Dr Seymour picked up her pen, indicating that the consultation was at an end, and thanking her Beth made her way thoughtfully out of the building.

That night, back home in Minsden, she stared into the darkness, wrestling with her conscience. What she planned was deception, but was it so terribly wrong to avoid hurting someone you loved? What would she achieve by unburdening her guilt, except to perhaps blight two people's lives? Surely the burden was hers, not Michael's?

Then eventually, as the dawn light filtered through the curtains, Beth prayed for forgiveness, knowing that she had finally come to a decision. She would keep her secret.

Chapter 17

Two weeks later, Beth sat watching with delight as several fashionably dressed mannequins paraded between the restaurant tables. When Sylvia Rushton had suggested that they meet for lunch in Hanley's leading and exclusive department store, she'd been at first intrigued and then glad of an opportunity to get to know her future mother-in-law better.

Mum would love this, she thought, as a model paused at the table where she was waiting for Sylvia to arrive, inviting her to handle the fabric of her skirt. Beth put out a hand and stroked the soft camel cashmere. The suit was beautiful, but way out of her price range. Then as her eye was caught by the exquisite diamond solitaire sparkling on her finger, she realised that this would soon no longer be the case and she smiled to herself, hardly daring to believe her good fortune. Not only was she to marry the man she loved, but her whole lifestyle would change. No more worrying about bills, no more fantasising before shop windows only to turn away . . .

"You bitch!" The words were hissed at her and, stunned, Beth turned swiftly to face Ursula, elegant in a navy and white polka dot dress, her face twisted with hatred.

"You conniving, scheming little bitch!" Ursula spat out the words with such venom that Beth recoiled.

"Ursula –" she began to protest.

"Don't you Ursula me! Why you're nothing but a gold-digger! You tried toadying up to me at school, but once I got wise to you, I soon put a stop to that! I thought you'd have learnt your lesson, but no, now you've set your cap at Michael. Quite the social climber, aren't you? But you won't get him to the altar, not if I've got anything to do with it!"

Astounded at the other girl's animosity, Beth retorted, "You mean you think I became your best friend at school because you were well off? I had no idea your background was so different from mine, not until your birthday party."

Ursula looked at her with contempt. "Of course, that's what you would say." Her eyes glinted with jealousy as they focused on Beth's magnificent engagement ring.

"I think you're the bitch, Ursula, not me!" Beth said, her voice tight with anger. "Go on. Tell me. Why do you hate me so much? I really would like to know."

"Why? Because you made me look a fool, that's why." Ursula tossed back her long blonde hair, oblivious to the fact that the clarity of her penetrating voice was making her the object of curious stares. "Inviting you home as though you were one of us!"

Beth's face grew hot with anger and embarrassment. She lashed out, "One of you! What the hell do you mean, 'one of you'? You know, Ursula, I must be a very bad judge of character, because I liked you, I really did. So now I know! You threw away our friendship because you're nothing but a lousy snob! Who on earth do you think you are anyway?"

Ursula gave an arrogant shrug, infuriating Beth even more.

"You had your chance with Michael," she said icily, "but he could obviously see right through you because he chose me. Do you know something? I feel sorry for you! You're all bitter and twisted. As for my marrying Michael, there's not a thing you can do to stop me!"

Their eyes locked in mutual hostility, then horrified to feel the threat of treacherous tears, Beth looked away, blinking rapidly. There was no way she'd give that cat the satisfaction of knowing she had the power to upset her.

"Why, Ursula, how lovely to see you!" The sound of Sylvia's light musical voice as she approached provided the spur Beth needed to bring her emotions under control, and she managed a bright smile as her future mother-in-law joined them and planted a light kiss on Ursula's cheek. "I can't apologise enough for being so late, Beth, but a friend called just as I was coming out."

"I thought I'd better get a table. It was beginning to fill up," Beth said. She raised her chin, her expression hardening. "Ursula has an urgent appointment. In fact she was just leaving." Her tone was deliberately curt and dismissive and, picking up the menu, she pointedly studied it.

"Oh, well, give my love to your mother," said Sylvia. "Tell her I'll be in touch soon."

Ursula smiled sweetly at Sylvia and then said, "Goodbye, Beth, and once again congratulations on your engagement. I was so sorry to miss the party, but you know how it is when you have flu."

She was charm itself, obviously for Sylvia's benefit, and Beth wondered whether Michael and his family had ever seen the other side of her.

Flu my eye, she thought, knowing that Ursula and her parents had been told the news before the official announcement. Just sour grapes and another snub.

She watched Ursula make a graceful exit and then,

meeting Sylvia's discerning gaze, lowered her eyes.

"Right, Beth, have you decided what you'd like to eat?"

Sylvia ordered their meal while Beth, still smarting from Ursula's vindictive words, struggled to regain her composure. She desperately wanted this first tête à tête with Michael's mother to go well, and they politely exchanged small talk, until Sylvia paused and then said, "Have you and Michael settled on a definite date yet?"

"No, we're waiting until we've found a house."

"Well, I don't think you'll have much difficulty in finding somewhere you both like." Sylvia broke off as the waitress placed bowls of minestrone soup before them.

Beth took a bread roll, wondering what was coming next. She was sure there was an ulterior motive behind Sylvia's invitation. She didn't have to wait long.

"I wanted to talk to you about the wedding, Beth. This is a little bit awkward, which is why I wanted to speak to you on your own."

Beth, outwardly calm, began to spoon her soup.

'It's just that, well, I know your mother is a widow . . . oh, by the way I was so so sorry that she and your grandmother couldn't come to the party. Is your grandmother better?"

"Yes, she's recovering very well." Granny Platt's bout of pleurisy couldn't have come at a worse time, and on the night of the party, Rose had refused to leave her side.

"Good. Well, to come back to what I was saying, I know it's normally the bride's family who stand the cost of the wedding, but do you think your mother would mind if we departed from tradition?"

"You mean . . ."

"Yes, I do. I'm sure you'll realise, Beth, that with a prominent family like ours, the wedding of our eldest son is bound to cause some interest, both socially and among other business people in the area. I'm sure your mother would do her best, but would she be able to cope with over 200 guests?"

Beth drew a sharp breath.

"No, of course she couldn't," Sylvia said briskly. "So I'm suggesting that you leave all the arrangements for the wedding to us, and you concentrate on finding a house that you like."

Beth's heart sank. There was sense in what Sylvia said, she was enough of a realist to know that. There was no way they could afford such a huge expense. It was just that she didn't know whether she wanted a huge society wedding – she'd thought it would just be both families and a few friends.

"And then there's the matter of the church,"

Sylvia continued. "Have you and Michael discussed it? I know you're a Catholic but St Hugh's where we attend is very High and it's such a picturesque church. It would look lovely on the photographs."

Beth stared at her. "Are you suggesting that we should get married in a Protestant church?"

"Would it matter so very much? You see, we'd thought of having the reception at Sutherland Hall, and St Hugh's would be so convenient." Sylvia smiled encouragingly, confident that she'd be able to organise everything in a way which would meet with Robert's approval. He was being so obstinate about the whole affair, still convinced it was a flash in the pan, but she knew Michael. Once he'd made up his mind, there was no moving him.

Beth took a deep breath. Oh, no, she'd have to stand her ground on this one!

"I'm sorry to disappoint you, Mrs Rushton, but I couldn't possibly get married in a Protestant church."

Sylvia raised one eyebrow. "Have you discussed it with Michael?"

"No," Beth said. "To be honest we haven't looked that far ahead, but I don't think you understand. It really is important to me to be married in a Catholic church."

Sylvia lapsed into thoughtful silence as the waitress cleared away their soup plates.

"Well, naturally it's a matter for you and Michael to decide. But Beth, have you considered that he may not want to get married in a Catholic church?"

"I didn't think he was particularly religious," Beth countered.

"Maybe not by your standards, but he was christened and confirmed Church of England. I'm not making an issue of this, Beth, but I do think you need to sort it out, and soon. We can't do anything until the church is booked."

"I will," Beth promised. She leaned back to let the waitress begin to serve her roast pork and vegetables, and then Sylvia suddenly smiled.

"I'm so glad we can talk like this, Beth. You know I've never had a daughter, and Giovanna lives so far away. I hope you and I will become good friends. I know I can be a bit managing at times, or at least so I'm told. However, from what I've seen of you, I think you'll stand up for your rights." She gave Beth a shrewd look.

"I've had to," Beth replied.

She looked appraisingly at the older woman, noting the quiet elegance of her grey suit and pale pink blouse, her beautifully set silver hair and carefully made-up face. She could learn a lot from Sylvia, and was suddenly aware that she would need such a valuable ally after she was married. She was under no misapprehension about her future life; it was going to be totally different from her mother's and grandmother's.

"I appreciate what you've just said, Mrs Rushton, and I warn you I'll probably be coming to you for advice," she said smiling.

"I'll be there when you need me," Sylvia assured her.

Unlike your husband, Beth thought with resentment.

The rest of the meal passed in casual conversation, and afterwards, her emotions still raw after the row with Ursula, Beth wandered around the shops, finding it a novelty to be in town on a weekday. With some misgivings, she'd reluctantly submitted to Michael's wishes and resigned from her job a week before his birthday party. For 'personal reasons' she'd said at the time, giving rise to much curious speculation and her request that there should be no collection had been considered eccentric to say the least. However, when she'd rather self-consciously gone into the factory on the Monday following the official announcement of the engagement in the local paper, her colleagues were full of ecstatic congratulations, together with much ribbing about being a 'dark horse'. Beth had borne it all in good humour, and then had toured the factory showing the girls her engagement ring, knowing they'd all be dying to see it, not caring that Michael's father would undoubtedly disapprove.

Pausing in the doorway of a shoe shop, she glanced at the ring for the hundredth time, its tangible presence a reassurance that the whole affair wasn't a dream and she'd suddenly wake up to reality.

Rose, on the other hand, was only too well aware that she faced the prospect of living alone, and later that week sat reflecting sadly that if only Beth had married someone of her own class, then she might have settled within walking distance. That would have been a comfort, close enough to pop in for a cup of tea, or a chat, or when the children came along, to share in their lives. As it was, there was no chance that Michael would buy a house in Minsden; it would probably be miles away in the so-called 'green belt'. Green belt! Another name for where moneyed folk lived, in her opinion. How was it she'd brought up two children, and neither of them lived close? She could remember the time when families were born, married, gave birth and died, if not in the same street, then at least within a mile radius of where they were born. What was it they called it, a more mobile population? Well, it didn't augur well for family life in the future. Anyone could see that.

Oh well, she might as well do something useful, she thought, and gathering together her hoard of Green Shield stamps from the kitchen drawer, settled herself down to stick them in the empty books. Every time she went shopping she intended to do it straight away, but she never did, and they all became tangled up together.

No, she might as well admit it, it wasn't just that Beth was getting married and leaving, that was natural and only to be expected. She was afraid, that was it, afraid of losing her. She was worried that she'd change, that she'd become influenced by her new affluent life, and the views of the people she'd mix with. Sometimes, she wondered whether it was a good idea to send these working-class children to grammar schools. It set them apart from their own, and yet they were often not accepted by the middle-classes either. Betwixt and between, Rose called it, and didn't envy them at all. Look at Beth, not an ounce of snobbery in her, and yet she knew that some of the neighbours considered her 'stuck up' because of the way she spoke.

Suddenly glancing at the clock, Rose tutted as she realised she was missing *Crossroads*, and got up to switch on the TV. At least she didn't have to cook for Beth – she was going to Michael's for the evening as his parents had gone on holiday to the south of

France. It must be lovely to see such places . . . still, she mustn't grumble she told herself firmly. She had a lot to be thankful for.

At Linden Lodge, Beth and Michael lay curled in each other's arms on the leather chesterfield in the drawing-room, savouring these rare moments of privacy.

"I can't wait until we're married," Michael murmured. "Then we can be alone whenever we wish – can you just imagine it?" His hand gently caressed Beth's leg as she snuggled up to him.

"Your mother wants me to talk to you about the wedding," she murmured.

"What, already?"

"She says she can't do anything until the church is booked, and she wants a decision by the time they get back." Beth lifted her head. "Michael, would you mind if we got married in a Catholic church?"

"Mind? I haven't really thought about it," he said. "I've been too busy scouring the estate agents. Which reminds me I've got some particulars of houses for you to look at, only I've gone and left them in the car."

"Oh, I can't wait!" Beth said, thrilled at the thought of choosing her own home. "I've got something for you too, the Beatles number one, 'From Me to You'."

"Great!"

"But we do need to get this matter of the church sorted."

"Well," Michael said, "I don't suppose you'd be willing to get married at our parish church?"

"No. I wouldn't feel married unless I got married in a Catholic church."

"Well, we can't have you feeling you're living in sin. Go on then, we'll get married in your church, but don't think you'll get everything your own way," he teased.

Beth breathed a sigh of relief and then said tentatively, "There are a few conditions."

"Such as?"

"The priest will want you to promise to bring up any children in the Catholic faith."

"Will he indeed?" Michael fell silent, and Beth waited, her stomach fluttering. What if Michael refused? Oh, it would have been so much easier if they'd both been of the same denomination.

"Are there any other conditions to marrying a Catholic?" Michael asked.

"Well," she flushed. "The church doesn't believe in artificial birth control."

"What sort does it believe in?"

"Natural methods, what it calls the safe period."

"And what is that exactly?" Michael began to feel

irritated. What business was it of anyone else what he and Beth decided to do about a family?

"Well," Beth began to explain, "there are certain days in the month when a woman is more likely to conceive, and during those days it's suggested that a couple should, you know, abstain. It's called the 'rhythm method'." Her cheeks flamed and she was glad that Michael couldn't see her face, held as she was with her head against his chest.

"You mean, I couldn't use anything, or you couldn't go on this new contraceptive pill?"

"That's right."

Again there was a silence.

"And do you go along with their thinking on this?" Michael eventually asked her.

"As a practising Catholic I'm supposed to, but I do have reservations. To my mind, if they accept the principle of birth control, the method isn't important."

"So, if we particularly wanted to avoid having a baby, you'd agree to do something about it?"

Beth thought carefully and then said, "I certainly wouldn't insist on doing anything in our married life that you weren't happy with. Although, perhaps the 'rhythm' method would work – it does with a lot of people."

"I don't care whether it works or not," Michael

said grimly. "I'm not having anyone dictating to me when I can make love to you. Good heavens above, we'll be married! It's bad enough restraining myself now."

Beth bit her lip. "What about bringing the children up to be Catholics?"

"I've no particular argument with that," Michael reassured her. "Many of the best schools are Roman Catholic. Just as long as you'll agree that when they're old enough they can choose for themselves – that if they want to join the Church of England, or the Methodists, or anything else for that matter, you'll not put any pressure on them."

"It's a bargain." Beth hesitated. "Does that mean you'll agree to get married in my church?"

"I will, my pet. Although if a few moments ago you'd given a different answer, we'd have had problems."

Beth looked up at him.

"Just remember. I'll have no priest telling me what to do, either now or after we're married!" Michael's tone brooked no argument, and any reply Beth might have made was silenced as his lips came down to hers and then he whispered, "I can think of far more interesting things to do than talk – we'll look at the brochures later."

On their return, Robert and Sylvia reluctantly

accepted their decision, not without some muttered expletives from Robert about Rome and its influence.

"Don't be silly, Robert," Sylvia admonished him. "You forget, I was educated at a Catholic convent school and no one tried to brainwash me."

"I still wish he'd married Ursula," Robert grumbled.

"Don't you like Beth?"

"Oh, she seems very pleasant on the surface, but I have to tell you that John Dawes has warned me to be on our guard. Apparently, Ursula told him she's a right little gold-digger – she remembers what she was like at school, always toadying up to the rich kids!"

"Ursula said that?"

"So he says."

"You know, I can't help wondering whether Ursula has her own axe to grind, Robert, and I do object to her spreading malicious rumours like this. Surely Sister Veronica would have mentioned it if it was true. No, I think it's a case of sour grapes – I sensed an atmosphere between them that day at lunch."

"Well, I hope you're right for all our sakes. I still think he'd have been better marrying Ursula."

"Oh, for heavens sake, Robert, give it a rest!" Sylvia said crossly. "What I need to know is which church it will be. Beth says her own parish church is far too small for the numbers we're thinking of. I don't suppose you've got any ideas?

"How would I know?"

"No, you only go to our own church for weddings and funerals. At least Beth has religious convictions, and stands up for them too, a rare thing among young people these days. Anyway, they're both going to see her parish priest this weekend."

Robert didn't answer, immersing himself in the *Financial Times*, a gesture he found useful when he'd tired of a topic.

Father Daly was affability itself as he ushered the young couple into the shabby sitting-room at the presbytery.

A pale, thin, bespectacled man, he ran the parish with great efficiency, endearing himself to the pious, and striking the fear of God into any who neglected their Christian duty. Once, he'd even berated the Catholic Mothers' Union from the pulpit, accusing them of endangering their immortal souls by indulging in malicious gossip which was injuring one of his parishioners. Beth felt a great affection for him, knowing that he unselfishly devoted his life to caring for his flock. He was, however, not a man to deviate from what he saw as his duty.

"It's no problem at all, Beth. I'll have a word with

Father O'Rourke up at Our Lady of Good Counsel in Newcastle. Sure and the church is a barn of a place, plenty of room for all your guests."

"I'd rather hoped you could marry us, Father," Beth said.

"I'd have been mortally offended if you hadn't asked me," he smiled. "Of course I'll marry you. It's a fine wife for yourself you'll be getting, Michael, I hope you realise that?"

"I do indeed, Father," Michael said feeling a little awkward using the term.

"So what do we do next?" Beth asked.

"Well, I'll get a date for you, in September if possible, and then of course you'll both need to come for instruction."

Michael's eyes narrowed. "Instruction? I haven't said anything about turning a Roman Catholic."

"Have I asked you to? Of course, if you were interested . . ." Seeing the antipathy in the young man's face, Father Daly suppressed a sigh, and said, "I'm talking of a few informal chats to prepare you both for the sacrament of marriage."

"Of course. That won't be a problem, will it, Michael?" Beth said.

"No, I suppose not," he replied, feeling slightly annoyed. He hadn't bargained for anything like this! Oh, he was willing to sign a bit of paper saying he'd bring up the children as Catholics if he had to, but sit and listen to a celibate priest lecture him on his marital role, it was a bit of an imposition, and he'd tell Beth so when they got outside.

"It's just normal, Michael. Gordon and Valerie had to go, just the same," she protested.

"Well, I warn you. I'm likely to get angry."

"No, you won't. Father Daly's used to it. He'll be very diplomatic."

"He'd better be!" he said grimly, "Oh, by the way, I've asked James to be best man, and Guy's agreed to be onc of the ushers." He steered her over to the car. "Come on. I've had enough of wedding plans. Let's go for a drink – I could murder a gin and tonic."

As Michael drove out to find a country pub, Beth remained silent. James and Guy would be at the wedding, of course, she'd expected that, but what of the others? John Forrester, Alan Slater, Peter Harris and Tony Morrison, those names which were forever engraved on her memory? They were bound to be on the invitation list. Was it possible that seeing the group together would trigger some form of recognition? She could remember vaguely the height and build of the three youths as they swayed in the doorway. They were of a similar build – no one stood out from the others. James and Guy were of the right height but surely the others must vary? That would at least eliminate one or two of them.

She felt nauseated as she became aware of the irony: it was almost certain that the man who'd raped her and fathered her child would be a guest at her wedding. Was she never to be free of his shadow?

Chapter 18

The church was full to capacity when Rose, last to arrive as tradition demanded of the bride's mother, paused at the entrance. Her initial nervous impression was one of a scented profusion of flowers and a sea of festive hats. Pretty pastel ones, smart navy ones, trimmed ones, plain ones, cartwheels bedecked with ribbons, the variety of colours and shapes swam for a moment before her eyes; then, taking a deep breath to steady her nerves, she stepped forward.

The aisle seemed endless as, summoning all the dignity she possessed, she walked alone towards the altar, conscious of a rustle of interest as heads turned to watch her progress before she slipped thankfully into her allotted seat in the second pew.

Michael, looking distinguished in his grey morning

suit, turned and caught her eye, giving her an encouraging smile. That must be James next to him and Rose looked at him with surprise; the two brothers were not at all alike.

She turned to whisper a greeting to her mother, sitting stiffly in a beige costume and proudly wearing a turban hat in coffee and cream swirled tulle. The middle-aged man next to her smiled his own slightly crooked smile, and Rose's heart filled once again with gratitude at Michael's generosity. On realising how sparse the number of guests on Beth's side would be, he'd immediately sent her Uncle Cyril the air fare and now here he was, having flown all the way from New Zealand especially for the occasion. It was said that money didn't bring happiness but, it did bring power, though from what she'd seen most folk didn't use it right.

Glancing across the aisle she met Sylvia Rushton's eyes as she smilingly inclined her head in acknowledgement. Beautifully dressed in pale grey silk, Sylvia's hat was a exquisite confection of pink roses, but Rose decided her own outfit of navy and white was far more practical, and her white hat with its small brim edged with navy was smart without being over fussy. No, she was quite happy with her choice.

There was a stir of expectancy as Father Daly

moved to the centre of the altar steps, and the elderly lady organist began the opening bars of Lohengrin's 'Bridal March' signalling Beth's arrival.

Beth waited as her Matrons of Honour arranged the folds of her elaborate train, and then with a tremulous smile placed her hand on Gordon's arm.

"Ready?" he whispered.

She nodded and followed by Valerie and Giovanna, one so fair and the other so dark in peach satin with flower garlands in their hair, she began her slow procession. There were a few sharp intakes of breath as she passed by, a vision in white Nottingham lace, her priceless veil a Rushton family heirloom, her bouquet a cascade of red roses and stephanotis.

Michael turned as she approached, his eyes alight with wonder and pride, and then they both took their places before the priest as he began to intone,

"Dearly beloved, we are gathered here today in the sight of God and before this congregation to witness the marriage of Michael and Beth . . ."

"Who's that with James?" Beth whispered to Michael much later, when at last they found a moment to talk. The huge number of guests to be greeted at the reception had been overwhelming, and eventually she'd abandoned hope of remembering who anyone was – they were just a blur of faces to be smiled at.

"Where?"

"In the corner, they're just looking at the table plan."

"Oh, that's Peter Harris and Alan Slater. Why, do you know them?"

"No, I don't think so – it's just the tall one reminded me of someone," she lied.

"Oh, that's Peter. He must be six feet three at least – he was jolly useful as a goalkeeper when we were kids. I haven't seen him for ages."

Beth swiftly eliminated him from her list. To even think of such things on this wonderful day seemed disloyal, but the temptation was too strong. There would never be another opportunity like this, to see the young men together, hopefully to see them standing together. Only then could she shortlist three of them.

She stared at Alan Slater. Could it be him? Smaller than James, he was already losing his sandy hair, and looked a bit of a wimp, but she thoughtfully committed his appearance to memory.

The guests took their places in the huge private room, with its casement windows overlooking green parkland, and then Michael led his bride to their seats in the centre of the top table, to tumultuous applause. Beth smiled, her eyes suddenly misty at the realisation that she was finally Michael's wife.

“Just start from the outside,’ she whispered to Gordon, who was looking in consternation at the variety of cutlery.

“I didn’t realise there’d be so many people,” he said, perspiring slightly.

“Are you still worrying about your speech?”

“I shan’t be able to relax until it’s over,” he muttered. “I’d rather do guard duty any day!”

She laughed, and later felt proud at Gordon’s few words which were delivered with an air of confidence she knew he was far from feeling. It felt so good to have all her family together, and looking along the table she saw Rose’s happy face, and received a loving smile from Granny Platt. She could hardly remember her Uncle Cyril, but his delight in being there only added to the occasion.

“Happy, darling?” Michael murmured, and she smiled radiantly.

“We’re going to be so happy!” she said.

“The happiest couple in the world.” He leaned over and kissed her gently on the lips, and for a few moments they were oblivious to anyone other than each other.

Later, mingling with their guests they became separated, and Beth eventually found herself before one of the casement windows and in a position to survey the crowd. Her eyes searched the room, and then found James, his arm around Giovanna, talking to a young man with horn-rimmed spectacles. Seeing Guy passing with a drink for his latest girlfriend, she caught his arm saying, "Guy, who's that with James? He looks familiar."

"John Forrester, you mean. Oh, he's one of the old gang, not that we see much of him now. He's shortly to be ordained as a Methodist minister. Not one of your lot!" He grinned. "We always used to rib him about being against the demon drink."

"You mean he's always been teetotal?"

"Oh, absolutely."

So that was another one off the list! Now which was Tony Morrison? She scanned the crowd, but there were so many young men in that age range, it was impossible.

Amid many murmurs of good wishes she made her way over to the door and went out into the cool vestibule and to the powder room, relieved to find it empty, glad of a few moments of peace and quiet after all the attention. As she was repairing her makeup Ursula entered and her heart sank. Apart from a cool conventional greeting on arrival, the other girl had so far avoided her.

"Well, if it isn't the new Mrs Michael Rushton!" said Ursula with sarcasm.

Beth ignored her.

"You may be winning so far, sweetie-pie," Ursula drawled, "but he'll soon tire of you. Michael needs a wife who can wine and dine the cream of the county, and I can't exactly see you fulfilling that role, can you? Meat and potato pie, and grilled oatcakes won't exactly fit the bill. Now, I've a diploma in cordon bleu cookery – much more suitable, don't you think?"

"Then since you're the perfect choice, I wonder why he didn't marry you?" Beth snapped.

Ursula's green eyes narrowed. "A temporary lapse. He'll come to realise his mistake. I give it twelve months, and I'm warning you now I'll be waiting to pick up the pieces."

"Then you'll wait a long time," Beth retorted angrily, but was prevented from continuing as Sylvia came in.

She looked from Beth's flushed fact to Ursula's pale one, and said casually, "I thought I saw you follow Beth in here, Ursula. Are you enjoying the wedding, dear? Perhaps, Beth, you could throw your bouquet in Ursula's direction – I'm sure we'd all like to see her happily married!"

With a thin smile, Ursula said in a forced tone, "I'll have to try and catch it. Ah well, I'll return to the fray." Opening the door to leave she said, "I'll see you both later."

Not if I can help it, Beth thought with bitterness.

Even on her wedding day, Ursula couldn't leave her alone.

Sylvia looked in the mirror and began to tidy her hair, her expression thoughtful. "You know Beth, I'm not a fool, I know there's some hostility between you and Ursula. I just want you to remember that you're a Rushton now, part of our family. You don't have to cope with anything alone."

Beth looked at her gratefully, and on an impulse leaned over and kissed her cheek. "Thank you, Mrs Rushton, but I think I can fight my own battles. Still, it's nice to know I can turn to you if I need to."

"Good, and don't you think you could call me Sylvia now? Or you can call me Mother if you prefer?"

"No," Beth said quickly. She couldn't do that no matter how nice Sylvia was. "I think of you as Sylvia actually, so I'll stick to that if you don't mind."

"Right, that's settled. So, come on, daughter-in-law. Let's face the multitude."

Michael watched them smilingly return to the room, and glanced at his watch. It was time for them to change before going away, and suddenly he'd had enough of the festivities. He wanted to be alone with Beth, in anticipation at last of the night to come.

The hotel had reserved two adjoining bedrooms for the bride and groom to use as dressing rooms, and in one of them, while Beth took off her headdress and veil, Valerie wandered around fingering the rich brocade drapes and admiring the ruched pink satin eiderdown and velvet chaise longue. Seeing the expression on her face, Beth said gently, "It's only the icing on the cake, you know, Val. You and Gordon have the cake, that's the most important thing. All this means nothing without that."

"I know," sighed Valerie. "But you can't help being a bit envious. Mind you, Gordon looked the part, didn't he, after all the fuss he made over wearing a top hat and tails. I could have fallen for him all over again. Anyway," she cheered up, "now he's got his qualifications he's hoping to be made up to sergeant. It was all due to my help of course!"

Beth laughed. "Go on, we all know you're the brains in the family. I still think it was a crying shame you never went to the grammar school."

"I know," Valerie said reflectively. "Mind you, I'm saying nothing against Gordon. His skills lie on the practical side. He's very well thought of in the unit. You know, if we get posted back to England next time, I think I'm going to go to night school, perhaps do some 'O' levels or something, what do you think?"

"I think that's a fantastic idea." Beth said.

"It'd be great if we were stationed at Lichfield again, particularly if you started a family soon – then the kids could play together sometimes." Valerie looked archly at her sister-in-law.

"You're fishing!" Beth smiled. "OK, just between ourselves, we've decided we'll let nature take its course. After all, we both want children, and there's no reason to wait. I mean we haven't got to save up or anything."

"Lucky devils. Babies cost a fortune. Still, I wouldn't be without Paul for anything. It must be wonderful not having to worry about birth control. It's a right pain."

"I'll let you know." Beth blushed as Valerie gave her a playful push.

"Go on then. I know it's been a secret, but you can tell me now – where are you going for your honeymoon?"

"Madeira for two weeks, but we're spending the first night in London, and," Beth turned to face her, "Michael's promised to take me to Carnaby Street tomorrow morning."

"Ooh, you lucky thing!"

"I know. Come on, Val. We'd better get a move on! You're supposed to be helping me get ready, gasbag!"

They giggled, for a moment back in their teens, and then Beth stepped out of her heavy wedding-dress and began to brush her hair and repair her make-up.

A few minutes later, there was a quiet tap at the door and opening it Valerie ushered in Rose.

"Are you nearly ready, love?"

"I won't be long," Beth promised.

Valerie glanced at them both, and then murmuring something about having to see Gordon, quietly left.

Rose sat on the chaise longue as Beth fastened a white pleated skirt over her navy silk blouse, slipped on a pair of high-heeled shoes, and a beautifully cut navy jacket. A white pillbox hat with just a hint of veiling perched jauntily on her head.

She turned to her mother.

"How do I look?"

"Like a million dollars." Despite her initial misgivings when Michael had suggested that he give Beth an advance wedding present of a large cheque to help out with her trousseau, Rose had to admit it had been a godsend. With a glow of pride, she got up and kissed Beth gently on the cheek.

"I'm not much good at this sort of thing," she said awkwardly, "but about tonight. Just relax, Beth."

"Oh Mum, I'll be all right. Just you look after yourself." Beth hugged her, her eyes filling with tears.

"Hey, what's all this?" Michael asked, as he gave a quick knock on the adjoining door and came through. "Come on, you two. This is supposed to be a happy occasion. I'll take good care of her, Rose. I promise."

"I know you will. Go on, the pair of you. Everyone's waiting," she chided.

Beth picked up a bouquet of flowers which was an exact replica of the one she'd carried that morning, and she and Michael descended the thickly carpeted staircase overlooking the reception area which was crowded with wedding guests waiting to see them off. She saw Ursula at the back of the group standing slightly apart with her parents, and taking careful aim flung the bouquet directly at her. Ursula caught it awkwardly, her face flushing as people cheered, and Beth's eyes fleetingly met the amused ones of Sylvia.

Running through a shower of confetti, they climbed laughingly into Michael's Jaguar, to which some wag had stuck 'L' plates and a '*Just Married*' banner. Michael groaned as he spotted a tail of tin cans, and then shrugged and switched on the ignition.

"Right then, Mrs Rushton, we're off."

They both turned to wave goodbye, and then Michael grinned. "Just look at those three! They've obviously been at the champagne."

Beth followed his gaze and then froze as she saw the three figures swaying together in the doorway of the entrance to the hotel. Suddenly, the years slipped away and she was back in that darkened bedroom seeing the same outline, three young men, all the worse for drink, all the same height and of a similar build, and she knew with absolute certainty that she was seeing them again. One was Guy, another James and the third . . .?

"Michael," she said faintly, "who's the third one?"

"Tony Morrison. Not very keen on him myself, he's more a friend of James."

The colour drained from Beth's face. So, now she knew. After all these years she finally knew the identity of her attacker. It had to be this Tony Morrison. It had to be. It was unthinkable that it could have been either James or Guy! She stared desperately at his face but of course it meant nothing. He was just an ordinary young man with brown curly hair, looking rather foolishly drunk. For a moment she sat dazed in a welter of conflicting emotions, and then on an impulse seized a camera from the glove compartment and pointing it carefully at the group, clicked the shutter.

As the car drew away from the well-wishers, she replaced the camera and with a conscious effort deliberately consigned the incident to the back of her mind. She was determined not to let anything overshadow these long-awaited first hours that she and Michael were to share as man and wife.

"You didn't forget to put my other bouquet in the boot?"

"It's all done."

Five minutes later, after parking the car beneath a large oak tree, Michael handed her the flowers. "Do you want me to come with you?"

Beth shook her head. In her high-heeled shoes, she picked her way down uneven steps into the deserted sunlit churchyard, and walked along the weed-encrusted path.

The small headstone was in a corner shadowed by a thick yew hedge and, as she halted, Beth read again, as she always did, the simple inscription.

"Harry Sherwin, loving husband of Rose, and a devoted father."

"I got married today, Dad," she whispered. "I've brought you my bouquet." She stood cradling the red roses in her arms, her eyes misting with tears. "You'd have loved the wedding. Mum looked really smart, and Gordon gave me away. I wish it could have been you, because if I hadn't had the education you insisted on, I wouldn't even have met Michael, let alone marry him. Remember, I told you he was one of the Rushtons? He's the best thing that's ever happened to me, Dad. I love him so much." Bending, she gently placed the bouquet on the grassy mound.

As Beth moved away, she gave one backward glance and then looked up at Michael waiting in the car and walked towards her new life.

Chapter 19

"Well, they couldn't have had better weather if they'd got married in June," Sylvia said, as the Bentley purred its way along the quiet tree-lined road to Linden Lodge. "You must admit, Robert, it all went exceedingly well – and didn't she make a lovely bride?"

"Yes," admitted Robert. "She did! Several people commented on it. I have to concede she looked the part."

"She's good socially too," Sylvia mused. "I watched her mingling with the guests. If you hadn't known, you'd never have guessed she came from such a different background."

"I suppose we've got the nuns to thank for that," Robert muttered, as he swung into the drive.

"Give the girl some credit, can't you!" Sylvia protested in exasperation as she got out of the car. Stepping inside the front door, she stood for a moment in the cool oak-panelled hall. It was uncanny. The house already felt different, empty somehow.

"Is there anything to eat? I'm starving," demanded Robert as he came in and slumped wearily into an armchair in the sitting-room.

"I told Mrs Hammond to leave some cold meats and salad in the fridge." Sylvia kicked off her shoes and padded into the kitchen, returning with a tray which she placed on a low coffee table.

"I'm shattered," she said. "How James and Giovanna have the energy to go off socialising, I don't know."

"I'm glad Giovanna's driving. James was in no state," Robert said, looking disparagingly at his plate. "You know I hate salad."

"It's good for you." Sylvia closed her eyes for a few minutes, and then opened them as Robert spoke again.

"I suppose it could have been worse."

"What could?"

"Michael's choice."

"Robert, what exactly did you expect him to do? Come and say 'Please, Father, I want to get married. Who do you suggest?' Honestly, you do annoy me at times."

"I'm well aware of that. You make it quite obvious," he bristled.

"Oh, don't start! Suppose you explain to me just why you're so disappointed – surely it's not pure snobbery? Because if so, I wish you'd let it drop."

Robert looked at her with impatience. "You're being short-sighted, Sylvia. It's a sure sign you don't run the business. Just think for a moment: who holds a large percentage of shares in the firm? Yes, Ursula's father. Now if Michael had married Ursula, and I know she'd have had him, then eventually those shares would have reverted back to the family. Get it?"

Sylvia stared at him in disbelief. "You're talking about people's lives and feelings, not a damn balance sheet."

"Someone has to think about balance sheets. How else do you think the Rushtons have remained so prosperous? Now James, for instance, did have the good sense to marry the only daughter of a prominent businessman, even if she was Italian, so eventually her inheritance will increase the family fortunes. Perhaps you can tell me what Michael's wife will contribute? I know you like her, Sylvia, and I'm not denying she's a nice girl, but money should marry money – that's how dynasties are founded."

"And that's your ambition in life, is it, Robert? To found a dynasty."

"Now that we've become industrialists, yes. We're a very old family. We can trace our line right back to William the Conqueror."

"Then perhaps Beth's contribution will be a drop of healthy peasant blood," Sylvia said tartly. "I suppose you wouldn't have married me if I hadn't been well connected."

"But you were," he countered. "And beautiful with it. You still are – there wasn't a woman there today who could hold a candle to you."

Sylvia softened. "Go on with you."

Robert leaned over and kissed her cheek. "No, I mean it. I'm a lucky man, and I know it."

"And as for that champagne, I'd rather have a nice glass of milk stout any day!" Gordon grinned as he closed the back door behind Mrs Ward and going to the window chuckled,

"Look at her, straight across to Mrs Allen's. She'll dine out on today for weeks!"

"Aye, it'll be the one topic of conversation for ages," Rose smiled. "Still, you have to admit this street's never seen a wedding like it."

"No, you should have seen the neighbours' faces, when Beth came out of the front door! There was quite a crowd. Of course, I bet they'd never seen a Rolls Royce before either."

"You looked right handsome today yourself, our Gordon," Rose said, easing off her shoes and gratefully wriggling her toes. "Valerie looked a treat. I was proud of the pair of you. Just pass me those slippers. There's a good lad."

"Now are you sure you'll be all right?" he said. "I really ought to be getting along. I'd like to see Paul before he goes to sleep."

"He was no trouble then?"

"No, Val's Auntie Vera said he was as good as gold."

"Did Valerie's parents enjoy the wedding? They were a bit quiet?"

"I think they were a bit overwhelmed by it all, and to be honest having us stay has been a bit much for her mother – she's not been too well lately."

"Yes, I know. Well, next time you're on leave you'll be able to stay here for a change – there'll be a bit more room now. So love, what time do you have to leave tomorrow?"

"About half past eleven. We'll pop along after we've packed up. We said goodbye to Gran before she left." Gordon wandered restlessly around the room, and then stood fiddling with the chain on the cuckoo clock.

Sensing his impatience, Rose said briskly, "Right then, love, you go. Don't worry about me. I've put the immersion heater on, I'm going to have a nice bath and an early night."

"OK. Goodnight then, Mum." Gordon bent and kissed her cheek, and then let himself out.

With the need for pretence gone, Rose stayed sitting in the armchair for several minutes, closing her eyes as she felt the energy draining out of her. She felt so tired, the hectic build-up to the wedding and the emotional day had taken their toll, more than she cared to admit. I feel old, she admitted to herself, old and worn out. She thought of Sylvia Rushton, glowing with good health, her skin lightly tanned from a recent holiday, her hands and nails beautifully manicured, and looked down at her own work-roughened hands with distaste. It's just the anti-climax, she told herself firmly. You'll feel better if you do something, and going upstairs to her bedroom she hung her navy suit in the wardrobe.

Slipping on her quilted dressing-gown she paused on the tiny landing and then opened the door to Beth's room, ruefully surveying the inevitable chaos the wedding preparations had left. That could wait until the morning. It would give her something to do. Already the room felt different, as though it had been discarded, just like the boxroom, which had never felt the same since Gordon had left home.

She slumped on the bed. So, was this it then? Was

this how her life would be from now on? Long empty evenings, no one to care for, to cook for? All her life she'd cared for people, her mother after she was widowed, Grandma Sherwin, Harry with his bronchitis, and then struggled to bring up the children. Now, her son was serving in another country, she rarely saw her only grandchild, and Rose was under no illusion that her importance in her daughter's life would remain the same. Beth now had her own life to live, a husband to look after, a home to furnish. She knew it was the natural order of things, all mothers had to accept that, it was just that . . . oh, if only Harry were still alive. Rose wondered whether he knew that Beth had crossed that drawbridge he'd talked of between 'them and us', in a way he could never have imagined. Her shoulders sagged as a solitary tear began to trickle down her cheek and she brushed it away with impatience. She'd always refused to give in to self-pity and she wasn't going to start now! Straightening, she went downstairs to the poky bathroom behind the kitchen and turned on the taps. A good night's sleep, that's what she needed. She'd feel better in the morning. As Rose bent to swish the water her thoughts turned to the newly married couple.

God bless them, let them have a good life, she prayed.

Chapter 20

Later that night, hunched miserably under the bedclothes, Beth lifted a shaking hand to brush away scalding tears of humiliation and shame. There was complete silence in the dim curtained room, but her nerves were so taut she could sense Michael's every breath. Since he'd flung himself away from her in violent anger just after midnight, he'd been sitting motionless in the armchair near the window, occasionally lighting a cigarette, and stonily refusing to speak or even look in her direction. There was still anger emanating from him, Beth could almost taste it, and she felt a cold trickle of fear. She wouldn't blame Michael if he never forgave her.

The evening had begun with them both in high spirits, Michael in a teasing laughing mood, and Beth lighthearted and like a child in a sweetshop as she exclaimed in delight at the luxury of their suite at the expensive London hotel, and the palatial bathroom complete with everything down to fluffy white bathrobes. Michael ordered room service for their meal, and she had to refrain from pinching herself as the waiter wheeled in the trolley.

"It's just like on the films," she breathed.

She refused any wine or champagne, feeling she'd drunk enough at the wedding, and Michael agreed.

"I think we're both on a high already, and we want to save our energies for later," he whispered, running his finger down her spine, and she'd smiled.

Yes, she had, she'd smiled, looking forward like Michael to the consummation of their love, convinced she'd long overcome her fears. Then how could she have let it happen, for it was all her stupid fault, hers alone. She clenched her fist and punched the pillow in tearful frustration. Oh, if only he hadn't gone downstairs to fetch those damn cigarettes. When he'd been gone some time, she'd imagined they were out of his brand and he'd had to pop out, but it wasn't that at all.

"Sorry I've been so long," he apologised as he came into the room. "Only I was just passing the bar, and fancied a long beer. It must be all that champagne at the wedding, I felt as though I was dehydrating."

"But you never drink beer," she said.

"I know, strange isn't it? Still, it was just what I needed."

But that one act proved a catalyst. Beth turned lovingly to Michael when at last they shared a double bed, with no other thought than that this was their long-awaited wedding night. There were no taboos, now no need for restraint and at first they'd lain quietly, not kissing, just touching and stroking, discovering each other, revelling in the intimacy and privacy. Michael gently removed her white silk nightdress and began a trail of sensuous kisses along the outline of her body, and as their passion flared and at last he moved to straddle her, she opened like a flower to receive him. It was at that crucial moment, as his lips came down to hers, that she smelled the stale beer on his breath.

Beth turned her head aside, frantically trying to avoid his mouth, as the taste on his lips brought with it nauseating blanked-out memories. She felt Michael's weight, and suddenly she was back in that darkened room, and in terror began to thrash about on the bed, struggling to prevent her body being violated. The memory of the pain, her fear of being ripped apart again was overwhelming, and in panic she lashed out, fists flailing at Michael's chest, desperately thrusting him away as he tried to enter her.

With an expletive, Michael had flung himself away from her and out of the bed, grabbing his robe to cover himself, and slumped into the armchair, his fists clenched. For two hours he had refused to speak, the strain and tension in the room lying like a leaden pall on the air.

Eventually, Beth could bear it no longer.

"Michael," she pleaded in a hoarse whisper. "Michael, speak to me please."

He ignored her.

"Michael, please." She felt a choking sensation in her swollen throat. "Michael, we've got to talk sometime."

He turned angrily and lashed out at her. "Talk! What is there to talk about? After that demonstration you've very plainly shown your feelings. I don't know whether it's your religion or what it is, but I assumed you knew what marriage was all about. Or are you expecting to remain a virgin, like that statue you're so fond of!" His voice was heavy with sarcasm.

Beth winced. "It's nothing to do with religion," she whispered.

"Then what is it to do with, or do you find me so repulsive you have to fight me off? What did you think I was doing, trying to rape you?" His words were clipped, tight with hurt, and Beth's heart went out to him.

Should she tell him? Floundering in her misery, the urge to confess and plead for his understanding and forgiveness warred with a conviction that it would be suicidal. She could still feel the heat of his anger and who could blame him?

"It was nothing to do with you. You know I love you –"

"You've got a strange way of showing it," he snapped.

"Please Michael, let me explain." She sat up, leaning towards him imploringly. "It was the beer, I know it sounds trivial and ridiculous, but if only you hadn't had the beer!"

"What the hell are you talking about?"

There was no alternative. She'd have to lie, anything to make him understand.

"Ever since I've been a child, I've never been able to stand the smell of beer, and if it's on someone's breath it makes me retch. That's why I was pushing you away! I was afraid I was going to be sick."

"Then why didn't you just say so!"

"If you remember you were kissing me at the time. Afterwards, well, you were just so angry," she wailed in anguish.

"Are you sure that's all it was, Beth?"

She nodded, wishing she had the courage to tell him the whole truth. She longed for there to be no secrets between them, longed for his understanding, his reassurance, but instinct told her this was not the time.

Michael looked at her, sitting forlornly in the middle of the large double bed, the sheet drawn up around her shoulders, and began to soften. Even in the dim light he could see the tearstains on her face. What a bloody start to their marriage! He felt terrible – the nervous strain of the day, the long drive down, the enormous shock and hurt of Beth's rejection coupled with lack of sleep – it was no wonder he felt exhausted.

Rising at last out of the chair, he went to the bathroom, while Beth waited in an agony of uncertainty. She breathed a shuddering sigh of relief when a few minutes later Michael slipped into bed beside her.

He lifted his arm and drew her head down to his shoulder.

"Don't you ever do that to me again – I've never been so angry in my life." His voice was still tight with resentment.

"I won't," Beth promised. "If only you hadn't had that beer it wouldn't have happened."

"How was I to know?"

"It wasn't your fault. It was mine. and I'm sorry. I really am."

"Come on," he said wearily. "Let's forget it and get

some sleep. We did promise for better or worse – it can only get better!"

Closing her eyes Beth offered a prayer of thanksgiving that she'd been granted a second chance. I'll make it up to him, she vowed. I'll never hurt him like that again.

Despite the excitement of their visit to Carnaby Street the following morning, relations between them remained strained, and they were both quiet during their four-hour flight. However, the warm sunshine and beauty of Madeira, so aptly called the "floating garden" acted like a balm to their troubled relationship. Beth had been wide-eyed with disbelief when they first arrived and she realised that their hotel was the world-famous Reid's. As soon as they were shown to their beautifully furnished bedroom and she'd seen the balcony overlooking a shimmering blue ocean, her spirits had risen. It was the perfect honeymoon setting. Surely here, amongst such beauty she and Michael would somehow find the answer to their problems.

They spent the first two days exploring the lovely town of Funchal just fifteen minutes' walk away, wandering around its colourful flower market and narrow streets, then sitting and relaxing at a pavement cafe sipping long iced drinks and watching the world go by before lunch. In the afternoons they swam in the hotel pool and lazily sunbathed in the exotic gardens before bathing and dressing for dinner.

It was idyllic, but each night when Michael simply kissed her goodnight before turning over to sleep, Beth's inner turmoil grew. She yearned to make amends for her rejection, to prove to Michael just how much she loved him. Yet one part of her felt relief, for her old fear that she was frigid had resurfaced. What if it happened again? She couldn't expect Michael to forgive her a second time.

Michael lay quietly on his side, every fibre aware of Beth's anxiety. But it was too soon. His own resentment was still simmering. He couldn't trust himself yet to handle the situation in the right way. Maybe Beth did have an aversion to the smell of beer, but he was remembering the days when they'd first met. It had taken weeks of patience and tenderness to coax her to respond to him – she'd been like a frightened faun. At the time, he'd blamed it on her Catholic upbringing, had been reassured by her growing passionate responses, for she loved him deeply. He knew that.

Had she no idea now difficult it had been for him to wait, respecting her religious views? Michael groaned inwardly. How would he cope if his wife proved to be frigid? What sort of marriage would that be for either of them? He loved her so much, and feeling the warmth of her soft body beside him, his loins began to stir. But no, not yet. He'd know when it was the right time, for his timing was crucial if they were to have any chance of happiness together.

They had been on honeymoon almost a week, when one balmy evening, strolling through the scented gardens, Michael said casually, "It's such a lovely night. Why don't we go up early, have some champagne and watch the sunset?" He lit a cigarette as he waited for Beth's answer, trying to sense her reaction.

Beth looked up at his tense profile and said quietly, "I think that's a wonderful idea."

Later, after the waiter had left the ice bucket, Beth stood by the rails of the balcony, gazing at the whispering ocean. So it had come. This time, there must be no mistake. She must remain in control, must try to be the wife Michael deserved.

She turned as he handed her a glass. "I do love you, so much."

"I know, darling, and I love you."

They remained close together watching the breeze play among the trees. Michael placed his arm loosely around Beth's shoulders, absently stroking her bare arm, and then the nape of her neck. She turned to him and raised her lips to his for a tender, fleeting kiss.

Gently, Michael caressed her as they stood together, his hand slowly moving over her body as they sipped their champagne. He kissed her again, this time a deeper, more intimate kiss, and then sensing it would be unwise to prolong the preliminaries, led her gently to the silken-covered bed.

Beth trembled as Michael turned to her, but he held her close, murmuring words of love, and all the time he stroked and caressed her, gradually soothing her fears. Slowly, she began to relax as her body responded, and then joy surged through her as, desire mounting, she found she wanted Michael, wanted to be one with him, to give all of her love. It seemed the most natural thing in the world to reach out to him, draw him towards her, and Michael, who had restrained his own passion with difficulty, felt a sense of overwhelming relief as at last they consummated their marriage.

Emotional but happy, Beth lay for a while cradled in Michael's arms, then he refilled their glasses.

After a few minutes, he turned and looked down at her questioningly, saw the answer in her eyes, and he lowered his lips to her breasts. Beth stroked his dark, tousled hair, exulting as desire rose once again within her. They made love again, slowly at first and then with urgency, each responding to the other's need, each longing to give the other pleasure.

Afterwards, Beth lay utterly relaxed and content, her mind at ease, listening drowsily to Michael's even breathing. All her worries and anxieties were behind her, the long nightmare was at last over. She reached out a hand and touched her husband, aware of how lucky she was. All this and they had another ten days of heaven before them.

"Another couple of hours and we'll be home," Michael murmured as the car sped along the busy road away from the airport. The night was turning chilly, and he leaned over and switched on the heater.

"So, Mrs Rushton, what will you say when people ask how you enjoyed your honeymoon?"

"I shall tell them you're sex mad!" she teased.

"Who wouldn't be with a wife like you, you temptress!" he retorted with a grin. "But seriously, it has been pretty wonderful, hasn't it?"

"Michael, it's been out of this world."

"And I know you liked Madeira."

"Oh, I did," Beth said dreamily.

She'd never forget these two weeks. The island was so beautiful, so full of contrasts. Astounded at the proliferation of honeysuckle, mimosa and poinsettia growing wild on the roadsides and hills, she'd loved everything, even the tiny lizards scuttling along every crevice. A guided tour of the island had revealed stepped vineyards, remote mountains and dramatic waterfalls, and everywhere they'd experienced the warm hospitality of the people.

"Mum would love it," she said wistfully.

"Well, there's no reason why you couldn't take her one day," Michael smiled.

"That would mean leaving you," she protested.

"Oh, we'd organise it for a time when I was away on business." He peered in his wing mirror and then accelerated effortlessly past a slow-moving long-distance lorry.

"One of the first things we must do is to get you some driving lessons. An intensive course would be best I think, and with a bit of luck you might pass your test first time. How about if I buy you a little Mini for Christmas? You'd be able to pop down to Minsden then whenever you wished, or fetch your mother up for the day."

"Oh, Michael, could I really? That would be absolutely perfect. I know she's going to miss me and I wouldn't seem so far away." A car of her own! Beth still couldn't get used to the idea that money was no object, that she only had to express a desire for something, and it was within her grasp. You'll have to watch yourself, my girl, she told herself, or you'll become spoilt!

Chapter 21

"What's it like then, now it's all finished?" Granny Platt asked Rose a few weeks later. They'd just had Sunday tea and were relaxing before a glowing coal fire, glad of the warmth on the chill November day.

"What? Oh, Beth's house. Well," Rose considered, "it's difficult to describe really . . . it's very big, there's five bedrooms! It's different, all modern and open plan."

"Open plan? You don't mean one of those silly houses where there aren't any doors? Who wants all the cooking smells wafting through everywhere, and as for being draughty! Anyway, I like the door closed when I'm settled in for a chat. I'd have thought our Beth would've had more sense!" she snorted.

"No," Rose said. "I've seen one of those. There's a

show house on that new estate in the village. I wouldn't have one for a gift! No, Beth's is different, it was individually designed for them by an architect. She's got a door on her kitchen – oh, you'd love that, Mum! Compared to our tiny sculleries it's a palace. There's a large study as well – that's got a door. But the rest of the downstairs is open plan. You go into a square hall with a lovely parquet floor and then the lounge and dining-room are split level, overlooking the garden. You should see the land they've got. Michael's having a landscape gardener in to plan it all for them."

Rose's mother lifted her tweed skirt to let the fire warm her arthritic knees, rubbing them gently.

"I was surprised in a way they went for a brand new house."

"Well, between you and me, Michael's father wanted them to buy a house in their road, and I think that's what made up Beth's mind. She said she didn't want a re-run of their lives, so they opted for a new one."

"A bit different than yer dad and me – we were glad to get a couple of furnished rooms! Still, she's the first one in our family to own her own home and I'm proud of her. Anyhow, when am I going to see it?"

There was a querulous tone in her voice and Rose hurried to reassure her. "Beth said she'd fetch you up for Christmas. She wants everything to be perfect before you see it. Eeh, you should see the carpets, Mum, pure wool and everywhere fitted, even the bedrooms. No patterns though, all plain colours. Mind you, I do agree with her, they go well with all that modern furniture."

Rose paused. Beth had been so busy since the wedding. It was understandable, of course, with that great house to furnish, but she'd missed her terribly.

"Something a bit more solid's more to my taste, and she won't find plain carpets very practical. They'll show every mark," Granny Platt sniffed. "Put the kettle on, Rose. I think I'll just have another piece of that fruit cake afore I go."

"It won't be that long before Cyril comes home now," Rose called from the kitchen. To the family's delight, Michael's promise of a job at Rushton's had been all her brother had needed to tempt him to come back to England. Still single, he hadn't any real roots in New Zealand and one look at his mother's increasing frailty had finally convinced him.

"Aye, it'll be grand having someone to look after again."

"I should think he'll be looking after you at your age," Rose chided, carrying in the teapot and placing it beneath a blue and red striped cosy.

"Go on with you. I'm not that old and I can still

make as good a dinner as the next!" the old lady bridled.

"You're nearly eighty, Mum. I hope you won't go wearing yourself out waiting on our Cyril. After all, he's fended for himself all these years. He's quite capable." Rose pursed her lips as she put the milk and sugar in the cups and cut a slice of cake.

"Don't you go worrying about me! What about you, our Rose, have you thought about yourself?" Granny Platt turned her head to one side to surreptitiously remove her false teeth. "Sorry, luv, but the seeds get under me plate."

Averting her eyes, Rose said, "How do you mean?"

"Have you ever thought of marrying again? I mean now you've got Beth off your hands?"

Rose flushed. "I don't know. I don't think I could be bothered, to tell you the truth. I'm not denying it'd be useful to have a man about the house but," she looked up at the photograph on the mantelpiece, "well, I'd never find another Harry."

"You've never been interested in anyone else?"

"No, but then I don't really go anywhere to meet anyone. I don't go to pubs or anything like that."

"No, you never were a one for drinking. Can't think where you got it from – I like a drink meself never mind what the Methodists think."

A few minutes later she drained her cup, rose stiffly

out of the armchair and began to change into her shoes. "I'd better get ready, or I'll have Mr Salt here."

"It is good of him to bring and fetch you on a Sunday."

"Oh, well, it doesn't take him long, and I always make him a nice apple pie as a thank-you. You see, I can still get me way with a man, even at my age," she chuckled.

"You've not lost your sense of humour. I'll say that for you." Rose smiled as she helped her on with her coat.

"Well, you're lost without one, that's for sure. Here he is. Goodnight, lass, I'll see you next week if you don't find time to pop down afore."

Rose waved goodbye from the window, and then set about washing the dishes and tidying the living-room. Stoking up the fire she switched on the television, ready for *Sunday Night at the London Palladium*, and thought about her mother's question. No, she just couldn't imagine herself sharing a bed with anyone else but Harry. It wouldn't seem right somehow. Not that anyone had ever asked her! She shrugged her shoulders. She was well over the change anyway, far too old to start that sort of thing again.

"I'll fetch them, Beth. I'm a more experienced driver than you," Michael insisted as they both peered out of the lounge window at the arctic conditions outside.

"Are you sure it's safe?" Beth worried. It would happen! Their first Christmas and the winter was already being designated 'the Big Freeze'.

"Well, what's the alternative? Leave your Mum and your Gran sitting waiting with their coats on? You know what they're like. They'll have been ready for the past hour. I tell you one thing, Beth. I'm having a phone put in for both of them after this lot, and don't say they can't afford the bills either – it's for our convenience as much as theirs, so I'll see to it."

"Oh, do be careful, Michael!"

"I've got a good car, and I'll go steady," he promised, and wrapping a warm scarf around his neck he opened the front door and braved the icy winds.

Beth watched him go, her heart in her mouth as she saw him almost lose his footing on the treacherous drive, and then went back into the kitchen to check on the turkey. Secretly she was relieved that Robert and Sylvia had flown over to Milan to spend Christmas with James and Giovanna this year. Not having to impress them with her cooking took much of the pressure off. She smiled with content as she basted the succulent bird and checked on the pudding steaming gently on the hob. In the dining-room the table was set, complete with her own festive flower arrangement as a centrepiece, the drinks were set out, there was a log fire burning brightly in the lounge, and she had never been happier.

She wondered how Jacqueline Kennedy was feeling and those two little children, Caroline and John. What sort of Christmas would they be having? She'd never forget the day she'd heard the newsflash. The fatal shooting in Dallas of the young American president had shocked the world. Never had a politician reached so many hearts; he and his glamorous young wife had seemed a beacon of hope, a new beginning. Why on earth God had let it happen, the first Catholic president too, she just didn't understand.

She put the potatoes to roast in the oven and over the next half hour paced back and forth to watch anxiously out of the window. She went to pick up some pine needles which had fallen on the pile of presents underneath the tinselled Christmas tree, and thought of Rosemary. She'd be eight years old now. Perhaps she'd be having a doll's house, or a nurse's outfit. Beth hoped her adoptive parents would buy her books, remembering her own longing for them even at that age.

Thinking of her lost child, her happiness dimmed and she went into the study and took the wedding album from a drawer. Turning to the photograph of James, Guy and Tony Morrison, grinning foolishly at the camera, she searched yet again for any resemblance on Tony's bland face to the tiny baby whose puckered features she'd never forget. No, nothing, there was no spark of recognition, no gut reaction, nothing. She sighed and put the album away. This was a happy day – what was she doing allowing the past to overshadow it?

Returning to her vigil at the window, at last she saw Michael turn safely into the drive and breathed a sigh of relief. This was her life now, here with Michael, and conscious of the extent of her love for him she was finally convinced that she'd been right not to tell him about the rape and Rosemary. Never must she allow anything to come between them

Chapter 22

"I've told you before, Michael, I won't have Ursula in my house!" Beth stalked out of the hall as Michael replaced the telephone receiver, her face pale and set with anger.

"What else could I say?" Michael followed her into the lounge and caught her arm. "It's no use, Beth. You can't avoid it forever. It's been well over a year since the wedding, and never once have the Dawes set foot in this house. It's become an embarrassment both to me and my parents."

"How can you ask me to have her here after all I've told you?" Beth demanded.

Michael drew her down on to the sofa, trying to find the right words without upsetting her.

"Honestly, Beth, don't you think you might have

been a bit over-sensitive and have exaggerated things? After all, I've known Ursula longer than you have and I find it difficult to believe she could be as spiteful as you say, and as for those silly threats you say she made at the wedding, she'd probably just had too much to drink."

Beth shook her head impatiently. "No, Michael, I haven't exaggerated, and she was perfectly sober. She hates me for some reason, and I wouldn't put it past her to deliberately try to cause trouble. That's one reason I don't want anything to do with her."

Michael frowned, trying to control his irritation. "Well, I'm afraid you're going to have to. Father asked me straight out if it would be all right to bring the Dawes and Ursula when they come to dinner on Saturday. I couldn't give him a concrete reason for refusing."

"Your mother knows how I feel!" Beth said defensively.

"Yes, well, Mother's like you; she doesn't consider all the implications. It's bad for business to antagonise them and that's an end to it."

Beth knew when she was beaten. When it came to financial affairs Michael was like his father: the company came first. It was one lesson she'd had ample opportunity to learn over the past fourteen months. Cultivating the right people in case they could be useful, giving carefully orchestrated dinner parties in the hope of securing orders. To Michael it was just a way of life he'd always known, but Beth hadn't yet overcome her feelings of insincerity knowing there was an ulterior motive behind their hospitality.

"You want to look after those shares of yours, don't you?" Michael teased, in an effort to lighten her mood. Really, it was ridiculous of Beth to think that Ursula had designs on him – they often encountered her socially and she was always perfectly charming.

"Of course I do. You know I really appreciate your father agreeing to my becoming a shareholder."

"Well, I thought it would make the perfect anniversary present." Michael smiled and kissed the tip of her nose. He knew she'd see reason eventually. "I'd better be off, or I'll be late for Rotary."

Resignedly, Beth watched him go. It was a way of life with the middle classes, she shrugged, this social expediency. The need to mix in the right circles, make good contacts. It was all so different from her own kind. The people in Minsden either liked you enough to want to be friendly or kept their distance. Wasn't it Oscar Wilde who said, 'Comparisons are odious'? But she found it difficult not to compare the two different outlooks on life.

She'd found herself ill-equipped and out of her depth at first. Ursula's sarcastic taunt about her culinary skills had rankled, particularly because she knew it was true. Determined to remedy her ignorance she appealed to her mother-in-law for advice, and seizing the opportunity to cement relations between them, Sylvia entered wholeheartedly into the project, delighted to have someone to whom she could impart her expertise. Their shared hours of achievements and hilarious disasters had not only provided the bonus of forging a warm bond of affection, but Beth had discovered she had a flair for creating imaginative dishes.

She made her menu plans for Saturday with elaborate care, determined to show not only Ursula, but also Mr and Mrs Dawes, just how wrong they'd been about her all those years ago. Unsuitable, she fumed silently! I'll show them.

On Saturday morning however, she couldn't resist teasing Michael.

"What do you think about having a theme for the meal tonight?" she said with an air of nonchalance.

"Good idea, what have you in mind, French cuisine or something like that?" Michael yawned, and closed his eyes as he lay sprawled on the sofa. "I really shouldn't have had that extra gin and tonic last night."

"No," she threw him an impish grin. "I thought we'd make it a peasant evening. I could do a huge meat and potato pie . . . ouch!" She squealed as Michael threw a cushion at her.

"Definitely not, you little monkey!" he laughed.

But Beth's relaxed mood was short-lived. As the day went on she was unable to prevent nervous tension from building up inside her, inwardly fuming with Michael for inflicting this ordeal on her. Mrs Dawes she found cold, while Ursula's father was well known on the potbank as an arrogant bastard. Still, she muttered resentfully, as she clattered pans in the kitchen, he's a wizard with accountancy, and after all that's all that matters to some people.

By the time they were due to arrive her nerves were at razor edge. Taking special care with her appearance, she selected a classic black cocktail dress. I'll beat them at their own game, she vowed, as she fastened a string of pearls to match her drop earrings. She smiled grimly. Now let them dare to patronise me in my own home!

Michael gave an appreciative whistle as Beth came downstairs.

"You look stunning, darling. Want a drink?"

"I could murder one."

Michael glanced up sharply at her tight voice. "You okay?"

"Yes, I'm fine." Beth sipped at her gin and tonic and looked nervously at the clock.

"Food smells good."

"I hope they like coq au vin."

"Cooked the way you do it, I'm sure they will. Everything looks great, Beth, table, flowers, the lot! Just relax. It'll be fine."

Beth glared at him. Just relax! It was easy for him to say that. All he had to do was pour a few drinks, while responsibility for the evening's success rested firmly on her shoulders. Then, before she could retort, the doorbell rang.

"I'll get it," Michael said, and Beth stood up, smoothing down the fabric of her skirt.

Gritting her teeth, she made a tremendous effort to play the perfect hostess, and to her overwhelming relief the evening was a great success. Ursula was charming and witty, while her parents appeared relaxed and at ease. Robert beamed approvingly at everyone and Michael, watching, felt sure that any tensions between the two families were buried once and for all. His hope was that Beth and Ursula could become good friends again. He knew Beth had been very fond of the other girl at one time.

"You were great, darling," he said, after they'd left. "The meal was absolutely fabulous."

"It was good, wasn't it?" Beth agreed, secretly gloating over the look of chagrin on Ursula's face.

There had been one potentially explosive moment,

when Ursula had followed her into the kitchen. Away from the others, she dropped her social mask and her eyes gleamed with malice.

"It's all very modern!" she drawled. "Of course, I suppose if you haven't grown up surrounded by good taste, you would go for the latest fashion."

Beth seriously considered throwing the coffee-pot at her, then exercising rigid self-control, turned and smiled sweetly. "Your green streak's showing, Ursula. I should watch that if I were you. It's most unattractive in a woman, you know."

Ursula shot her a glance of pure hatred, then to Beth's relief Sylvia joined them.

Glancing from one to the other, she murmured, "Why don't you go back to the others, Ursula dear? I'll give Beth a hand."

Now Michael put his arms around her and nuzzled his face in her neck.

"Leave the clearing up. Mrs Hurst can do it in the morning. Come on. Let's go to bed. I'm feeling randy."

"You always are," she giggled, and twisting away raced up the stairs and flung herself on the bed, pretending to fight him off as he followed and pinned her down.

"I do love you, Mr Michael," she said.

"Then do as the boss says," he murmured, bringing his lips down to hers.

After their lovemaking Beth lay feeling replete

and drowsy, hoping that this time she would have conceived. Perhaps she was being impatient for a baby, but Michael was an ardent lover and they never bothered with any birth control. Her last thought before she slept was that according to her secret chart, she was in her ovulation period. It would be wonderful if they could become a real family.

"Her father said what?" Beth looked with astonishment at Michael as she poured them both a cup of tea the following morning.

"Pass me the marmalade, darling. He said Ursula was seeing Tony Morrison. You know, he's the other bloke in that photo of James and Guy at the wedding. He was away on holiday or she'd have brought him last night. Why?"

"Oh, nothing, I wouldn't have thought he was her type, that's all." Beth felt the blood drain from her face. Tony Morrison of all people!

"I thought we might ask them over some time," Michael suggested.

"I thought you weren't keen on him."

"Well, no, I wasn't – but perhaps he's changed. People do as they get older. In any case, he's a solicitor now and it always pays to keep on the right side of our friends at court."

"You sound just like your father." Beth began to

clear away the breakfast things, while her brain rapidly digested this new turn of events. She stood motionless as she ran the hot water into the sink. Why was she hesitating? It was a golden opportunity to get to know her attacker.

She thought for a few moments and then said. "We could have them over for drinks before we go to the works' Annual Dance at the end of the month, if you like."

"Good idea, I knew you'd come round to my way of thinking. Old Ursula can be quite good company when she wants to be." Michael smiled at her complacently. "So, you're off to Mass then?"

"Yes – are you sure you won't come?" Beth paused hopefully.

"No, not this morning. I'll just slob out and read the papers. I'll keep out of Mrs Hurst's way.

"Well, don't forget we're going to Mum's for lunch," she reminded him.

"Don't worry I won't. I wouldn't miss her baked custard tart for anything." He grinned and went to settle himself down in the lounge.

With a guilty look at the chaos of the kitchen, Beth went to get ready for church. Initially, she'd resisted Michael's insistence that they have a daily help, not wanting to share the privacy of her home with another woman.

"I'm not working," she argued. "I can do my own housework."

"I'm sure you can, but then you wouldn't have time to socialise. There'll be coffee mornings, bridge afternoons, oh all right," he laughed, seeing her horrified face, "no bridge. But seriously, darling, we'll be doing quite a bit of entertaining, not to mention that I'd like you to come with me sometimes on business trips. You may want to take up golf, join the Inner Wheel, or do charitable work. Anyway, I don't want my wife looking like a drudge. I want you to enjoy your allowance and spend it all on looking beautiful just for me."

Beth smiled, but seeing her still doubtful expression Michael played his trump card.

"Look at it like this, Beth. Having money carries responsibilities. You can afford to give someone a well-paid job – wouldn't it be a bit selfish not to?"

So, Mrs Hurst, a middle-aged widow from the council estate a mile away came in for three hours every morning. A cheerful, hardworking woman who genuinely enjoyed cleaning, she and Beth took to each other immediately, and the arrangement proved a great success.

Picking up her black lace mantilla, Beth called goodbye to Michael and getting into her red Mini drove thoughtfully to church. After Mass she remained behind as always to light Rosemary's candle in front of the statue of Our Lady. Never once in the eight years since Rosemary's birth had she missed the small ritual of prayer to keep her child safe and happy, believing that in some way the act served as a link between them.

Afterwards, driving home, she wondered fleetingly whether Ursula might be in danger, but she had no real proof that Tony Morrison was the man who'd raped her all those years ago. Anyway, he'd hardly be likely to rape Ursula. It would be tantamount to social suicide and the end of his career. She was certain of one thing however; one of those three figures in that photograph was responsible, and everything pointed to Tony Morrison. It just couldn't have been either Guy or James. Guy had become a good friend. She'd liked him from the very first time they'd met at the New Year's Eve party at Linden Lodge. James, well James was Michael's brother. She was genuinely fond of him and of Giovanna – no, the concept was unthinkable.

She spent a long time on her appearance on the night of the Dance, not because of Ursula or Tony Morrison, but because she knew she would be the centre of attention for most of the employees.

She'd decided to wear a rich coral evening dress. The neck was fairly high, so with the thought of Morrison's company uppermost in her mind, she deliberately wore her locket with its lock of Rosemary's hair. Superstitious perhaps, but she felt desperate to feel something, an instinct, an awareness that this was the man, that between them they had created a new life.

She outlined her lips carefully with a brush. It had taken her ages to master the knack, but the result was far more professional. She had found very early in her marriage that such attention to detail gave her confidence. She fastened the diamond earrings Michael had given her for her birthday and gave herself a nod of approval.

When Ursula arrived with Tony in tow, Michael kissed her warmly on the cheek while Beth watched uneasily. No matter what Michael said, she still didn't trust Ursula where he was concerned.

"You've met Tony, of course, Beth," Ursula said.

"I don't think we actually had a chance to talk at the wedding," Beth replied, her eyes anxiously meeting his pale blue ones. But there was no sign of recognition, just a polite acknowledgement. She hadn't really expected anything else. Neither Guy nor James had ever given any sign that they'd seen her before, but then what would they remember after eight years? Just a dishevelled teenage girl lying in a shadowy room, holding her aching head, her face almost totally obscured. The actual rape had taken place in total darkness. But it was unnerving to think that this guest in her house could be the man responsible and it was with a forced smile that she ushered them both into the huge lounge.

"Mm, something smells nice," Ursula commented.

"It's the logs. They're applewood. Lovely, aren't they."

"Right, you two, what are you drinking?" Michael busied himself at the cocktail cabinet, while Beth sat in a chair which gave her a good vantage point.

As Michael began to chat to their guests, she took the opportunity to study Tony closely. A typical solicitor, she thought in his navy pin-striped suit. His appearance was nondescript, his brown hair already receding, his lips thin and without humour. Her overall impression was one of coldness. She couldn't understand whatever Ursula saw in him.

At the Dance, once they joined the others on the directors' table, Beth found herself separated from Ursula and Tony, and decided to concentrate on enjoying herself.

"How's he treating yer then?" bawled Ivy, with her usual lack of ceremony as Beth and Michael waltzed past her on the crowded dance floor.

"Oh, he only beats me twice a week," she retorted laughing.

"That's a new word for it!" Ivy cackled, and Beth blushed.

"You walked right into that one," grinned Michael, as he steered her away and into the stream of dancers. "How does it feel, seeing everyone again?"

"Oh, I'm really enjoying it. I do wish you and your father weren't against my coming in to the works sometimes," Beth said, as she smiled and nodded to former fellow workers.

"It just wouldn't do, believe me. They'd only think you were patronising them anyway. You don't really miss working, do you?"

Beth considered. "Not now. I did a bit at first, but I enjoy my voluntary work at the hospital, particularly taking round the library trolley. I'd much rather do that than spend my time playing bridge or gossiping over the teacups!"

Her tone was disparaging, and Michael laughed. "Still my little socialist, aren't you, underneath all that expensive make-up."

"I think I always will be," she said.

As the evening wore on she surreptitiously watched Tony, dreading the inevitable moment when he would ask her to dance. How would she feel, how would she react when he actually touched her, held her in his arms? Surely her body with some deep unerring instinct would know, would confirm her suspicions. But it was not until after the interval when Michael took Ursula on to the floor for a quickstep, that Tony leaned over and said, "May I have the pleasure, Beth?"

Her throat closing with nerves, she could only nod.

"*Mr Sandman*," the vocalist sang as they walked on to the floor and then Beth turned nervously as Tony put his arm around her waist and took her hand. His palm was clammy with perspiration and with distaste she made herself lean closer as they quickstepped around the ballroom, hoping that physical contact would confirm her suspicions. When another couple suddenly bumped into them, forcing Tony's body to jerk clumsily against her own, Beth tensed. She waited, her breath coming in gasps, but to her dismay she felt nothing. No reaction at all. Reluctantly, she had to accept that dancing with Tony Morrison was no different than dancing with any other acquaintance.

As they circled the room, Beth caught glimpses of Michael dancing with Ursula. Anger and jealousy grew inside her as she saw the other girl laughing up at him, whispering intimately into his ear, drawing his head closer to hers.

First to return to their table, she watched the couple return, Ursula clinging to Michael's hand, her bright eyes mocking Beth's.

"Thank you," she said huskily, then with a

triumphant glance slipped into her chair next to Tony.

Beth glared at him. What a wimp! Surely he could see what she was up to? Ursula was supposed to be his girlfriend, for heaven's sake.

Later in the cloakroom, Beth was repairing her makeup when Ivy sidled up to her.

"I should watch that blonde bit, if I were you," she muttered.

Beth stared at her.

"After our lad, inna she? Not the first time either. She's been setting 'er cap at 'im for years. You watch out, Beth. The fact he's married won't stop 'er!" She turned. "All right, Glad, I'm coming," she yelled as one of the paintresses popped her head round the door. "It's the Gay Gordons. I never miss that! Now you remember what I said . . ."

Beth nodded. So it was as noticeable as that! Perhaps it was time she had a word with Miss Ursula Dawes. As for Michael, he obviously couldn't see an inch in front of his nose. She supposed knowing Ursula since she was a child blinded him to her true nature. Not that she was worried: Michael loved her and she loved him. But a certain person needed to have her card marked, and not before time.

"Want to come back for a nightcap?" Michael suggested at the end of 'Auld Lang Syne'.

"Lovely!" Ursula's eyes lit up.

Beth frowned. She wished Michael would check with her first. The last thing she felt like was making polite conversation. On the other hand, perhaps this could be her chance!

It wasn't until an hour later that she managed to get Ursula alone. After watching the other girl once again blatantly flirt with her husband, Beth was growing more and more incensed. What the hell was Michael playing at, letting her toady up to him all the time? She glanced at Tony with contempt. He really was a cold fish! She was finding it more and more difficult to believe he had enough passion in him to have raped anyone!

Michael gradually became aware of the anger in Beth's eyes and groaned inwardly. Why couldn't she relax and let go a bit?

"Have another drink, darling," he suggested, going over to the cocktail cabinet.

Beth frowned at his slightly slurred speech, but knew better than to suggest he'd had enough when other people were present.

"No, thanks," she said shortly. "Why don't you show Tony your plans for a billiard room extension?"

"Hey, what about it, Tony?" said Michael with enthusiasm.

"Fine." Tony carefully replaced his drink and followed Michael to his study.

Beth got up and swiftly closed the door after them.

She sat opposite Ursula and leaned forward intensely.

"Right, Miss, just listen to what I've got to say and remember it."

Glittering green eyes met determined blue ones, and Ursula curled her lip.

"I can't think of anything you have to say which would interest me in the least."

"Well, try this for size! If you ever make up to Michael again like you've done tonight . . ."

"You'll do what?" At Ursula's patronising tone Beth almost lost control. Oh, how she'd love to slap that supercilious face! But that wouldn't achieve anything, pleasurable though it would be.

She held the other girl's gaze, and her expression hardened. "I'll personally make sure that every woman in our circle knows that their husband isn't safe when you're around. Don't think other people didn't notice your behaviour tonight. They won't find it difficult to believe. How would you like to be a social outcast, no dinner parties, no invitations for drinks, no tennis parties?"

"You cat!" Ursula hissed.

"No, Ursula, just defending myself. I'm telling you, just one more time –"

Beth turned as Michael came back.

"Ursula's ready to go," she said sweetly.

A few minutes later, Michael closed the door behind their guests.

"Great evening," he grinned.

"You certainly seemed to enjoy yourself!" Beth plumped up the cushions furiously.

"Didn't you?" She turned to glare at him, but Michael was already yawning and heading for the staircase. What's the use, she thought, he'll never see her through my eyes.

"What are you doing today?" asked Michael a few days later as he shrugged on his warm overcoat. "It looks a bit overcast."

"Oh, I'm meeting your mother for lunch and some Christmas shopping. With James and Giovanna coming over, there's lots to do."

"Well, have a nice time." He kissed her, and then put a finger under her chin. "Don't take it to heart, sweetheart. There's plenty of time."

"I know." Sadly she watched him reverse the Jaguar out of the garage, and leave for work. She'd been so hopeful this time, but she'd awoken to find the usual tell-tale bloodstains. Resignedly, she marked a circle in her diary and reminded herself that everyone said up to two years was normal to wait for a baby, and after all it was only fifteen months.

In an effort to distract her train of thought, she

dwelt yet again on the night of the Dance and the disappointment of her lack of reaction to Tony Morrison. Going over every nuance yet again, she suddenly came to a decision. She would make a concentrated effort to remove the emotion from her thinking and analyse the whole situation.

"Could you give the cooker a good clean," she called to Mrs Hurst, in an effort to gain some peace and quiet. It was wonderful to have a daily help, but sometimes her habit of singing as she went about her work made serious thought impossible. Today was obviously a Gracie Fields morning – they'd already had 'Bless This House' and 'Wish Me Luck As You Wave Me Goodbye'. Hopefully, she was hardly likely to sing with her head inside the oven.

Beth went into the book-lined study and sat in the winged chair, resting her feet on the matching green leather footstool. She leaned her head back and closed her eyes, and after a few moments of absolute silence painfully opened the dark part of her mind that she tried to keep secret even from herself. She was seventeen again, at the teenage party, drinking that fatal fruit punch. She distinctly remembered how ill she'd felt when she'd stumbled upstairs to lie down thankfully in the darkness of one of the bedrooms. She recalled how her brain had been fuddled, her limbs refusing to obey her, that the room had spun round and round, that she'd been fighting nausea. She saw again the hazy outline of the three masked youths swaying in the doorway. Think, she told herself. Use your intelligence. It was over eight years ago; it was dark; we were both the worse for drink. If he can't remember your face, how can you expect your body to recognise his?

She had to face it. She was never going to find out the truth. Brooding on it would only spoil the happiness she had now. Let it go, Beth, she told herself. Let it go, and get on with your life.

Chapter 23

"What do I need with a fridge?" Granny Platt protested to Beth and Michael. "My pantry's as cold as any fridge! Anyhow, I bought a quarter o' boiled ham from across the corner shop last week, they've got one and there wasn't a bit o' taste in it."

"Oh, Gran, you're as bad as my mother," Beth said in exasperation. "She says milk that's been in a fridge makes the tea cold! The Americans have had refrigerators for ages. Why shouldn't we? I find mine very useful."

"I daresay you do," grumbled the old lady. "Anyway, where would I put it?"

"It would go nicely inside your pantry – I've measured it. Oh, do say you're pleased, Gran. We thought a fridge would be the perfect Christmas present for you and for Mum!" Beth pleaded.

"I'm not sayin' I'm not grateful, Beth, but I've managed all these years without one . . ."

"Then all the more reason you shouldn't have to manage now," interrupted Cyril. "Come on, Mother. Don't be so set in your ways. You have to move with the times. She'll be glad of it after a couple of weeks, I promise you, Beth."

Granny Platt darted a resentful look at him and then queried, "Your mum's having one then?"

"Yes, she took some persuading too," Beth complained. "Honestly, you can't help some people."

"Oh, all right," Granny Platt capitulated. "I'm not promising I'll keep everything in it, mind!"

"So long as you find room for my bottles of beer!" Cyril joked.

Beth laughed.

"That's settled then! Now you know you're both going up to Mum's for Christmas Day, don't you? Do you want me to organise a taxi for you?"

"No, lass, I'll see to that," Cyril insisted. "You have a nice day with your in-laws. You'll be looking forward to seeing your brother and his wife, Michael."

"Yes, they're flying over on Christmas Eve. But you'll both be coming to us on Boxing Day afternoon, won't you, so you'll see James and Giovanna then. I'll pick you up about four."

Michael caught Beth's eye and glanced at his watch, impatient to be off. He found the tiny cluttered parlour claustrophobic. How people managed to rear large families in these poky terraced cottages was beyond his comprehension.

"We'll be going then, Gran." Beth leaned over and kissed her cheek. "Thank you for the presents. I'll put them under the tree."

"I'm really looking forward to seeing James and Giovanna," Beth said as they drove home. She shivered and snuggled deeper into her camel cashmere coat. "It seems ages since we saw them in June."

"Yes, it was a good trip, wasn't it?" Michael commented, peering through the windscreen. "This fog's coming down. I'll be glad when we get home. You don't mind too much not seeing your mum on Christmas Day?"

"Well, it can't be helped, can it? After all, they all came to us last year. Anyway, she'll have Uncle Cyril to fuss over."

"That's true."

"How's it going?" whispered Michael on Boxing Day afternoon as he came into the kitchen to collect some clean glasses.

"Oh, as you'd expect," Beth said. "Gran and Uncle Cyril are hardly saying a word, and Mum's so self conscious she seems like a different person. Why can't they all relax and enjoy themselves?

"Give them time. They'll loosen up with a few more drinks inside them," Michael said, with more optimism than he felt.

"Mum won't, 'cos she'll only ever have one small sherry," Beth pointed out.

"Yes, but your mother's on edge because the others are – once they relax she will."

"I hope so."

Beth carried in a tray of warm mince pies and sighed as she saw her family sitting stiffly side by side on the sofa. Robert didn't help with his pompous and patronising attitude, although Sylvia was doing her best to keep some form of conversation going. Perhaps things would improve when James and Giovanna eventually joined them.

"I can't think where they've got to," Robert grumbled.

Beth and Michael exchanged glances, guessing that the young couple had taken advantage of an hour of privacy, a view which was borne out by Giovanna's flushed face when they arrived half an hour later.

"Not the most stimulating gathering," yawned James, after the others had left later that evening. "Sorry, Beth, I didn't mean . . ."

"It's all right, James, I know exactly what you

mean," Beth said. "They just haven't got anything in common with your family, that's all, and to be honest your father can be a bit intimidating."

"I think my wife would agree with you at times," James grinned.

Later when she was showing Giovanna some new furnishings in one of the bedrooms, Beth said, "Are you having problems with Michael's father?" Somehow, even after over a year of marriage, she still couldn't bring herself to refer to her father-in-law by his Christian name.

"No, not problems, but," she blushed, "he keeps looking at me, you know, to see if I am pregnant."

"Oh," Beth smiled, "you mean this obsession he has with founding a dynasty. Well, I suppose he thinks you're more likely to be first as you've been married two years longer than us."

Giovanna's eyes clouded. "And you, Beth, you want children, yes?"

"Yes, of course. Don't you?"

Her lovely face downcast, Giovanna sat on the bed. "I am, how you say, frightened."

"Frightened? You mean of having a baby?"

She nodded. "My cousin, she die and the baby too." She looked up at Beth, her eyes clouded with anxiety.

"Oh, I'm sorry . . . but that really is very rare these days. Does James know how you feel?"

Giovanna shook her head. "He wants us to start a family." Giovanna bent her head, her fingers ruffling the pile of the green candlewick bedspread. "I cannot tell him, Beth. I feel ashamed."

"Do you like children?" Beth asked gently.

"I think so. I was the only child, you understand."

Beth sat by her on the bed. "Honestly, Giovanna, I'm sure all these fears would go away once you were actually pregnant. I'm not saying you wouldn't be a little nervous, everyone is the first time, but once you held your baby in your arms . . ." Her voice trailed off as tears rolled down the Italian girl's face. Why, she's really terrified, Beth thought, and you're nothing but a hypocrite. Why don't you tell her that you've been through it and what it was really like. But even as the thought came Beth quickly suppressed it, knowing she couldn't take the risk.

Giovanna turned her head away as the door opened and James came in.

"Come on, you two, what's this? A mothers' meeting?"

"Hardly!" Beth laughed, moving in front of the bed to give Giovanna time to compose herself.

"Ah, well, it's only a question of time," he joked. "You haven't forgotten, girls, that we promised to meet Guy and Sue for a drink?"

"Oh, I had," Beth said. "To be honest, James, I feel too tired."

'I know, so do we, but we've tried phoning and they must have already left."

"OK." She resigned herself to another late night. "Where are we meeting them?"

"The White Unicorn – it's on the Whitmore road." He turned to go, "You two powder your noses, while we warm the cars up. We'll each take our own then it'll save messing about afterwards."

"Are you all right?" Beth whispered to Giovanna. She nodded. "Just remember. Millions of women have been through it."

Giovanna didn't reply, and then there was little time for further conversation as they both hurriedly got ready and joined the others out on the drive.

"Brrr, it's nippy," called James. "Come on, Giovanna, and close the door. You follow us, Michael. I know where it is."

"Have you had a good Christmas, darling?" Michael asked, as they followed the red MG along the almost deserted roads.

"Yes, it's been lovely."

"You seem to get on well with Giovanna, I must say."

"I do. I'm very fond of her and of James," she replied, fiddling with the car radio. She leaned back into the leather upholstery and relaxed, closing her eyes as the soft, velvety voice of Nat King Cole filled the air.

They travelled in companionable silence enjoying the gentle music until suddenly Michael slammed on the brakes. Beth was thrown forward as he struggled desperately to control the car as it swerved and skidded off the wet road before shuddering to a halt, its bumper embedded in a hedge.

"Christ almighty!" Michael swore. "Are you all right, Beth?"

She straightened up slowly, feeling dizzy, and putting up a hand could feel a lump beginning to form on her forehead. "I think so. What happened?"

"Some idiot came hurtling out of a side road – didn't you hear the crash?" He closed his eyes and put a trembling hand to his forehead, then shouted hoarsely, "James, for God's sake, James!"

He flung open the door, scrambling out of the car and ran into the darkness. Beth struggled to open the heavy passenger door, forcing her shaky legs to follow, and as her heart hammered against her ribs she prayed desperately that no one had been hurt. Battling against the freezing wind, she managed to reach the road only to see the red MG crumpled grotesquely against another vehicle, and Michael wrenching at the door, trying to get it open.

She rushed forward to help but came to a standstill frozen in a nightmare of horror as she saw Giovanna. Thrown through the windscreen and on to the bonnet, her pale oval face and long dark hair looked as beautiful as ever, the only difference being that blood seeped from a jagged hole in her skull and her dark eyes stared blankly into space.

Transfixed with shock, Beth heard herself begin to scream, and then Michael was shaking her. "Stop it. You've got to pull yourself together!" He turned her round to face the other way. "Look, there's a house over there. See the lights? Go on, quickly. Get them to dial 999 – I think James is still alive." His face was ashen and at first Beth could only stare at him numbly without comprehension, before she began to run, to run as fast as her court shoes would allow, across the wet road, squelching over grass verges, the muddy ground sucking at her high heels and impeding her progress. In desperation she dragged her shoes off and ran in her stockings, heedless of the sharp stones that tore at her feet.

Stumbling up the drive to the front of the isolated farmhouse she slammed the palm of one hand on to the doorbell and banged on the door with the other.

"Hurry up," she sobbed. "Oh, please hurry up."

A man's voice yelled angrily, "What the hell! All right, I'm coming!" And suddenly the oak door opened, and she almost fell into the hall.

"Help!" she gasped, her breath coming in short painful sobs. "Dial 999. There's been an accident."

Shivering with cold and exhaustion, she clutched the doorpost for support as the man peered beyond her down the road.

"Bloody hell! Mary, Mary!" he shouted, and a middle-aged woman appeared wearing a floral housecoat. "There's been an accident! Dial 999 and then bring some blankets!"

Beth suddenly remembered the other car – who knew what carnage it contained?

"We may need more than one ambulance," she whispered.

The man grabbed a duffle coat from the hallstand and not bothering to change his slippers took Beth's arm and hurried her back down the drive. "Come on, lass. Let's see if there's anything we can do."

Beth stopped to pick up her discarded shoes and, slipping and sliding on the wet grass, struggled to keep up with him until they reached the wrecked vehicles. Another car had drawn up, and with the help of the other two men Michael managed to lift James out of the car and lay him on the ground. Covering him with his jacket, Michael cradled his brother's head in his arms.

"James, James, can you hear me?" He bent his head and listened to his chest. "I think he's breathing. Hang on, James. Hang on. There's an ambulance coming."

Beth crouched down beside him, struggling to

loosen James's collar. "Don't move him, Michael," she said anxiously, her face blanching as she saw the extent of his injuries.

"What about the other car?" the man from the house asked.

The other man drew him to one side. "Just one bloke. He's in shock and he's got a few cuts and bruises but that's all. He's the worse for drink as well. Typical, isn't it? It looks as though it was his fault, and he gets off scot-free. God, what a mess – that poor girl – Christmas as well."

He turned away in distress as the woman from the house joined them, awkwardly carrying a bundle of blankets and her husband covered Giovanna's body with one and tucked the other around James.

James stirred, trying to speak. "Gio . . . Giov . . ."

"Don't worry about Giovanna. Just lie quiet." Michael looked up at Beth, his face gaunt with strain, and she put her arm around his shoulders, her eyes brimming with tears. How could Giovanna be dead, her young vibrant spirit wiped out in a few seconds?. "Eternal rest grant unto her, O Lord," she wept, and then there was the sound of sirens in the distance and a few seconds later the police and ambulances arrived.

Beth and Michael stood in the bitter cold watching as both casualties were examined. Giovanna's body was quickly removed. James was transferred carefully on to a stretcher and lifted into the ambulance.

"You and your wife go with him, sir," a police officer said. "We'll see to everything else."

Michael thanked him and they climbed in the ambulance and sat huddled together, stunned by the enormity of the tragedy which had overtaken them.

Chapter 24

At the Infirmary, they waited in an agony of apprehension in the busy Casualty Department. Michael sat with his head down, his hands hanging loosely between his knees. He felt so helpless, so impotent. Apart from asking for a consultant and private facilities, there was nothing more he could do. He groaned. If only they'd set out a few minutes later, or Guy had been in when they'd phoned to cancel the outing. But he knew such thinking was futile, nothing could change what had happened.

Wearily, Beth leaned her head back against the wall, and closed her eyes. Please God, let James be all right! A sob rose in her throat. Never, as long as she lived, would she forget the grotesque sight of Giovanna sprawled lifeless across that car bonnet. Poor, beautiful Giovanna! Struggling to control her tears, Beth glanced at Michael with concern. He looked dreadful. She must get a grip on herself, must try and be strong for him.

"Do you want to try your parents again?"

He nodded, and went to the payphone, only to return a few minutes later, his face grey with worry. "No, still no reply. They must have called somewhere on the way home." He began to pace up and down restlessly. "The other driver was drunk, did you know that?" His voice was thick with suppressed anger.

Beth nodded.

"Oh, God, I can't believe it!"

She put out her hand and drew him down beside her.

"Are you OK?" Michael suddenly noticed Beth's pallor and the purple swelling on her forehead.

"My head hurts, and I feel sick," she confessed.

"We'd better get them to have a look at you." He began to rise.

Beth clutched at his arm, "No, I'm not moving from here until we hear about James."

He sank down beside her. "Someone's going to have to notify Giovanna's parents." His voice broke and, struggling for control, he turned his head away. The senseless tragedy would devastate the devoted Milanese couple whose only daughter was their life.

"Mr and Mrs Rushton?" A doctor in his mid-thirties, his tired face grave, approached them.

They stood up.

"I'm Dr Farrar, the Senior Registrar. Would you like to come with me?"

Beth, limping painfully on her lacerated feet, followed Michael as the doctor ushered them into a tiny, sparsely furnished room. He sat facing them and, leaning forward, spoke in a low voice, "I have to tell you that your brother has regained consciousness."

Michael and Beth exchanged glances of relief.

"However," he continued, "I'm afraid he has suffered extensive internal injuries. We're doing everything we can but I must warn you that it's unlikely he'll survive the night. I'm so very sorry."

Michael drew in a ragged breath as his mind absorbed the finality of the doctor's statement, and pleaded, "What about a specialist? I told them at the desk it doesn't matter what it costs. No reflection on you, Dr Farrar, but isn't there anything . . ." He fell silent as the doctor shook his head.

"Mr Rushton, no one, I repeat no one, can do any more for your brother. It's a wonder he wasn't killed outright. As I've told you, he is conscious at the moment, so my advice to you is to make the most of whatever short time he has left. Have you notified your parents?"

"I'm trying to," Michael said, his voice tight with strain.

"Right, so if you'd like to come with me I'll take you to him. Remember he's heavily sedated."

"Does he know. . .?" Beth asked.

The doctor shook his head.

James had been taken to a small side ward where a nurse, at a sign from the doctor, rose as they entered and left quietly.

Michael stared down at his brother's ashen face, at the still, forlorn outline of his body beneath the hospital sheets, and sat by the side of the bed in despair. Oh, God, that it should come to this!

"James," he whispered, taking his brother's hand in his own.

James opened his eyes.

"Michael . . ." He struggled to speak, his voice weak. "Giovanna's dead, isn't she? No, tell me the truth."

Michael could only nod, his head bowed.

Beth moved to the other side of the bed and leaned over. "She didn't suffer, James. She wouldn't have felt a thing." Her voice caught in her throat as she saw the utter misery in his eyes.

Dr Farrar said softly, "I'll leave you with him. Press that buzzer if you need the nurse."

They nodded.

"Have you told Mum . . ." whispered James. He turned his head to one side as weak tears coursed down his cheeks.

"I'm trying to reach them, but there's no reply," Michael said heavily.

James clutched at his hand. "I know I'm not going to come through this." He tried to smile at Beth, but his lips twisted. "You're the expert. Is there really such a thing as heaven and hell?" He broke off, fighting for breath.

Beth's eyes brimmed with tears. "Oh, James, I shouldn't think you have anything to worry about."

He lay quiet for a moment. "But I have, something I've never . . . forgiven . . . myself for." Michael leaned forward, his voice hoarse with emotion. "Don't upset yourself – save your strength, James. We're none of us saints."

James closed his eyes, and Michael whispered tensely, "I'll try the phone again. They must be back now!"

"Would you like me to go?"

"This is one job I can't delegate," he said grimly, and went to the payphone, hoping yet dreading that someone would lift the receiver. There was no reply.

Beth looked up as he came back in and shook his head in despair.

"I think he's asleep," she said. "I'll just go to the loo. I won't be long."

A few minutes later, James stirred and murmured, "Has Beth gone?"

"Yes."

"Something I want to tell you . . . been on my conscience." He struggled to speak. "That party years ago . . . we gatecrashed . . . not you . . . the night before your National Service –"

"Yes, I know. Take your time. Don't tire yourself," Michael urged. For heaven's sake, what did it matter? What did anything matter?

"No, I need to tell . . . I've never told anyone. There was a girl . . . drunk . . . we all were. I thought she was fair game . . . but she struggled and after . . ." His mouth trembled, "Oh God, I think I raped her."

The shocking words hung in the air between them, and then Michael was leaning forward, shaking his head in denial, desperate to ease the agony he saw in his brother's eyes.

"No, James. I'm sure you're mistaken. You're torturing yourself for nothing." Hadn't James suffered enough on this nightmare of a night, without baring his soul?

"No . . . there were signs . . . you know. I've never forgiven myself, never."

He closed his eyes again in exhaustion, while Michael sat and watched him. All these years. He'd thought they were so close, and yet he'd never seen the troubled spirit behind his brother's laughing, carefree facade. How well do we ever know anyone, he thought sadly, until it's too late.

Unknown to them both, Beth stood motionless inside the doorway. Neither of the men had sensed her return as she slipped quietly into the room. Her face drained of colour, her mind struggled numbly to grasp what she had just heard. James had raped her? All those years ago, in that darkened bedroom, it had been James? For God's sake, it was him! The brother-in-law she'd laughed with and hugged. She'd become so fond of him, had been grateful for the way he'd welcomed her into the family!

Her legs began to tremble, and she tried to steady herself. It was such a profound shock. All through the years, not once had she imagined that the drunken youth she remembered with such bitterness could have regretted his action. In her mind she had built up a picture of an uncaring monster, and now to discover it was James! James, who having lost the young wife he adored, was shortly to lose his own life. She felt such pain that she was unable to stifle a cry, and Michael turned and saw her.

"I'll try the phone again," he said in a strangled voice and walked quickly out of the room.

Beth moved to take his chair. She looked at the sick man lying so still on the narrow bed, lines of pain etched upon his pale, freckled face, and her heart filled not with hatred, but with compassion. His painful confession had shown that he'd carried his burden just as she had carried hers. He was so young to die. How could she let him go on suffering such guilt.

Suddenly, she knew what she must do and without hesitation she bent over and put her lips close to his ear.

"James, it's Beth. Can you hear me?"

Slowly, he opened his eyes.

"James," she said urgently, "I heard what you were saying to Michael." Treacherous tears filled her eyes, and she brushed them away, clutching at his hand. "James, listen to me. I want you to know something. I was that girl."

He stared at her dully without comprehension.

"All those years ago, I was that girl at the party. You know, when you dressed up as a Lone Ranger." She willed him to understand. "Michael doesn't know. No one knows!"

His eyes slowly widened in horror, and she said intensely, "I want you to know that I forgive you. You were very drunk and very young. We both were. You're a good man, James. I can't bear to think of you torturing yourself like this."

His eyes beseeched her, his mouth moving

convulsively, and she leaned forward and kissed him gently on the forehead, whispering, "After all this time wondering, I'm glad I found out it was you, and not one of the others. Oh, James," she said brokenly.

As his eyes closed and the precious minutes ticked away, Beth anguished over her next words. Should she tell him? Tears caught in her throat. There would never be another chance. Surely, despite everything, she owed him the truth?

"James . . . listen to me . . . James!"

Slowly, with a tremendous effort, he opened his eyes.

"There's something I have to tell you . . . want you to know . . ." She struggled to get the words out. "I had a baby, your baby, a little girl called Rosemary. Oh, James, she was so beautiful . . ."

As understanding gradually dawned, James clawed at her arm.

"Where . . .?"

There was a sudden noise out in the corridor as a porter wheeled a trolley, and Beth glanced nervously over her shoulder before bending nearer. "I had to have her adopted." Her voice shook. "I'm sorry, James. I really am. There was nothing else I could do. But I promise you one thing," her eyes fastened on his, holding his gaze, willing him to struggle to remain conscious. "If I ever find her, I'll tell her she had a father to be proud of."

Weak, helpless tears began to trickle down his face, and Beth tried desperately to comfort him.

"It's all right, James, honestly. Everyone's allowed one mistake . . ."

But slowly his eyes drooped and closed, his breathing became shallower, and what little strength he had began to ebb. Sensing he was lapsing into unconsciousness, Beth hurriedly pressed the buzzer for the nurse.

When Michael joined them, he looked ten years older. Grey with exhaustion, he looked down at his dying brother and told her, "They're on their way."

It was then that the room began to blur and as the nurse came forward murmuring something about concussion, Beth felt herself falling into merciful oblivion.

Chapter 25

Beth stood by Michael at the side of the open grave, her eyes brimming with tears, as first Robert and then Sylvia sprinkled a handful of soil down on to the oak coffin containing the body of their younger son. Then Michael moved forward in his turn, his head bowed with grief.

When at last the vicar turned away, the crowd of mourners began slowly to disperse, sobered by the stark reminder of their own mortality. They filed in procession out of the cold windswept cemetery, anxious to regain the familiar warmth of their cars. There were many in attendance at the funeral, for James had been popular, and several local dignitaries and prominent businessmen were there to pay their respects, deeply shocked by the tragic circumstances.

The Rushton family remained forlornly behind until eventually Beth touched Michael's arm.

"We should be going. People will be waiting at the house," she whispered.

He nodded and, moving between his parents, took each one by the arm and supported them back to their car, Beth following a little distance behind, her face pale and drawn, knowing that tomorrow she and Michael were to fly to Milan for yet another funeral as it was the wish of Giovanna's parents that their daughter be buried in her own country.

"You're going to have to be strong for them all, lass. Are you sure you're feeling better?" Rose whispered later, as she kissed Beth goodbye.

"I'm all right, Mum," Beth said quietly.

Eighteen months later, Beth drove her new white Cortina into the drive of Linden House, and walked quickly up to the front door where Sylvia, on the alert for her arrival, stood waiting.

"Where is he?" Beth whispered.

"In the drawing-room. He just sits there, staring into space. This can't go on, Beth. He won't go into the works; he doesn't take any interest in anything around him; he won't even play golf. I'm at the end of my tether." There were lines of strain around Sylvia's eyes which now filled with tears, and Beth put her arms around her and held her close.

"Don't worry. We'll get it sorted," she promised with more conviction than she felt. She'd seen this coming for months, had watched her powerful and domineering father-in-law slowly disintegrate beneath his overwhelming grief. Strange, she would have expected that he'd be the strong partner, but it had been Sylvia who, after the initial devastation, had persevered in trying to rebuild her life. Now, her carefully built defences were being shaken yet again, as she watched her husband sink ever more deeply into depression.

"I don't know how. He refuses to see the doctor," she said in a weary voice. "If I as much as suggest it, he bites my head off."

"Couldn't you have a word with David yourself?" Beth suggested. Their family doctor and, in fact, the other members of their medical practice were all known to them socially.

"I have," she admitted. "David says Robert needs to acknowledge that he has a problem and to consult him but his temper is so unpredictable, I daren't mention it. Look, you go in to him. I'll make up some coffee."

Beth entered the drawing-room and crossed over to the winged leather armchair where Robert was sitting in a slumped position, his hands hanging loosely between his knees, his eyes vacantly staring.

She was shocked to see the man whose clothes were always immaculately co-ordinated, dressed in an old pair of trousers, unshaven and without a tie. He gave no sign that he'd even noticed her entrance.

"Good morning, Father-in-law," she said, taking the seat opposite. "It's a lovely day, don't you think?"

He slumped further into his chair, ignoring her.

She suppressed a feeling of irritation. "I'm surprised you're not going into the works. Isn't it today that the Japanese delegation is coming?"

Her words fell emptily into the void between them. She sat looking at him, feelings of compassion warring with impatience. A slow anger began to build inside her as she thought of Sylvia's strained nerves, of Michael's worry and frustration. She made a sudden decision. Someone had to pierce the armour he'd built about himself, and what had she got to lose? He'd never approved of her anyway.

"Don't you think you're being rather selfish?" she said.

He didn't reply, his gaze focused on some unseen point.

"I said, don't you think you're being rather selfish?" she repeated, this time raising her voice and speaking sharply.

He slowly refocused his eyes to meet hers. "What do you mean?"

"I mean, not acknowledging what is happening to you. You're suffering from depression, Robert, following a bereavement. Don't you realise that by refusing to see a doctor you're causing distress to everyone?"

He stared at her, his attention caught at last.

"Aren't you interested any more in the firm? If not, then retire or resign," she said brutally, "and let Michael appoint another director to relieve him of some of the responsibility. You can't expect him to do two men's work for ever, you know. It's beginning to affect his health."

"Resign!" For a split second there was a spark of indignation in his eyes and she seized her opportunity.

'Yes, resign. Retire, make way for someone else with fresh ideas. After all, you were always saying 'expand or die'. Or appoint Sylvia and me as directors, and we'll do your job between us."

At this suggestion, as she'd hoped, his face suffused with anger, and he exploded. "What!"

"Well, what's the alternative?" Beth countered. "You won't run it, Michael can't do your job and his own for ever, you refuse to bring in anyone else! What do you suggest?"

He looked hopelessly at her and then to her horror she saw his eyes fill with tears as he sank back into his chair.

With a rush of sympathy, her voice softened.

"Look, there is a solution. Swallow your pride and let David come and see you here. A few weeks on anti-depressants could work wonders, and no one would know, only ourselves. Please, Robert, for all our sakes!"

Sylvia, standing in the doorway, oblivious to the weight of the tray of coffee she was holding, held her breath.

Robert sat in silence for a few minutes, and then said, "No one need know, you say?"

"No one. Will you let Sylvia phone?"

He nodded, turning his head away to hide his deep shame that this young woman who used to be one of his employees should witness his weakness.

"They think it's all over. It is now!" As Kenneth Wolstenholme's words captured the hearts of the nation a few weeks later, Michael and Guy leapt to their feet in euphoria, while Beth laughingly went to fetch a bottle of champagne from the fridge.

"We've won, England's won the World Cup! What's more, we beat Germany! I can't believe it," Guy said, pacing up and down the room in excitement. "What a game, what a team, and Geoff Hurst got a hat trick!"

With a huge grin, Michael popped the cork with a loud bang and poured the frothing golden liquid into champagne flutes.

"Here's to Geoff Hurst. May he someday play for Stoke!" he proposed.

"Here's to good old Nobby Stiles!" said Guy, raising his glass again.

"To Captain Bobby Moore!" Michael picked up the bottle in readiness for a refill, as he added, "And our intrepid goalkeeper – I give you Gordon Banks!"

"Hold on. Are you two going to toast the whole team?" Beth joked.

"You bet we are. What did you think of that third goal?"

As the two men began a postmortem on the match, Beth escaped into the kitchen, placing her glass on a working surface while she cut some chicken sandwiches. It was wonderful to see Michael so full of joy again. With all the extra stress at work he was short-tempered and irritable these days.

Anyway, she thought, as she piled the dainty sandwiches on to a doyley-covered plate, and put some sausage rolls to heat, she was hoping to have her own reason for celebrating. She was already two days late with her period, which had never happened before. She hugged her excited anticipation to herself. They'd been married nearly three years now, three years of longing for a child. Surely this time. . .

She thought back to Giovanna and their conversation just before the accident. The poor girl never had the chance to face up to her fear of childbirth. Her own forgiveness of James on that terrible night had brought with it a sense of inner peace, an easing of the bitterness she had carried for so many years. Her sadness at parting with Rosemary would always be with her, but she had at last achieved a calm acceptance.

However, at seven thirty the following morning, she emerged from the bathroom tearful and sick with disappointment. Michael took one look at her face and took her in his arms.

"It's not the end of the world, sweetheart."

"Do you think there's something wrong?" she asked, not for the first time.

"Well," he admitted, "I know I've been against it before, but perhaps it is time you went to see the doctor. Have a word with David. Perhaps it's only something minor."

She nodded, dreading the moment when she would see the knowledge dawn in the doctor's eyes that she'd already conceived and carried a child to full term. But she couldn't go on like this, hoping and praying from one month to another. Her longing for a baby was beginning to overshadow everything else in her life. Just the sight of a pram or a pushchair brought her heartache. Anyway, she'd have to see their family doctor sooner or later – after all, if she did become pregnant, she would need antenatal care. She would just have to pluck up courage and go.

The following week, before her resolve could falter she nervously presented herself at the surgery.

After examining her, David remained silent for a few moments before asking, "Does Michael know?"

She looked at the man who was a friend, who had dined at her table, who played golf with her husband. "No."

"And the child?"

"Adopted." She kept her answers short, praying that he wouldn't press her further.

"Well, I can see no reason at all from what you've told me and from a physical examination why you haven't conceived. Of course the next step would be to do tests, to see whether your fallopian tubes are blocked or there's a problem with ovulation. You could have them done privately if you prefer."

She nodded.

"Right, I'll arrange an appointment for you. And Beth," he looked into her troubled eyes, "anything that happens in this surgery is confidential, you know."

She gave a small embarrassed smile. "Thank you, David."

A few weeks later, Rose sat in her armchair gazing at the electric fire sitting in pride of place before her new cream-tiled surround. It might have a coal effect, she mused, but it wasn't the same as the real thing, and she did miss the old fireplace and fender. There were no dreams in watching a light bulb flicker. Still, as Beth and Michael had persuaded her, she didn't have to rake out the ashes every morning or fetch in the coal, and you couldn't have everything.

Thinking of Beth and Michael, she frowned uneasily. There was something amiss there, she could sense it. That last time she'd visited them, there had been a distinct atmosphere. Come to think of it, Beth had been looking a bit strained for some time, but she didn't like to probe. The lass knew she was always there if she wanted to confide in her.

Now there was Val's news about the new baby to tell her and she was a bit apprehensive as to how she'd take it. Rose sighed. She just couldn't understand it. A couple like that with everything to offer a child and still no sign of a family. "Look at some people," she muttered, as she got up to make a pot of tea. "Don't want them, won't look after them, and yet they breed like rabbits!" God certainly moved in mysterious ways – she just couldn't fathom him out at times. Look at Aberfan, all those little children suffocated to death under a sliding mountain of coal slurry. What sort of a God could let a terrible thing like that happen?

She lifted a corner of her apron to wipe a tear from

her eyes and then heard a car pull up. That would be Beth now – you could set your clock by that girl.

"Don't you think you've had enough?" Beth said quietly one evening, as she watched Michael cross over to the sideboard and pour himself another glass of whisky.

"No, I don't, and I don't need you to tell me what to do," he snapped, returning to his armchair to stare morosely at the television.

Beth got up and silently left the room, knowing from past experience that if she stayed while he was in one of his moods then Michael would find some way of provoking yet another row. It was all they seemed to do these days, either that or live their lives in a chill distance from each other.

She went upstairs and sat on the bed as tears of hurt and frustration stung her eyes. No matter how she tried, he turned away from her. It was weeks since they'd made love. If only Michael would talk to her, really talk, tell her how he felt, then they could share the problem, discuss it, help each other. But no, ever since his fateful visit to the specialist's consulting room, he'd shut her out, returning from work each evening to find what solace he could in the whisky bottle.

She went over to the dressing-table and began to

brush her hair, wearily aware of her pallor and shadowed eyes. If only the fault had been hers, then perhaps they would have coped better, but Michael had reacted as though the fact that he had an abnormally low sperm count was a reflection on his manhood. She'd never forget the expression in his eyes when he'd told her that it was unlikely he would ever be able to give her a child.

Chapter 26

Michael parked his car under the wet branches of an ancient oak tree near Linden Lodge and, placing his elbows on the leather steering wheel, rested his head dejectedly in his hands. His throat constricted at the thought of what he knew he must do. He could only pray that his father, now back at work and recovering from his depression, would cope with the knowledge that there would be no dynasty, no heir to the family fortune.

But he had to tell them, they had a right to know, and at least it would put an end to Robert's heavy-handed hints and speculative looks, which were increasingly causing Beth intense embarrassment. He remembered James telling him that he used to do the same with Giovanna. Poor old James. That had been the worst night of his life, having to watch his brother die in grief and racked with the burden of guilt. He'd often wondered how long Beth had been in the doorway and whether she'd heard James confess that many years ago he'd raped a young girl. He shook his head; he still found the concept difficult to believe.

He sat in the silence for a long time, thinking back over the past two years. The accident had scarred all their lives; he knew he'd never been the same man since. His relationship with Beth was becoming ever more strained, and he knew it was his mainly his fault. He still couldn't bring himself to make love to her. It was as though he carried inside him a block of ice; the very act seemed futile. It was psychological he knew and completely unfair to Beth, but he found it impossible to talk to her about it, even though he could see the hurt in her eyes. Their hopes had been so high – they'd hoped and planned to have at least three children.

He stared out at the rain for a while and then taking a deep, ragged breath, straightened his shoulders and switched on the engine.

Half an hour later, Michael sat opposite his parents before a crackling log fire in the drawing-room hardly able to bear the pain in their eyes.

"Are you sure?" Sylvia whispered.

"I've told you exactly what the specialist said."

"Oh, Michael, I don't know what to say." Sylvia's face was pale with distress.

"I thought you both had the right to know," he said.

Robert sat stunned, unable to speak.

"How has Beth taken it?" Sylvia asked quietly.

"It's been a shock to her, of course," he answered, and she looked at his troubled eyes with perception. She'd guessed something was wrong between them, but this bombshell! Dear God, how would Robert take it with his fierce pride in his family history, his hopes for the future? She glanced at him with impatience. Surely he could say something for heaven's sake? It was an even bigger tragedy for Michael and Beth and his son needed support and reassurance.

But Robert just sat in grim silence, his face like granite.

"If you and Beth wished to, you could always adopt," she began in a soft voice.

"Adopt!" Robert suddenly sprang into life. "No adopted whelp is going to inherit my business!"

"For God's sake, Robert, people want a family for more reasons than inheriting money," Sylvia said sharply. "You and your precious bloodline. There are other considerations, you know! For example, how about a bit of understanding for how Michael feels?"

Robert had the grace to look ashamed, and said

gruffly, "Yes, of course. It's a rotten deal you've been given."

Michael shrugged, his face bitter, saying, "I need another drink – how about you two?"

Before they could answer, there came a loud ring at the door. With an exclamation of annoyance Sylvia got up to answer it.

"I don't want to see anyone," Robert snapped, and Michael followed his mother into the hall to see her greet Ursula who was busy apologising for her dripping umbrella.

"It's absolutely filthy out there. Why, Michael, this is an unexpected pleasure!" Her face lit up as he approached to kiss her cheek. "I haven't seen you for ages! Where have you been keeping yourself?"

"Oh, it's just been a busy time," he said evasively.

"I've brought this file for your father. Daddy forgot to give it to him, and apparently he needs it for a meeting in the morning."

"Thank you, dear," Sylvia said, casting a despairing glance at Michael.

Seeing her dilemma he said quickly, "I was just going down to the pub, Ursula – do you fancy coming for a drink? That's if you've got time?"

Her eyes widened with surprise and pleasure. "I'd love to," she replied quickly. She turned to go, her green eyes gleaming with anticipation. "Bye, Sylvia, see you soon."

"Goodbye. Take care, Michael. Tell Beth I'll ring." Sylvia murmured, her expression thoughtful as she watched them hurry down the drive to Michael's car.

"Beth not with you, then?" Ursula said curiously.

"No." Michael swung his long legs into the driving seat of the Jaguar.

"So, I've got you all to myself, like old times eh?"

He smiled. "Yes, I suppose it is."

He drove carefully along the dark wet roads towards the pub in the village, and parked.

"Come on then. I might even play you darts!" he offered in an effort to throw off his dark mood.

"I could always beat you," she laughed, tucking her arm companionably into his.

Gradually, over the next couple of hours, Michael began to relax. He'd forgotten what good company Ursula was, and as they reminisced he realised with a pang just how long it was since he'd been so lighthearted.

"Are you still seeing Tony Morrison?" he asked eventually.

"On and off."

"It's not serious then. I'd have thought by now you'd have been snapped up," he smiled.

"Oh, I've had plenty of offers, but," she touched his hand for a second, "the man I wanted married someone else." Her eyes met and held his for a long moment before he looked away and, glancing at his watch, drained his glass.

"I'd better be going."

"Yes, me too."

They walked back to the car and then, as Michael switched on the engine, Ursula turned to him and murmured, "I did enjoy that, Michael. We must do it again some time."

He turned and looked at her. "Yes, I enjoyed it too," he said quietly, and then as Ursula leaned tentatively towards him, her lips soft and inviting, he kissed her. Just a fleeting kiss, a friendly kiss, he told himself.

"Then let's do it again, just the two of us. After all, we are old friends. There's no harm in it."

"Why not?" he agreed, and letting in the clutch drove back to where her car was parked in his parents' drive.

Beth was reading in bed when he arrived home, the scene one of cosy domesticity in the soft light of her bedside lamp. She looked up anxiously as he came into the bedroom.

"How did they take it?" He'd been such a long time. She wished he'd taken her with him, but Michael had been adamant that it would be better if he went on his own.

"As you'd expect, it's not the sort of news anyone wants to hear from their son!" he answered curtly, and went into the dressing-room to remove his clothes.

Incensed by his dismissive tone, Beth nevertheless held back an angry retort. He was bound to be feeling upset after his visit – she really ought to have more patience. It was all she seemed to do these days, make excuses for Michael's moods, but she desperately wanted an end to the tensions between them, to get back to their old happy, loving relationship.

Michael came back into the bedroom and, without speaking, climbed into bed beside her. She put out a tentative hand to hold his, but he merely gave it a brief squeeze before turning his back and settling down to sleep.

There was no need to mention about going out for a drink, he decided. Beth had always been a bit paranoid about Ursula.

Over the following three months, without really planning it, he ran into Ursula on several occasions, and gradually their meetings, usually in some pub or other, became a regular part of his life. Michael rationalised that there was no need for Beth to know. After all, it was no different than his meeting an old male friend for a drink and a chat. If, each time as they said goodbye, Ursula raised her face for his kiss and that kiss became gradually warmer, then surely it was only affection and no threat to his wife?

Beth was immersed in her own problems. Ever since the initial shock that it was extremely unlikely that she would ever bear Michael's child, she'd realised that Rosemary was the Rushtons' rightful heir. How could she deny her own daughter her birthright, and Robert and Sylvia their only grandchild? She miserably reminded herself that she had forfeited all rights to Rosemary when she'd agreed to have her adopted, and it would probably be impossible to trace her. However, the fact remained that she did exist and she had no right to keep that information to herself. Unable to come to a decision, she spent much of her time wandering aimlessly around her immaculate and expensively furnished home, feeling ever more isolated. Michael was often out in the evenings either at Rotary or on business, and time lay heavily on her hands.

She tried to explain this to Michael but her suggestion that she should take an interest in local politics met with instant disapproval.

"You can't mean you want to join the Labour Party?" he asked in a scandalised tone.

"Well, if I hope eventually to serve on the Council, I can hardly stand as a Tory with my views!"

"It's absolutely out of the question," he insisted.

"You're forgetting, you're a Rushton now. Besides don't you think my father's got enough on his plate without everyone knowing he's got a socialist daughter-in-law?"

Robert was a worry to them all. The knowledge that the Rushton name would finish with Michael had caused him to slip back into an even deeper depression and he was once again becoming a sullen recluse. But even so, she thought bitterly, why should my life be curtailed through closed minds and snobbery?

"What happened to the man I married?" she flung at him. "At one time, you would have had a more tolerant and liberal view, and supported me."

His jaw tensed and he turned away, running a hand wearily through his hair. "What's for dinner?" he asked, indicating that the discussion was at an end.

"Coq au vin," she replied, although anger was rapidly dissipating her own appetite.

"I'll have a drink while I'm waiting."

Beth watched him lift the whisky decanter and pour a generous measure.

Even though she knew her timing was bad, she blurted out, "Michael, have you thought any more about adoption?"

"Not now, Beth," he said shortly, and switched on the television set for the evening news. As the noise of the set blared out, she turned angrily and went into the kitchen. The time was never right apparently, and in her frustration she screwed up a tea towel and flung it violently at the wall. He was becoming impossible!

Michael slumped miserably in the armchair, trying to ignore the sound of Beth slamming around in the kitchen. The only time lately he felt at all at ease was when he was with Ursula, and glancing at his watch he decided that after dinner he'd drive over to the White Swan. There was a fair chance that he might see her there. Then, for a couple of hours at least, he didn't have to feel guilty all the time, to feel that he'd ruined his wife's life.

Chapter 27

Michael pushed open the heavy oak door into the lounge bar of the White Swan and glanced quickly around the crowded tables. No, there was no sign of Ursula and, disappointed, he turned to order a large gin and tonic only to feel a few minutes later a touch on his shoulder.

"Hi!" Ursula kissed his cheek lightly.

"Hi, yourself. What are you having, your usual?"

She nodded, and went to find them an unobtrusive table in a corner.

"You always seem to be in here. I'm beginning to wonder if you're a secret boozer!" he laughed as he brought over their drinks.

Ursula flicked back her long blonde hair and her eyes avoided his as she said, "Oh, it's a favourite of mine, and it gets me away from the parents."

"Yes," he said curiously. "I'd have thought you might have wanted your own place by now."

"I have thought about it. It is restricting living at home," she admitted. "Gosh, it's warm in here." She slipped off her summer jacket, revealing a strapped dress, its cleavage drawing his eyes like a magnet, and he suddenly found himself aware of her sensuality.

"Talking of parents," she murmured, "mine are away on a cruise as you know. Do you fancy coming back and having a drink there? It's getting so crowded in here."

She waited, her eyes watchful, as Michael hesitated for a moment, and then he said, "Why not?" Beth wouldn't miss him, he thought. She'd mentioned about going down to see her Gran, refusing his half-hearted invitation that she should accompany him.

"No, you go and talk football in the bar, or whatever it is you men talk about," she'd said, obviously still resentful of his refusal yet again to talk about adoption.

He followed Ursula's red MG and ten minutes later they arrived at the house. She flung her jacket carelessly over the oak balustrade and led the way into the sitting-room.

"We've got the place to ourselves – the housekeeper's away for a few days, so you'll have to forgive the untidiness."

He laughed. "You women are all the same. There's not a thing out of place."

"There would be if you'd take your jacket and tie off – you must be sweltering," she smiled.

He obeyed and settled himself down on the soft cushions of the chintz sofa as she poured them a couple of drinks. She then began to regale him with an idiotically funny story she'd heard at the golf club. Her wit, as usual, was spiced with malice but as always Michael found her sense of humour irresistible.

"Here, let me get you a refill," she giggled.

"OK, but go steady on the gin this time – that last one must have been a treble."

"So what? You can always get a taxi home," she murmured, and going over to the radiogram switched on a Sinatra long-playing record. "Come on, how about a dance? We used to make quite a couple in the old days."

Feeling pleasantly muzzy, he smiled and getting up took her in his arms. They circled slowly around the floor to the crooner's seductive rendering of 'Strangers in the Night'.

Ursula nestled against him and, aware of the headiness of her perfume and her soft hair beneath his chin, his pulses quickened. He remembered the many intimate moments they had shared in their youth, and for a moment the years fell away. As the music faded before the next number, they both reached silently for their drinks, holding each other's gaze as they drained their glasses, and then Ursula drifted back into his arms, her body warm and pliant as they swayed to the music.

Putting her arm around his neck her lips sought his, parted and inviting, and almost before he knew what he was doing, Michael was kissing her, not just once but many times, long, deep, passionate kisses as her mouth became more and more demanding, inflaming his senses.

Taking his hand, she moved slowly away and whispered, "Come upstairs. I've champagne on ice."

Still bemused by what had just taken place, he followed her unsteadily up the carpeted staircase to her bedroom – curtains drawn, softly lit and complete with ice bucket at the side of the bed.

"Do you always keep champagne at your bedside?" he asked, as he automatically began to unscrew the cork.

"It's been there, darling, every evening since my parents left and I've had the house to myself," she purred. She swung her long slim legs up on to the peach satin coverlet, and lay back languidly, her eyes gleaming with triumph. "I knew you'd be in the White Swan sooner or later – surely you don't think that all our meetings have been by accident?"

"I hadn't really thought." Dimly, Michael became conscious of a sense of unease as he popped the champagne cork and poured the frothing liquid into crystal glasses.

Ursula leaned forward to take her glass, her full breasts straining against the thin material of her dress and she began to slip down the straps seductively. Patting the bed, she held out her hand to draw him down beside her. "You and I are made for each other – I knew you'd realise it eventually," she murmured.

Michael paused, glass in hand.

"You planned all this, didn't you?" he said thickly.

She didn't answer, merely looking at him through lowered lashes while her hand began to caress his thigh, slowly moving upwards towards his zip.

Michael froze. Struggling to think clearly, he carefully placed his half-empty glass of champagne on the bedside table, and with an effort moved away from the bed, muttering,

"I won't be a moment."

Half-stumbling along the landing to the bathroom, he closed the door behind him and going over to the washbasin, stared with bloodshot eyes into the mirror above. Bending, he put his head under the cold-water tap and turned it on to full pressure for a few moments before reaching for a towel.

He sat on the bathroom stool, holding his head in his hands and asked himself what on earth he thought he was doing – and whatever had she put in that gin?

Half the damn bottle? All those chance meetings, this whole evening, it had all been a set-up! Beth had been right all along: Ursula was out to break them up. She was a bitch, a calculating bitch. To think he'd nearly fallen for it, had nearly, in his self-pity, betrayed Beth's love and loyalty. Hot shame swept over him as he remembered those kisses downstairs, was conscious of the intimate scene in the bedroom. He'd come so close – if she hadn't revealed her hand, would he have been unfaithful? He groaned. No, please God, no matter how much he'd drunk, he wouldn't have gone that far!

What a bloody, stupid fool he'd been, and now he'd have to get himself out of this, and if he knew Ursula she wouldn't make it easy!

By the time he returned to the bedroom, it was obvious that Ursula was on her third glass of champagne. Her dress was now flung into a corner of the bedroom and she lay on the bed in suspender belt and stockings in a pose of complete abandonment.

"Have another drink, darling," she coaxed. "I'm way ahead of you."

Michael went over and picked up her dress and, averting his eyes, handed it to her.

"I'm sorry. I shouldn't have let it get this far. I think we're both forgetting something, Ursula. I'm married."

She sat up, her green eyes glittering with spite. "Married! To that little nobody! She can't even give you a child after three years. You don't fool me, Michael. You don't love Beth, or you wouldn't have been sniffing after me these past few months!"

He winced. Old friends indeed. How naive could you get!

"I'll ignore that remark, except to say that I'm sorry if I gave you the wrong impression."

"Oh, no!" Ursula clambered off the bed, clutching the dress to her. "You don't get off as easily as that, Michael Rushton. I wonder how that po-faced wife of yours would react if she knew that you'd spent the evening smooching with me, had been here in my bedroom, on my bed drinking champagne?"

He blanched. "You wouldn't! Anyway, nothing happened, not really . . ."

"Oh yeah, and who'd believe you? It's your word against mine! Have you never heard the words, 'Hell hath no fury like a woman scorned'? You reject me tonight, Michael, and you've rejected me twice." Her voice softened, and she began to cajole, "Come on. Don't be silly. I know you want me," and dropping the dress began to sway towards him.

With distaste, Michael turned to go and said curtly, "Goodnight, Ursula! I'll send a driver for my car in the morning."

Descending the stairs, he grabbed his jacket and tie from the sitting-room, and opened the front door only to hear her screaming after him,

"I'll be on the phone, you bastard, before you get to the end of the drive!"

"Go on then. I'm sure you'll want Beth to know I repulsed you," he yelled back, nauseous bile rising in his throat.

Slamming the front door behind him, and taking deep gulps of the cool night air, he hunched his shoulders in despair as he began to walk quickly down the long deserted road. How on earth had he allowed himself to be manipulated like that? He felt humiliated as he thought of the scene in the bedroom, of his stupidity in even following her up the stairs. Beth had told him he was drinking too much – well, he'd certainly learned his lesson. What he needed now was black coffee, lots of it, and remembering there was an all-night transport cafe near the main road, turned off to the left, hoping desperately that Ursula's pride would prevent her from carrying out her threat.

Chapter 28

Beth could hear the persistent ring of the telephone as she got out of her car, and hurrying to the front door inserted her key in the lock and dashed to pick up the receiver. But it was too late – whoever was on the other end had rung off. Glancing at her watch, she frowned, and going into the kitchen switched on the kettle to make a cup of tea. Michael's car hadn't been in the garage, but he shouldn't be long. It was probably him, trying to phone. Since the accident, he usually rang to let her know if he'd been delayed, as otherwise her feverish imagination would have him on a mortuary slab and the funeral over by the time he arrived home.

Suddenly, the phone rang again, its intrusion startling her, and she answered it expecting to hear Michael's voice.

"Hello?"

"Beth? It's Sylvia!"

"Oh, Sylvia! Have you rung before?"

"Yes, I've been trying to get you all evening. Is Michael there?" Her voice sounded strained.

"No, he's not, but he shouldn't be long. There's nothing wrong, is there?"

"It's Robert. Oh God, I've got to talk to someone, no matter what he says. I can't make a decision like this on my own."

Her voice choked, and Beth said quickly, "Sylvia, what is it?"

There was a short silence and then, "I had to insist on calling in the doctor. Robert was in a dreadful state. He just sat there weeping, saying what was the point of it all, his whole life had been wasted, that it wasn't worth going on. I felt frightened, Beth, really worried."

"Oh, Sylvia . . ." Beth's heart went out to her.

"David rang Charles Meredith at home – you know, the Consultant Psychiatrist at the City General. He came straight away."

"What did he say?"

"He says Robert is suffering from reactive depression, with the threat of a nervous breakdown. He thinks he's come to terms with losing James, but the knowledge that he'll never have a grandchild has pushed him over the edge. He wants him to have that awful electric shock treatment, Beth – you know, where they put electrodes on to the head and –"

"Yes, I know, Sylvia," Beth whispered. She couldn't bear the thought of that proud, autocratic man having to submit to such a procedure.

"It's just that I have to give my permission, and . . ."

"Naturally, you wanted to talk to Michael about it. Look, Sylvia, I've no idea how long he'll be, but I want you to promise me something," Beth said urgently. "Don't decide anything until tomorrow. I'll come over as soon as I can."

"I promise."

Her voice was weary, and Beth reassured her, "I'll tell Michael as soon as he comes in, and get him to ring you in the morning."

"Thank you, dear. Sorry to burden you with it all, but I had to talk to someone."

"That's what I'm here for. Goodnight – try and get some sleep."

Slowly putting down the phone, Beth went back into the kitchen numbed by the implications of Sylvia's words. Pouring herself a cup of tea, she carried it upstairs and placed it on her bedside table. She sat on her lace bedspread and was soon deep in thought. Subconsciously, she'd always known that one day her secret would come out. Now she had to face it. There was no decision to make any more – it had all been taken out of her hands.

The alternative was to watch Robert travel down the dark tunnel of depression, to allow him to be subjected to a horrific ordeal, to deny him the knowledge that was rightfully his. She couldn't do it.

Wearily sipping her tea, she glanced at the alarm clock: eleven thirty. Michael was very late and she felt a niggle of anxiety, only to breathe a sigh of relief as she heard a car door slam and his voice bidding someone goodnight, followed by the sound of his key in the door. Curious, she hurried over to the window and peered out to see the tail-lights of a taxi disappearing down the drive.

Going to the head of the stairs she called down, "Michael, are you all right?"

"Yes, I just had a bit too much to drink, that's all. I did try to ring but the phone was engaged," he answered in a tense voice.

"Yes, it was your mother. Do you want some coffee?"

"No, it's OK. I've had some. I'll come up later."

At the sound of Beth's normal tone, Michael went into the lounge and slumped exhausted into an armchair, overwhelmed with relief. Ever since he'd dialled his home number and heard the engaged tone, he had lived in fear of what he might find when he arrived home, imagining the disillusionment on Beth's face, her disgust, her misery. Now, with clarity, he saw that over the past few months his refusal to accept that he was flawed, that he couldn't father a child, had not only put a strain on his marriage, it had clouded his judgement.

He rested his head on the wing of the leather chair. He was so tired, but he daren't go to bed until he was sure Beth was asleep. He just couldn't face her, not yet.

That night was the longest of Beth's life.

She lay still and quiet, watching the minutes tick by on her bedside clock, dreading the morning, praying that she would find the right words, that Michael would understand and forgive her. She'd feigned sleep when he'd eventually come up to bed, deciding to give him Sylvia's message in the morning, when he'd sobered up. At last, as the luminous dial was showing five, her eyelids grew heavy and she dozed off, only to wake up with a jolt as the telephone rang.

Blinking at the time, she realised that she'd forgotten to set the alarm, and fumbled for the receiver.

"Hello?"

By her side, Michael lay absolutely still in an agony of apprehension.

"Oh, I'm so sorry. No, don't worry, you take as much time as you need. No, it's fine, honestly. 'Bye then."

She turned to him.

"It was Mrs Hurst – her sister's ill, so she won't be coming in for a couple of days."

Michael closed his eyes, feeling shaky with relief.

"Beth," he said, "do you think I could have a cup of tea?"

"Of course. I could do with one myself." She swung her feet to the floor searching for her fluffy mules, a sick fear in the pit of her stomach as the ordeal of her confession loomed. I'll get breakfast out of the way first, she decided. Perhaps something to eat would steady her nerves.

While she was gone, Michael lay staring unseeingly at the bedroom ceiling, and knew he was going to have to tell her. Otherwise, their marriage would be a sham. How could he listen to Beth's words of love knowing she believed him to be faithful? There had to be truth between them; their marriage was too important to be built on lies. In any case, he wasn't prepared to live his life jumping every time the telephone rang, always under Ursula's threat of emotional blackmail. He could only pray that she would forgive him, that his coldness towards her over the past few months hadn't ruined everything between them.

Hardly noticing how quiet Michael was, Beth struggled to eat a slice of toast and to control her rising panic, until at last she said, "Michael, there's something important I want to talk to you about. Is it possible you could take some time off work this morning?

He stared at her in surprise. He'd been about to suggest the same thing, and then his stomach knotted with fear. Could it be that he was wrong, that Ursula had phoned after all?

"I'd already decided to take the day off. I want to talk to you, too," he said, his face taut. "I'll go and ring the works."

Beth cleared away the breakfast debris. What did he want to say? He'd been so uncommunicative these past few weeks she hardly knew what was in his mind any more. Going into the lounge she took the chair opposite him, while the early morning sun streamed in through the large picture windows. He looked so pale and drawn, something must be drastically wrong and her stomach tightened with apprehension. He couldn't . . . no, there was no way he could know what she was going to tell him!

"Oh, your mother rang . . ." she suddenly remembered, but Michael held up a hand.

"No, Beth, that can wait. What I have to say can't." Any second that damn phone could ring.

Blast Ursula and her vindictive nature!

He leaned forward, "There's something I need to tell you." He swallowed nervously. "Over the past few months, I've been seeing quite a lot of Ursula."

Beth stared at him and then her stomach lurched. Oh, no, please God, no . . .

At her stricken intake of breath, he said hurriedly, "No, not like that, just the odd drink in a pub."

"Then why didn't you tell me if there was nothing to hide?" Beth's eyes narrowed with suspicion. And why tell me now, like this, she suddenly thought, unless . . .

"Because I knew how you'd react. Fool that I was, I thought her interest in me was purely a friendly one, but last night . . ." his eyes evaded hers, "I had too much to drink."

Beth paled at an image of Michael with Ursula, and hot jealous anger surged inside her. "You don't mean . . ." Was he trying to tell her he'd been unfaithful, and with Ursula Dawes of all people? "Go on," she said tensely.

Awkwardly, he told her of the whole humiliating episode, of how Ursula had planned a seduction scene, how he'd been weak enough to be tempted, of her threat of exposure.

"My only excuse, if it is an excuse, is that I was drunk but, thank God, not drunk enough!"

"You're right. It's not an excuse," Beth snapped. "I've been telling you for weeks you're drinking too much, but oh no, you wouldn't listen to me!"

"Don't rub it in, Beth." Michael said in a weary tone. "I'm well aware of how I've been these past few months."

There was a short silence, and Beth looked away, hot tears stinging her eyes. She felt bitterly hurt, angry and betrayed. How could he be such an idiot! As for Ursula, it was just what she might have expected from that scheming bitch. Then her heart sank. Why had Michael fallen for it, been so vulnerable? If their sex life had been as it should be none of this would ever have happened, and whose fault was that? Michael had been the one to turn away, retreating inside himself after his visit to the specialist. But then, perhaps if she'd shown more understanding, more patience . . .

"I just want you to know that I love you, even if I haven't shown it much lately," Michael said. "I'm sorry, Beth. I don't know how I could have been so stupid." Shakily, he lit a cigarette, inhaling deeply.

Beth stared at him, still stunned and disappointed that he could be weak enough to put their marriage at risk. Yet she knew that many men wouldn't have thought twice about taking what Ursula had so blatantly offered.

Eventually, her voice trembling, she said, "I love you too, Michael. You know that."

"Can we put it behind us? I promise things will be better from now on."

He waited, his eyes on hers pleadingly, until Beth said slowly, "I'm glad you told me. I don't want any secrets between us after today. Perhaps now you'll believe I've been telling you the truth about her all this time."

"I don't think we'll have any more trouble with Ursula Dawes," Michael said grimly.

They sat in silence for a few minutes and then he asked, "What was it you wanted to talk to me about?"

Beth hesitated, still shaken by what he'd just told her. God, what a day this was turning out to be!

"I'll make us some coffee first. Come and talk to me, and I'll tell you what your mother said."

While the coffee percolated, she told him what had happened, and how the psychiatrist had said Robert was on the edge of a nervous breakdown.

The proposal that his father should undergo electric shock treatment appalled Michael. "Surely that's too extreme? Surely it can't be as bad as that? He was always so strong, almost too damn strong at times. You ask anyone at the works!"

"Your mother was really upset," she said, pouring the coffee, and taking it into the lounge.

"It must be a dreadful strain for her. I'll go over later." He put his head in his hands. "I just can't believe what's happening to our family." He looked up in despair. "I've let everyone down. Why? Why on earth can't I have a child? I've ruined your life too. How do you think I feel, knowing that because you're married to me you'll never have a baby?"

Hoping it would steady her nerves, Beth took a gulp of the strong, fragrant coffee.

"But you're wrong, Michael. You haven't ruined my life." She panicked for a moment, fearful of the consequences of her confession – then, her mouth suddenly dry, moistened her lips and forced out the words. "I've already had a baby."

Her forehead beaded with perspiration as Michael looked at her in bewilderment.

"What did you say?"

"I said, I already have a child," she whispered.

"What on earth are you talking about?"

"Do you remember the night of the accident, just before James died?"

He nodded in puzzlement.

"James told you something, something which was on his conscience, about his raping a young girl at a party?"

"Yes, he did. I wasn't sure whether you'd heard," Michael said. "But I don't see . . ."

"I was that girl, Michael." Her eyes searched his face in anguish, seeing his expression change to shock and disbelief.

Stumbling over the words, she went on to tell him everything, how after Val was taken ill she went to the party alone, about the spiked punch, the darkened bedroom, the three drunken youths in their Lone Ranger costumes. When it came to the rape, her throat constricted and her voice died away, but Michael didn't need her to spell out what had happened.

"It was only when James was talking about the party that night in Milan, that I had any idea who was responsible," she said.

His own brother! The thought made Michael feel sick with revulsion.

"Let me get this straight," he said slowly, trying to marshal his thoughts. "Are you saying that as a result of that night you had a baby, and James was the father?"

She nodded. "Now you see why at last I had to tell you."

"What happened to it? Was it a boy or a girl?"

"It was a little girl. Rosemary. Oh, Michael, I had to have her adopted. I had to. I had no choice."

While Michael listened, his face tense, his eyes never leaving her face, she told him of her dilemma, of Rose's struggle with bereavement and financial problems, of the sacrifices she and Grandma Sherwin had made for her education.

"I don't know if you can understand the morality of the working classes, Michael, and the stigma an illegitimate child carries with it. I really thought it was the best thing for Rosemary too." Her eyes filled with despairing tears. "If you only knew how I've regretted it ever since."

She told him of her confession and how Father O'Neill had arranged for her to spend the summer at Westbourne.

"Are you trying to tell me your mother knew nothing about it?"

"She still doesn't."

Michael looked at his wife, his eyes full of pain. She'd lived with him, slept with him, shared his life for over three years, and yet there had been a part of her life, a devastating part, that he knew nothing about. "All this time, and you've never said a word, not even when we got married."

"I was afraid of losing you," Beth said, her voice breaking.

"You know, this explains a lot," Michael said slowly. "I always wondered why you didn't like to be touched when we first met. At one time I thought you were frigid. Then there was that disastrous scene on our wedding night . . ."

"I'm sorry, Michael," she whispered.

"And James never knew he had a child," Michael said, his face sombre.

"But he did. I told him, just before he died, that it had been me, that he wasn't to torture himself, that I forgave him. And I did, Michael – he was so very young. We both were." She looked imploringly at him, desperate for him to say that he understood, that he still loved her.

"You say the baby was adopted – have you any idea where she is now?"

She twisted her damp handkerchief in anguish, and shook her head.

Michael stood up and walked over to the window, staring unseeing into the garden. He thought of the frightened seventeen-year-old girl, the culpability of his own brother, and of the child who must be what, ten years old?

A silence fell between them, and Beth endured an agony of uncertainty and apprehension as Michael remained standing with his back to her.

"Michael?" she whispered, unable to bear the suspense any longer. She rose from her chair in the same instant he turned towards her and suddenly they were clinging to each other.

"I need you, Michael," she whispered.

"And I want to share all of your life, Beth, not just part of it."

Chapter 29

It had been many years since Rose had allowed herself the relief of tears, but that afternoon she wept copiously, her heart full of pain. Pain that her beloved daughter had suffered so much, heartbreak that she hadn't turned for help to her own mother.

"Why, Beth? Why didn't you tell me?" she whispered. "Were you afraid to, was that it? Did you think I'd throw you out?"

"No, Mum, of course not. I know you better than that," Beth said, her own face wet with tears. "There was never any doubt in my mind that you'd support me, that you'd help to look after the baby."

"Then I don't understand!"

"How could I bring such trouble on you when you were struggling to cope after losing Dad? You worked so hard to bring us up decently. And can you imagine what it would have meant to have another mouth to feed?"

"We'd have managed," Rose insisted, wiping her eyes.

"It wasn't just that – you know what people are like around here. Think of it, Mum, the shame I'd have brought on you, and not just you but Rosemary. Then there was all the money you and Grandma Sherwin had spent on my education, and the sacrifices you made. It would all have been wasted."

She looked with distress at her mother, seeing bewilderment and hurt in her eyes. "You think I did the wrong thing, don't you?"

"I can't take it in that all these years you've been hiding this from me. I thought we were close," Rose accused her. "I've always prided myself on being a good mother."

"Oh, Mum, you are. You're the best mother in the world. It was me! I was young and stupid, but I really did think I was doing the right thing. If you only knew how many times I've regretted it!"

Beth's voice broke, and Rose said, "Don't take on, love. No one's blaming you. It's just the thought of that little lass being brought up by strangers."

"They won't be strangers to her, Mum."

"No, but they won't be her own family, either."

Rose's heart was heavy as she looked with infinite sadness at her daughter. She found it very hard to accept that at seventeen Beth had undergone two of the most traumatic experiences a woman could be subjected to, both without her knowledge.

She looked down at Beth's gold locket nestling in the palm of her hand and stroked the tiny lock of silvery baby hair. To think that somewhere she had a little granddaughter. Eeh, it must have taken a lot of courage for Beth to tell her after all this time.

"I feel sorry for Mrs Rushton," she said suddenly. "To lose your son and then find out he did such a terrible thing."

"James wasn't a bad person," Beth said. "I became quite fond of him."

"Aye, well, you didn't know the truth then," Rose said grimly. "Drink!" she snorted. "It's been the ruin of many a good man!"

"I'm coming to that conclusion myself."

Later, Rose watched Beth's car pull away and slowly dropped the net curtain. As the cuckoo clock struck four, she took Harry's photograph from the mantelpiece, and sitting heavily in her armchair gazed at the familiar features.

"Did you hear that, Harry? Our Beth, who we thought so fragile when she was born a month before her time, to go through all that by herself! Do you think I was at fault, love, not realising she was pregnant? I know one thing. That baby wouldn't have been adopted if you'd been alive!"

Sighing, she leaned her head back on the white antimacassar. There's not a cat in hell's chance of finding that child, she thought, not if I know anything of how these things work. Then she pursed her lips, considering. On the other hand, I've always said money talks, and for once I hope I'm right. Ah well, it was all in God's hands.

Beth let herself in to find Michael prostrate on the sofa, his eyes closed in a shallow sleep, his face gaunt with strain. She tiptoed out and going upstairs ran a bath, sprinkling in a generous handful of lavender crystals as she wondered how Michael had fared.

That morning she'd been adamant that her first loyalty must be to Rose, despite the troubled situation at Linden Lodge.

"It's unthinkable that your parents should know about Rosemary before my own mother," she insisted. "Besides, I think you ought to tell your mother privately. It's going to be a tremendous shock, particularly about James."

So they'd compromised, Beth driving in trepidation to Minsden, while Michael went alone to Linden Lodge. And from the look of him, Beth thought, he's emotionally exhausted.

Undressing, she sank gratefully into the scented water and closed her eyes, thankful that at last after all these shadowed years, she was free of deceit.

A few minutes later, Michael stirred and forced open his eyes, his mouth gritty and sour. Levering himself off the sofa he padded into the kitchen for a glass of water, noticing as he went through the hall that Beth's car keys were on the table. Recognising the faint scent of lavender, he guessed she was taking a bath. He slipped on his shoes and wandered out of the French windows into the garden. Despondent, he savagely kicked a pebble along the path wondering whether life would ever be the same again.

Scarcely recovered from the shock of Beth's revelations, it had been one of the hardest things he'd ever done, to watch the colour drain from his mother's face as he told her that her youngest son had raped the daughter-in-law she doted upon.

God, what a bloody pig of a day! He went back indoors and lit a cigarette, glancing at his watch. He needed something to eat. They'd had nothing since breakfast, and going to the foot of the stairs he called, "Beth!"

There was no answer.

"Beth?" With an exclamation of annoyance, he ran up the stairs and knocked on the bathroom door. "Beth!" he said sharply. "Beth!" He knocked harder, his heart suddenly hammering against his ribs.

"Mmn, yes?"

"You stupid idiot, you've fallen asleep," he shouted,

anger escalating inside him. For a minute he'd thought . . . he couldn't believe what he'd thought. He went into the bedroom and sat on the bed, his hands trembling.

Beth came in, rubbing at the back of her hair with a towel. "I was so shattered I must have dropped off."

"Don't you ever do that to me again, do you hear?" His voice was like a whiplash, and Beth flinched, her nerves stretched to breaking point.

"I'm sorry. . ."

He took a ragged breath. "God, if anything happened to you . . ."

She put her arms around him, drawing his head against the softness of her towelling bathrobe, and held him close. "I love you, Michael Rushton."

"And I love you." His throat thickened with emotion as he held her tight against him. All day, he'd struggled not to give way, to be strong for her and for his mother, but now at last with his face pressed against Beth's body, his shoulders sagged and the difficult tears came.

"Oh, Michael!" Beth bent her head and rested her cheek on his hair. "I had to tell you. You do see that?" she whispered.

"Yes, of course I do. It's delayed shock, that's all. It was bad enough to think of you being raped, but for it to have been my own brother!"

"He was very young, Michael, and very drunk."

"Yes, well, alcohol seems to have a dangerous effect on the Rushtons," he said grimly. "I've learned my lesson, I can tell you."

"How did your parents take it?" Beth watched his expression with anxiety.

Michael told her that Sylvia had been stunned by the news of Rosemary's existence, and devastated about James. Convinced that she should be the one to tell Robert, she'd pleaded for time to recover her composure. He'd promised that he and Beth would go to Linden Lodge first thing in the morning.

"How about your mum?"

"I think she felt very hurt that I hadn't turned to her for help."

"I know how she feels. I still wish you'd trusted me, Beth."

"I'm sorry. Do you think you'll ever be able to forgive me?" she asked in despair.

Michael kissed her gently. "I think we need to forgive each other."

Later that night, in a mutual need for comfort, they slept in each other's arms. Beth knew it would take time for the scars to heal, but the day had shown that their need and love for each other was the bedrock of their marriage.

Chapter 30

The following morning, when they arrived at Linden Lodge, it was to an atmosphere of tension, Sylvia's eyes evading Beth's as she greeted them at the door.

"Your father's waiting in the drawing-room," she murmured, and Beth felt a sudden chill, sensing her mother-in-law's unease.

Michael took her hand and together they went in to see Robert sitting in a crouched position on the leather chesterfield. Not bothering to greet them, he went straight into the attack.

"Well, this is a pretty kettle of fish, I must say."

"What exactly do you mean?" Michael said.

"This," he spat out the words, "this wife of yours trying to palm off her bastard as a member of our family!"

Beth blanched. Of all the reactions she'd anticipated,

it had never entered her head that she wouldn't be believed.

"But . . ." she began, her stomach knotting with fear.

Michael put his hand on her arm to silence her.

"Would you mind explaining what you mean by that statement, Father," he demanded.

Sylvia went and sat by Robert, twisting her hands in anguish.

"Robert, please . . ." She looked up pleadingly at them. "Do sit down."

"Never mind the social niceties, Mother. I'm waiting for an answer." Michael's voice was hard, and he put his arm protectively around Beth's shoulders.

"Your father's not well. . ." Sylvia began.

"Don't make excuses for me. I know perfectly well what I'm saying," Robert snapped. "How do we know James is the father of this child? In fact, how do we know that Beth was the girl in question? We've only got her word for it."

Incensed, Michael glared at him. "Are you accusing my wife of lying?" he said coldly

"I'm not accusing anybody of anything. There's a lot at stake here, Michael, and I'm trying to get at the facts."

"You do accept what James did?" Michael asked.

"I find it hard to believe he could do such a thing,

but your mother tells me he confessed to you before he died," Robert said in a gruff voice.

"So what's the problem?"

Mulishly, he persisted. "You say Beth overheard? Well, considering she had an illegitimate child, it wouldn't take Einstein to realise how opportune that was."

Michael exploded in anger and stepped forward, shouting at his father. "You've surpassed yourself this time! Have you any idea of the courage it took for Beth to confess all this to me, and to her mother? She put her marriage on the line out of concern for you, and this is the thanks she gets!" He turned to Sylvia, "I can see the shock's brought him back to the land of the living, but if he's going to be so bloody-minded, I'd rather he'd stayed as he was!"

"You don't mean that, Michael." Beth spoke at last, and went to sit in a wing armchair, leaning forward. She looked at Robert with sadness, deeply shocked to realise that he distrusted her, and then she saw the fear in his eyes, the fear of a man whose whole world rested on the truth, and yet hadn't the faith to believe it. For all his bluster, the tremor in his hands betrayed his nervous state, his face was pale, his eyes shadowed.

"Michael, would you repeat to your parents, exactly what James told you?" she said.

Into the emotional silence, Michael repeated the words he'd never forgotten.

"It was a tremendous shock to me," Beth said. "You see, I'd always suspected Tony Morrison. I couldn't believe it might have been James." She paused for a moment and then said, "So, Michael, James never mentioned where this party was held or on what date?"

"No, just that it was the night before I left for my National Service."

"Which I don't know," Beth stated.

"No, there's no reason why you should."

"So, if I tell you that Rosemary was born on the third of August, would those dates tally."

Michael did a quick mental calculation. "Exactly. But you don't need to do this, Beth. You don't have to prove your integrity to me."

"Thank you, Michael," she said, loving him for his strength and support. She turned to Robert. "So, do you believe that I was raped?" she asked bluntly.

Robert winced, and Sylvia said quietly, "Of course we do. No woman alive is going to own up to a thing like that unless it's the truth. I can't tell you how sorry I am, Beth."

"That goes for me too," Robert muttered.

"So, the only issue is, was I raped by James?"

At Sylvia's intake of breath, she said, "I'm sorry,

Sylvia, this must be very painful for you, but if we're to get at the truth . . ."

"I don't see what you're getting at," Robert said.

Beth undid her handbag and taking out her diary tore off a sheet of paper. She scribbled on it and then handed it to Robert. "That's the address of the house where the party was held. James never mentioned it, and neither has anyone else."

"I've no idea where it was," Michael said.

Beth looked at him. "No, but Guy has. He was there, Michael."

"I see what you mean," he said slowly. "If Guy confirms the address then . . ." He turned swiftly on his heel and left the room, the atmosphere behind him almost unbearable in its nervous tension.

Beth remained silent, gazing out of the window, the minutes ticking slowly by until Michael returned, brandishing a piece of paper.

"I just caught him. He was on his way out. He can't remember the number, but that's the name of the street and he says it was the –"

"Only house with a tree outside," Beth finished the sentence in a tight voice.

"That's exactly what he wrote down. Here, you can see for yourself." Michael thrust the paper at his father, and came over to where Beth sat, perching on the arm of the chair.

They watched in silence as Robert carefully compared the two addresses.

"Satisfied?" Michael said bitterly.

Robert passed the pieces of paper to Sylvia, and looked at Beth, his expression one of acute embarrassment. "I think I owe you an apology. I've sadly misjudged you, my dear. You may not be a Rushton by birth, but you're stronger than any of us."

He sat back and closed his eyes, his brow wet with perspiration, and Sylvia nodded to them to follow her as she went into the kitchen to make some coffee.

"It will take time, but knowing he has a grandchild will make all the difference." She turned and drew Beth to her, kissing her cheek. "I never doubted you for an instant, but his nerves are in such a state that I thought it best not to oppose him."

She held Beth at arms' length for a moment, gazing steadily into her eyes.

"I want you to know that I'll never forget what you've done. You're a lucky man, Michael. I hope you realise that."

"No, Sylvia," Beth said quietly. "I'm the lucky one."

Epilogue

It was the following summer.

Beth waved goodbye to Granny Platt and, adjusting the sunshade on the expensive navy and white pram, wheeled her long-awaited adopted baby son out for an airing in Queen's Park.

Turning the corner, she looked down the hill at the landscape in the distance. Everything was changing, the old bottle kilns were disappearing, and many small family potteries were being swallowed up by larger companies. A new decade was approaching and as she walked up the steep hill to the park gates she wondered idly what innovations the seventies would bring.

Strolling through the flower gardens and past the bowling greens, she seated herself comfortably on a bench in the shade of an old oak tree. She watched a mother duck marshalling her chicks as they swam in a procession across the lake, and the antics of a baby squirrel a few yards away. She was at last happy with her life. Ursula, safely distant at a school in Sussex, no longer posed a threat, and now, with little Andrew and hopefully another child later, her world was complete.

If at times she wondered whether her brain was lying fallow, then she knew there would be no resistance to any political ambitions she might have. The Rushton family had long abandoned their efforts to mould her in their image.

For Robert, finding his granddaughter had become an obsession. Advertisements were still placed regularly in the personal columns of all the national and local newspapers, and he had vowed never to abandon the search.

Within Beth there was now a quiet certainty that one day, in God's own time, she and her daughter would be reunited. She would never forget the trauma of discovering that James was Rosemary's father, but with forgiveness had come healing. The canker that had eaten away at her for so long was finally appeased. Now she had a tiny ache in her heart for the pain of Andrew's natural mother but, smiling at her baby's fascination with the sun-patterned leaves fluttering gently in the breeze, she knew that her deep love for Michael had finally brought her fulfilment.

THE END

Acknowledgments

To all members of the Wednesday morning Writers' Workshop in Wellington Street, Leicester, not only for their constructive criticism which has been invaluable, but also for their friendship.

To my family for their encouragement and support, and to Poolbeg, for giving me the chance to hold my own book in my hand.

Escape to the world of the Stoke-on-Trent Potteries, with the next books in 'The Potteries Girls' series by award-winning historical romance writer, Margaret Kaine.

All can be enjoyed as a stand-alone story.

1. A MOTHER'S REGRET

Could the secret of her past risk her future happiness?

2. A DAUGHTER'S WISH

A lifetime of regret. One chance to be reunited.

3. A FAMILY'S BOND

Married life isn't what they promised it would be . . .

4. THE PRICE OF LOYALTY

Will she pick true friendship or forbidden love?

5. A LIGHT IN THE DARK

An unexpected baby. A life-changing decision . . .

6. A BROKEN HEART

Can she ever forgive the mother who abandoned her?

7. HOPE FROM THE ASHES

Alone in the world, will she have the courage to follow her heart?

Available to read in eBook now!

Read on for an extract from Margaret Kaine's captivating next novel, *A DAUGHTER'S WISH* . . .

Chapter 1

The dark brown stain of the teapot's contents trickled obscenely down the kitchen wallpaper. Brenda Latham was hysterical, out of control, her features contorted as she grabbed whatever was nearest to her and threw it at the door. Rosemary, who had only just missed being hit as the china teapot hurtled past her, stared in horror at her mother.

"Hey . . . watch what you're doing, for heaven's sake!"

Dodging her mother's flailing arms, she rescued the rest of the tea set which sat temptingly on the kitchen table.

"What good is breaking things going to do?" she yelled. "You heard what he said, he's gone. This isn't going tobring him back!"

Her young eyes brimming with tears, she stood glaring at her mother. Their eyes locked in a battle of wills and then Brenda crumpled, collapsing on to a kitchen chair as she gave way to her pent-up feelings. As her mother sobbed, Rosemary's shoulders slumped in despair.

Shakily, she filled the kettle and switched it on. There had been rows before, terrible rows, with tension in the house and strained relationships for days, but her dad had never before threatened to leave.

"Is there another woman?" Her voice cracked on the sentence, and she kept her back to Brenda as she waited tensely for an answer.

"What do you know about such things at your age?" Her mother's voice, though muffled with tears, was sharp, causing Rosemary to swing round in irritation.

"You might not allow any newspapers in the house, but I do live in this world, you know."

Noisily blowing her nose, Brenda got up and restlessly paced the kitchen. She glared at the slim, fourteen-year-old girl, whose lightly freckled face beneath untidy dark hair was wet with tears.

"I don't want to talk about it," she muttered. She wiped her swollen eyes on a damp handkerchief, and going over to the sink began to splash her face with cold water. Mutinous, Rosemary made the tea, putting a generous two spoons of sugar in each cup.

"When will you stop treating me like a child?"

"Some things aren't for young ears," Brenda snapped.

"Mum – it's 1970 for heaven's sake! Not that you'd

ever know the permissive society existed, living in this house."

"Don't be cheeky! You young people nowadays know too much, too soon."

"Maybe, but it's better than growing up in ignorance like your generation did!" Rosemary flung at her.

Brenda sat again at the kitchen table, cradling the warm cup in her hands. She didn't need an argument with her teenage daughter. She was emotionally drained, exhausted by the violent scene with Keith. It was unfortunate that Rosemary had been in the house; the walls were so thin, she must have heard every word. Wearily, she pushed back her greying brown hair from her forehead, surprised to find it damp with perspiration.

"Don't you get upset. It's our problem, not yours."

"It's a bit late for that," Rosemary said with bitterness.

All of her young life, for as long as she could remember, she'd been conscious of friction between her parents. Most of the time it had been barely concealed, their hostility revealing itself in subtle innuendos and barbed comments. Did they think a child was deaf to such things? At least when she was younger, they'd restricted themselves to glowering silences. Now, their emotion serupted at the slightest provocation.

So, her dad had got himself another woman! Her lip curled in contempt, as she wondered what on earth she could be like. Not that she cared that much. Her father had never shown much interest in her. She often wondered if he resented her very presence.

Rosemary looked at her mother, who was sitting slumped at the kitchen table, one hand scrabbling in her handbag for a pack of cigarettes. They both smoked incessantly, her mum and her dad. The house stank permanently of nicotine.

"Mum," she said, frowning, "you don't think he'll really leave?"

Brenda looked up at her as she inhaled, and then gave a ragged sigh. "That's what he says."

"But if he does, what will happen to us? I mean, how will we manage?"

Keith Latham had always been in work, but his heavy smoking and drinking ate a large hole in his wages. He'd once had a well-paid job as a sales representative, but that had been when Rosemary was a baby. She'd only ever known him to drift from one job to another. His latest was barman at the Dog and Gun, a popular pub frequented by day trippers on their way to the coast twenty miles away at Westbourne.

"God knows!" Brenda stared blankly at her.

"Couldn't you ask Father Kavanagh to talk to him?"

"Hah!" she sniffed. "Fat lot of good that'd be – he doesn't even go to Mass half the time. Anyway, he thinks Father Kavanagh's an old woman."

Rosemary bit her lip. "You could get a job, I suppose. And I could, as soon as I leave school. I don't have to stayon for my exams."

"You'll do no such thing!" Brenda bristled. "Not when you're top of your class. And why should I go out to work? It was agreed, when we had you, that I'd stay at home and be a full-time mother." She looked at her daughter, her expression hard. "If he wants to go and live with his floosie, let him. We'll soon see how he likes keeping two homes going."

She stood up and began to brush the cigarette ash from her jumper, her thin face pale and tense. "Come on, let's clear this lot up, then you can go and fetch some fish and chips. Just the two of us, mind! If he comes back, he can bloody well get his own!"

But Keith Latham didn't come back, and later that night Rosemary lay in her narrow, single bed and stared dismally at the grey cracks in the plastered ceiling. Like the rest of the house, her cheaply furnished room was in need of redecoration, but her dad was a man full of promises and not much action. It worried her sometimes that she felt so little for him. Often, cringing at his coarse humour, she would sit and stare at him, wondering how they could be so different.

She didn't take after her mum either, but at least she could relate to her. The small, bay-windowed semi tucked away at the end of a tiny cul-de-sac was Brenda's whole world. Rosemary remembered her saying once that a lousy husband was better than no husband at all. Despite her forced bravado, Keith's desertion would hit her hard.

Rosemary turned over, pummelling the pillow into shape, her shoulders hunching miserably under the bedclothes. One thing was for sure, life was never going to be the same again.

Love Margaret Kaine's stories?
Why not sign up for her newsletter!

Keep up with the latest books, exclusive extracts, and insider information from the author at:

https://signup.harpercollins.co.uk/join/6n7/signup-avon-margaretkaine

Or explore more wonderful historical romance novels at the Avon Publishers website here:
www.avonbooks.co.uk

We look forward to seeing you there!